TOWARD A NEW BEGINNING

Arkansas Valley - Book 1

r. William Rogers

Toward A New Beginning
Copyright © 2015: Robert W. Rogers
Cover Art by: Laura Shinn Designs
laurashinn@yolasite.com
ISBN-10: 1508413355
ISBN-13: 978-1508413356

Christy Award Winner

Toward A New Beginning was recognized as the winner of the prestigious Christy Award for: "Excellence in Christian Fiction."

Introduction

I am thrilled with my friend Bob Rogers' new western novel, <u>Toward A New Beginning</u>. It is evident that Bob has done his "homework." He has captured the joys, sorrows and adventures of those brave pioneers who left their homes east of the wide Missouri and journeyed westward in wagon trains to begin their lives all over again.

This captivating story has it all...unique personalities in the wagons, dangerous weather, raging rivers, hostile Indian attacks, hunger, water shortage, vengeance, courage, romance, biblical principals...and a story pivoting on the valor and ingenuity of beautiful Birdsong, a full-blooded Comanche woman.

If you want excitement and page-turning enjoyment, READ ON!

Al Lacy

Born in the Rocky Mountain West, Al Lacy was raised on a ranch in the foothills of the Colorado Rockies. He has written more than ninety novels, including the Angel of Mercy, Battles of Destiny, and Journeys of the Stranger series. He and his wife, JoAnna Lacy, are coauthors of the Mail Order Bride, Hannah of Fort Bridger, and Shadow of Liberty series. The Lacys make their home in the Colorado Rockies.

Although this is a work of fiction, it is as geographically and historically correct as possible. The author guarantees all contents are original and do not infringe upon the legal rights of any other person or work. The views expressed in this ebook are not necessarily those of the publisher.

Unless otherwise indicated, Bible quotations are taken from the King James Version of the Bible. Copyright © 1989 by Thomas Nelson Inc.

Foreword

The Louisiana Purchase of 1803 was the brainchild of then U.S. President Thomas Jefferson. For the price of about three cents an acre, the United States acquired, from France, territory that more than doubled the land area of the United States at that time.

The newly acquired "Louisiana Territory." extended from the Mississippi River in the east to the rugged Rocky Mountains out west, and from British North America all the way down to the Gulf of Mexico. This transaction was and still is referred to as: "The greatest bargain in American history."

Not only did this acquisition open up exploration of the Pacific Northwest via the Oregon Trail, but it additionally served as a basis for the establishment of a merchant route between the eastern trade markets and the western frontier; specifically all the way to Santa Fe, New Mexico.

The customary route snaked its way south from the Missouri River to the Arkansas. It then turned west and followed the latter through hostile Comanche lands to nearly its headwaters in what is now present day Colorado. There it turned south again, this time to Taos, New Mexico, and finally to Santa Fe.

Despite the rigors and dangers involved, the route was a

good one and its importance to the successful development of the eastward silver and fur trade, as well as the westward transporting of manufactured goods, was a contributing factor to U.S. seizure of New Mexico during the Mexican-American War.

Although the Mexican-American War was still being fought in late 1847, it was mainly a political war stemming from Mexican anger at the United States' annexation of Texas in 1845, as well as a dispute over whether Texas ended at the Nueces River (Mexican claim), or the Rio Grande (U.S. claim). The general consensus was that the whole disagreement was not much more than just a nuisance and would soon be settled.

It was finally settled in February of 1848, with the signing of the Treaty of Guadalupe Hidalgo. As a result of that treaty, huge land grants became readily available to those hardy souls who were resilient enough and who had strong enough desires and commitments to overcome the hardships involved in settling these vast new lands.

Use of the Santa Fe Trail increased and prospered under U.S. rule, especially after the introduction of mail delivery service via stagecoach in 1849. However, as is true with most good things, its use ceased altogether shortly after modernization began spreading west in the form of the building of the Atchison, Topeka & Santa Fe Railroad in 1880.

Independence, Missouri, was the "Jumping off spot." for folks with a "Hankerin' to head West." as they gathered there by the thousands and joined wagon trains before beginning their westward trek along the trail.

Folks who engaged in the attempt to realize their dreams by joining a "train" were usually an adventuresome, above average, spunky kind of folks with a yearning for the wide-openness and unpredictability of a new land.

One such man was a gent by the name of Sam Bartlett.

TOWARD A NEW BEGINNING
Arkansas Valley - Book 1

❧Chapter 1❧

"Are you sure, Sam? Are you really sure that's what you want to do?" Judith asked as she looked across the breakfast table at her husband.

The question remained unanswered while he toyed with a splinter that until then had been minding its own business along the top edge of the table. He appeared engrossed while he picked at it methodically. Finally, hooking it with a fingernail, he tugged and it came loose. He stuck it into the corner of his mouth and raised his gaze to meet hers.

His eyes were a soft hazel hue, seeming to change shades as his mood dictated. Right now, they were just a mite paler than usual, suggesting maybe a doubt or two with the issue at hand. His rugged features were chiseled to a handsome perfection, punctuated by a square jaw that indicated a man who was apt to stand up for what he believed. There was a genuine good-natured set to his mouth that implied a willingness to smile easily if something struck his fancy. His hair was thick, wavy, and a brown shade that was about the same as a desert sand dune right after a rainstorm. The color did justice to the warmth of his hazel eyes.

He removed the splinter from the corner of his mouth and

flicked it onto the floor. "Why don't you ask me an easy question?" he asked. "All I know for sure is that I can't seem to get the notion out of my head. It's like the Lord is telling me what to do." He responded with a subtle gentleness to the concerned look in her eyes by reaching a hand across the table and gently resting it on her forearm. "I'm truly sorry if this troubles you, Jay, but there's a real opportunity out there," he added tenderly.

"But we'd be doing pretty much what we're already doing right here in Independence. I guess I just don't see the sense in us pulling up stakes and traveling all that way to do something that we could continue to do right here where we are. It just doesn't seem to make much sense is all."

He sighed heavily. "You're probably right, sweetheart. I've been trying to sort through that very line of reasoning for the better part of an entire month now."

"And what reasonable justification did you manage to come up with?"

He lowered his eyes. "None, I guess," he said feebly. "It's just that..." The words trailed off as the foolishness of the proposed venture positioned itself right about the front tip edge of his brain. With some difficulty, he swallowed his uncertainty and looked into her troubled eyes. "I know it doesn't seem to make much sense at first glance, but it's something I feel a genuine calling to do. I'm not denying that we could do just fine by staying put. But there are folks out there on the frontier that need horses the same as folks right here do...maybe even more so."

The passion he was feeling began to take over and the excitement he was experiencing was evident in his eyes as he continued, "And not to mention the fact that there's army forts and trading posts being built out there that I'm sure also have a real need for good mounts." His gaze was focused on her troubled expression. He lightly touched the side of her face. "Just think of the help we would be giving to those folks," he coaxed gently.

The washboard of wrinkles disappeared from her forehead and her eyes returned to their normal state of loveliness. "And just where would you get all these horses? You wouldn't be thinking of driving them along with the wagon train, would you?"

His eyes lit up as his face broke into an enthusiastic grin. "Now *that's* the real beauty of the whole thing; the horses are already there!"

The furrows returned. "What do you mean, already there?"

Now more hopeful than ever, he quickly picked up the pace, "The countryside is chocked full of wild mustangs just for the taking. All a fella would need to do is build a few corrals and go out and catch 'em." He grinned that special grin of his—the one that never failed him.

"Do you honestly think it would be all that easy?"

His ace in the hole disappeared and his eyes changed to a slightly darker shade as they took on a faraway look. He spoke his answer slowly, "Nooo, but it sure would be an adventure."

"Sam, if you know in your heart of hearts that the Lord is calling you to pack up your wife and son and head out for wherever the—"

Her line of reasoning had been interrupted as she rested her gaze on their son, Tom, who was seated in his highchair along a third edge of the table. While she watched him playing with his food, she couldn't help but wonder at the hardships they would be faced with if they did indeed decide to join a wagon train and head west.

Her concerns were temporarily pushed aside as Tom scooped up a handful of mush from his bowl, and while managing to miss his mouth almost completely, deposited most of it on the tray in front of him, with a good portion of it slopping over the edge and onto the floor. "It sure doesn't seem worthwhile to set a spoon in front of you, now does it?"

She picked up the utensil and two-handedly wrapped his tiny fingers around the handle. "There. You'll no doubt have better luck with this," she said and guided his hand as together they dipped the spoon into the oatmeal. Once she had Tom back on an even keel, she picked up the dishcloth she kept handy on the tabletop and went to work on the mess that seemed to her to be just about everywhere.

Sam watched silently as she cleaned. Her tears didn't escape his notice, though, as they slowly worked their way down her cheeks. He fancied himself a pretty good judge of things and rightly figured that those tears weren't entirely as a result of Tom's antics. With all the tenderness he could scare up, he placed a loving hand on her wrist and said softly, "Sweetheart, look up here and listen to what I've got to say."

She managed to find a clean corner on the dishrag, and after positioning it just right, used it to dab at the tears.

He cupped a hand under her chin and raised her gaze to meet his. "If you're dead set against it, I'll not follow through," he said lovingly. "But if it's just the fear of the unknown, well then, I reckon we'll need to pray about it and see if the Lord will give you the needed strength."

She smiled her faith in this man that she loved with all of her heart and soul. "Sam, I expect it is just a fear of the unknown, as you say, but praying about it wouldn't hurt none either." She sighed resignedly. "If all goes well, when do you figure you'll be wanting to cart us off to that heathen infested part of the country?"

A smile lit up his face as her response once again reaffirmed her willingness to follow him wherever he led.

They had fallen in love almost at first sight. It had happened in upstate New York where he had been involved in a clothing factory venture with a gent from Syracuse.

Although Sam was at first an absentee partner in the

business, his colleague had wired him in Virginia requesting his immediate presence because of what he'd referred to as "A predicament."

As it turned out Sam's partner had, as a result of his love for playing cards at the local honkytonk, gotten himself and the business into a cash flow situation. Sam, being a born-again Christian, had no desire to remain in partnership with the fella after finding out he was a gambler and a carouser. With that in mind, he discretely bought him out and thereby solved both their immediate problems.

Because Sam was himself a gentleman with firm roots and substantial holdings in the Shenandoah Valley, he had little to no desire to remain in the Syracuse area and tend to what was now solely his business...especially after laying eyes on the previously unseen clothing factory.

Oh, it was a clothing factory all right, but the garments it turned out were ladies unmentionable undergarments. Once he had found that out, he was at first furious about how he'd been duped into investing in a sight-unseen business that dealt in such a scandalous product. But not being averse to turning a good profit, he calmed down long enough to realize some distinct possibilities and started looking for a buyer with maybe less propriety than he.

During the time while he searched for just the right person upon whom to unload his now undesired asset, he found the time to attend one of the local churches each Sunday morning.

Having a strong desire to listen to good preaching, he was pleased to have found a church and pastor to his liking. As fate would have it, that's not all he found that was to his liking. It was there that he first noticed and then later met, Miss Judith Van Sheckle — the soon to be Mrs. Sam Bartlett.

He was instantly taken by her tantalizing personality and extremely ladylike manners. She was also a little on the extroverted side, while at the same time able to remain extremely cordial and considerate.

Her beauty was a sight to behold. She was of average height, about five-five or six. Her hair was a light shade of auburn that reminded him of a sorrel filly playfully kicking up her heels in the slanting rays of the early morning sunlight. Her eyes were a captivating deep blue and portrayed an undeniable tenderness. The facial structure was long, but not too thin. Her nose and mouth were perfect...*absolutely* perfect.

They hit it off right from the start and their romance quickly blossomed into one of the whirlwind variety. It was barely a short two months before he proposed and she accepted; they were soon married in a similarly whirlwind fashion.

What with her being a bit of an upper crust debutante, she was at first unwilling to completely give up her accustomed lifestyle and succumb to his attempts at luring her back to the wilds of Virginia. He therefore did the only thing he could under the circumstances; he sold his holdings and properties in the Shenandoah Valley. With more time now available to him, and unable to readily find a buyer for the factory, he resigned himself, and despite his misgivings, concentrated his efforts on making a success of the garment factory.

Sam and Jay—as he liked to call her—were a happy couple right from the start. She quickly realized that there was more to life than debutante balls and ladies teas in the afternoons. She grew to love Sam more and more as time went by, and those affections allowed her to devote her every waking moment to making him as happy as she was capable of.

About a year went by, during which time he put up with the factory as best he could. But despite his honest to goodness and well intentioned efforts, he finally came to the conclusion that making ladies undergarments was definitely not for him. With that in mind, he decided to have a talk with Jay about it, and after locating her in the parlor, mustered up the necessary courage.

"Ahh...Jay?" he said almost sheepishly, while standing in

the doorway.

She looked up from her Bible, and seeing the seriousness in his eyes, tucked the lacy crocheted bookmark between the pages and closed it lovingly. "Yes, Sam. What is it?"

He crossed the room while clearing a frog that had suddenly decided to occupy a prominent spot in the back of his throat. He gazed down at her, and before his nerve abandoned him completely, he dove right in, "I've decided that I'm not at all cut out to cut out women's clothes." He smiled one of those genuine smiles of his. "I'll bet I couldn't say that again three times real fast without stumbling all over my tongue."

"No, I suppose not. But why did you say it in the first place?"

"Well, because I've decided to unload the factory for a song and go do something I'm better..." he smiled that smile again and continued, "cut out for...pun intended." He watched her eyes closely for a reaction. It came right away, but was a sight less than he figured it would be. She barely frowned as her eyes darkened only slightly.

"And just what might that be?" she asked suspiciously.

He had already made up his mind to not beat around the bush. "My true interests lie in raising horses," he said confidently.

Her surprise was complete and her eyes opened wide. "Raising *what*? Boy, just when you think you know a person," she said from under raised eyebrows.

"Sorry I didn't tell you before about this. It's just that I never saw the need before now."

"And now you do?"

"Ah...yes, yes I do."

"Go on."

"Uh...I've been reading the newspapers and..." He inhaled deeply while trying to get it all just right in his mind.

"And what?" she coaxed.

He looked her square in the eye, exhaled heavily, and blurted, "And I see a real need for the right man to set up a horse raising endeavor in Independence, Missouri!"

She appeared deep in thought, until, as her love for him won out, she allowed her expression of disbelief to change to one of resignation. "And just why do you feel you're the man for the job?"

Sam thought he saw what he hoped was an encouraging look in her eye. Hardly daring to believe that it might mean what he hoped it could, but at this point figuring he had nothing to lose, he said tentatively, "Wa-well, just because, I guess." He swallowed dryly before continuing, "Jay...I've been reading in the newspaper where folks are leaving out from Independence by the scores, and just good common sense would tell a man that all those wagons need either horses or oxen to pull 'em."

He sat on the arm of her chair and gently took her hand in his. He spoke softly, "Jay, I know I'm asking a lot, maybe even too much, but we've done well with the business and can afford to take a bit of a beating on a quick sale. We could then buy a good-sized herd down in Kentucky or Tennessee somewhere and drive 'em the rest of the way to Missouri."

His speech picked up to a more normal pace...and even a bit beyond as he began to get excited. "With a fair-sized investment we could buy a piece of land with a ranch already on it and set up housekeeping! That'd give us the start we'd need and we could commence right in with breeding the stock for selling to those folks in the wagon trains!"

As she watched his eagerness, she likened the excitement in his eyes to that of a little boy.

"What'dya say, Jay? I promise to take real good care of you out there!"

"How about our child? Do you promise to take care of our child, as well?"

His expression immediately changed to one of slight

bewilderment, then quickly transformed to one of total happiness as the realization of what she'd just said clicked in his brain. "You mean…you're…we're gonna—?"

"Yes, darling, we're going to have a baby."

&Chapter 2&

The move to Independence hadn't proved to be of a particularly difficult nature. Sam had purchased a prairie schooner that had also served as a chuckwagon of sorts. He had additionally been especially mindful of keeping Jay as comfortable as possible during the journey.

They had not only been lucky enough to have located a sizable herd for sale in Kentucky, and at a fair price, but were fortunate to have found and hired on four drovers to help get them all the way to Missouri.

The drive proved to be slow and exhaustive, but it was made without anymore than the usual mishaps that were a normal part of such endeavors. Only a minimal number of the herd had been lost to predators and by the grace of God the Indians that were inherent to the area had, for whatever reason, left them alone.

As soon as they arrived in Independence, Sam wasted no time and through the local bank readily found what he felt was a suitable spread. He and the owner quickly worked out an agreeable arrangement and the property changed hands in a matter of just two short days.

Sam was a diligent and hardworking sort of man. Him

being an honest Christian didn't hurt him none either when it came to furthering his reputation as a man who'd be willing to give a down and outer the shirt off his back if he were in need and found himself hardpressed to afford one of his own.

彡

The months flew by, while the business flourished and folks just kept on coming and going through Independence.

The excitement and enthusiasm of the many folks heading west was a blessing to Sam and he was able to at least temporarily satisfy himself with just the knowing that he was being a part of them fulfilling their dreams of settling what were the vast and untamed lands of the western frontier.

However, as fate would have it, he soon realized that he envied them, but not wanting to upset Jay, he managed to bite his tongue and keep those feelings to himself.

彡

"Sam?"

His attention returned to their conversation across the breakfast table as he realized he had been daydreaming. "Oh...sorry, Jay. Guess my mind was off somewhere else."

After having rid herself of the last of the tears, she held tightly to the dishrag and smiled weakly. "Which hasn't been too unusual as of late," she observed. She then allowed what had been a forced smile to disappear completely as a seriousness took over. She placed her hand atop his. "Sam...darling, I followed you all the way out here from New York, and that turned out to be a good choice. With that in mind, I guess I could continue to follow you...leastways until you lead me astray."

Sam smiled as he gazed lovingly into her understanding eyes. "The Lord has surely blessed me," he said with heartfelt tenderness, and leaned toward her.

Their lips met in a kiss filled with warmth and affection. "Thank you," he said softly, after they had parted. "I promise I'll take real good care of you out there."

೨೦

It had been a busy time for the both of them since they'd made the decision to head west. Sam had a ranch and a flourishing livestock business to sell, as well as wagons to buy.

Jay, on the other hand, because of space constraints, had spent the entire time laboring over which household items to take along and which ones to leave behind. Although they had been married barely five short years, she'd felt it necessary to save mementoes, knick-knacks, pieces of yarn, and anything else she had found a nook or cranny in which to fit her triflings. She was the type to not throw anything away and there were what seemed to her like mountains to sort through. Not only was she a pack rat of sorts, but she rightly reasoned that it just didn't make any sense to start completely all over again.

So, after a serious discussion with Sam, she found herself willing to compromise on the condition that he purchase an extra wagon in which to haul what items she could manage to squeeze into it. Besides, they could sell the wagon after they arrived at their final destination…wherever that turned out to be.

Sam, being eternally grateful for her agreeing to make the trip at all, eagerly consented to the second wagon. He felt that it was the least he could do. He figured he would be able to hire a driver from one of the young men who would already be making the trip. All he had to do now was find just the right person…if in fact one even existed.

೨೦

About three weeks had now gone by since the decision had been made to leave Independence. It wasn't until then that Sam was able to find a buyer for his stock business and an equitable price had been agreed upon. However, his efforts to sell the ranch had not as yet proven fruitful and he was forced to face the reality that maybe the ranch wouldn't sell before they were ready to leave. With that in mind, he made the necessary arrangements with the president of the bank, Jacob McMasters.

What with Jacob also being a Christian made it a whole lot easier for Sam to trust him with his legal matters, and after filling out a legal Power of Attorney, he turned the sale of the property over to the bank. Sam would be in touch after reaching their destination and would get word back as to where to send the proceeds once the sale had been made and finalized.

With that worry now out of the way, he concentrated his efforts on finding out as much as he could about the formation of the next train.

The word around town was that it would be leaving in less than a week. Because the number of spots were limited, anyone interested in joining up needed to make arrangements with the wagonmaster in order to solidify their spot in the final lineup.

Sam asked around and found out that the proposed leader of the train was a fella by the name of Hector Yallow—folks said that he was the one to see. It seemed that anyone who had an acquaintance with him held him in high regard as a no-nonsense kind of person and a fair man to boot.

It was a particularly delightful, warm Tuesday morning when Sam was finally able to catch up with the gent in front of the mercantile.

The description he had been given fit the grizzled oldtimer to a tee: weather beaten leathery features, short graying beard, hat folded up in the front, and walked with a slight limp that favored the left leg.

"You Mister Yallow?" Sam asked as he approached the gent on the boardwalk.

The oldtimer stopped and eyed the younger man until he decided to reply by first spitting a stream of amber tobacco juice in the general direction of the street. "Heck Yeah, at yer service," he said and wiped the dribble from the graying stubble that covered the bottom half of his face and nearly all of his neck until it just sort of blended in with the chest hair that shown through the buckskin lacing at the top of his shirt.

Sam extended a hand. "Pleased to meet you. My name's Sam Bartlett. I'm looking for a spot in your wagon train."

The wagonmaster took his sweet time while he assessed Sam and digested the request. "You any tougher'n ya look?" he finally asked.

Sam eyed the fella. Figuring that he was probably harmless, he shot back, "You any tougher then *you* look?"

A quizzical look flicked across the man's eyes and Sam wondered briefly if he had made a mistake by electing to give the gent a dose of his own medicine.

A crooked grin replaced the dubious expression. The wagonmaster then reached out and accepted the still outstretched hand of the upstart whippersnapper. "Nope. Fact is, I'm just a big ol' cuddly pussycat. Pleased to make your acquaintance, Mister B," Heck said from behind a now genuine smile as he applied a firm grip and began pumping the hand vigorously.

"That's...*Bartlett.*"

"I know that. I just don't cotton to rememberin' folk's names is all. It's a whole lot quicker an' easier to just put an initial to their features."

He released Sam's hand.

Sam wondered if any bones had been broken. "In that case what do I call you?" he asked as he clenched and unclenched his hand a few times just to be sure.

"Done told ya...Heck Yeah. That's short for Hector Yallow. The name come from somewhere over in Europe. Never did 'preciate it none. But I reckon a fella's gotta do with what the good Lord gives him."

"Amen," Sam said, nodding his understanding.

"You a religious fella, are you?" Heck asked.

"I'd say that'd depend on what your definition of religious is. If you're asking whether I'm saved by grace and washed in the blood, then I'd say I'm religious." Sam wondered where this was all headed. "But if you're asking—"

"Well, hallelujah! Now I ain't got no worries about us getting along. I know Jesus my ownself."

Sam felt relieved, and asked, "Good. Does that mean I get a spot in the train?"

"Yep, that it does. Ain't never turned down a good Christian family and never will...long as I still got a God-given breath left inside of me. Fact is...if I had my druthers, I'd make the whole danged train made up of nothing but Christian folks."

"Thanks, Heck, I appreciate the consideration. Now that we got that all settled, just where is your train heading? Some folks say you're going over the Rocky Mountains and some say you'll be stopping just short of them."

"Well, what it being late August already, we'd have no chance of climbing them mountains and gettin' to the other side before the snows was clean up to our eyeballs." Another small brown puddle formed in the street dust. "Nosiree...I'm saying this here particular train is gonna be stopping a bit short of them mountains. We'll be leaving come this Thursday morning right about sunup. We'll be meeting out at the west edge of town."

"Sounds good to me. Oh...and one other thing, I have *two* wagons. I hope that won't present any problems."

"Nope, no problem atall. They's still two more spots left open after yourn. Just make durned sure that they're both sturdy and in good enough shape to make the trip without holding the rest of us up."

Sam knew that both his wagons were sturdy and well equipped to make the trip, and because of that, he elected to not comment. He instead remembered that he needed to hire a driver for the other wagon. "Do you happen to know of anyone who might be interested in driving my other wagon? I'd be willing to pay him for his trouble."

Heck swept the sorry excuse of a hat off his head, revealing a receding hairline. He reached into his back pocket, pulled a mostly red, soiled handkerchief, and used it to rub his forehead dry of the sweat that had collected. "Let me ask around. I just might be able to help you out there." He then wiped the inside rim of the hatband and positioned the hat back onto his head, tilting it just a mite to the right in the process. He then stuffed the handkerchief back into his hip pocket.

Sam figured there was no other good reason for keeping the man from whatever it was that he had been doing, and said, "Well then, I'd say that that just about completes our business."

"Peers like."

"I reckon we'll be ready to go by Thursday morning then. In the meantime if you come across someone —"

"I'll do just that."

Their business completed, they shook hands and went their separate ways.

Sam was eager to find Jay and tell her the good news. Their ranch was just on the outskirts of town and he made good time getting home.

"Jay!" he called, as he pushed through the doorway and into the main house.

"I'm in here…in the bedroom!"

He entered the bedroom and greeted his son first. "Hi, Tom. You being a good boy today?"

"Uh huh," Tom said and held his arms up and out to his pa, obviously wanting to be hoisted up.

Sam lifted the boy and held him perched atop a forearm. "We got us a spot in the train," he said to Jay. "We're leaving this coming Thursday at daybreak." The look in her eyes was the same one he had seen when she had first realized that they were leaving their comfortable life in New York to relocate to Missouri.

"That soon, huh?" she asked and tiredly pushed her way up from her task of sorting through the personal items in the oversized cedar chest. She then approached her husband and said softly, "Put Tom down, Sam. I really could use a comforting hug right about now."

Sam lowered his son onto his feet and took her in his arms. He pulled her close.

"I'm scared, Sam," she said and buried her face against his chest. "I'm truly scared."

He patted her back tenderly and closed his eyes as he, too, wondered if they were indeed doing the right thing.

❧Chapter 3❧

Sam busied himself with hitching up the team while Jay went about putting the final touches on getting Tom ready to go. He knew that she would then say her final farewells to the ranch, vowing to never forget the fond memories it held for her.

Once he had completed the task, he pulled the schooner to the front of the main house where Jay and Tom climbed aboard.

Once she had settled into her place on the seat beside him, he snapped the reins along the backs of the lead pair, and as planned, they completed the short trip to the rendezvous point even before the sun had peeked its orange brilliance above the eastern horizon.

Heck had been true to his word and had found someone to drive the extra wagon for them. He'd come up with a young fella of seventeen by the name of Darrell Henderson. Sam had met with the youngster the evening before and had concluded that despite being a bit on the peculiar side, he was an all right sort.

After their meeting, it was decided that he would meet up

with them at the rendezvous the following morning with the Conestoga.

≫

He was tall and lanky, about two or three inches over six-foot. The slenderness of his frame gave the false impression that he was even taller than he actually was. On his head perched a shapeless brown hat, worn pushed back which allowed an unruly shock of blonde hair to escape and dangle over one of his intensely blue eyes. He wore a slightly tattered, gray, long sleeved shirt and a pair of gray woolen trousers that, not unlike the hat, had also seen better days. The whole thing was held together by a set of frayed, light brown suspenders.

"The wagonmaster said you were looking for a driver, that right?" the youngster asked from behind an unwavering gaze that Sam figured could have only come from a well-directed upbringing.

Sam focused his attention on the boy's face rather than his clothes. "Yeah. You applying for the job?"

"Depends."

"On what?"

He lowered his gaze and scuffed the toe of his boot in the soft dirt. He then started drawing small circles with it. "On whether or not me an' your horses will get along with one another."

"That doesn't make any sense."

"Does to me."

"You're saying—?"

"I'm sayin'...if I don't get along with the bunch I'll be driving, then I reckon I ain't driving 'em...simple as that." Darrell rested his gaze on the sturdy-looking Conestoga that occupied the area at the side of the main house. The canvas sides had been tied up, revealing the items that were stored inside. "That the Conestoga they'll be pulling?"

"Sure is. It's loaded with furniture and things that the wife seems to think she just can't do without. There's a schooner right behind it that'll be carrying me and my family."

The youngster nodded his understanding. He then reached back and latched onto the tail end of the dirty blue handkerchief that hung from his right hip pocket. He pulled it and wiped the sweat from his brow, pushing the shapeless hat even further back on his head in the process. "I wanna meet the horses," he said matter-of-factly. He adjusted the hat for a better fit before replacing the handkerchief.

"Never heard it put quite like that before. Folks generally say they'd like to *see* the horses."

"That's most likely because they don't know no better. I figger horses are about the same as regular folks are. Some are alright and some aren't. Reckon they all got their own fool notions to deal with."

Sam liked what he was hearing. There seemed to be a simpleminded freshness about this youngster that was setting real good way down deep inside. "You think you can handle that big of a wagon with a six-up pulling it?"

"Yep! Long as they like me an' I like 'em right back."

Sam grinned at the straightforwardness of the fella. "You say you want to see the horses, huh?"

"What I said was...I wanna *meet* the horses. But I reckon I'll meet 'em when I see 'em."

"Well, c'mon then."

Darrell lagged a bit behind, keeping his gaze intent on the animals as he and Sam approached the corral. He caught up and asked, "Can I have my pick?"

"Uh...sure. I don't see why not, doesn't make any difference to me. I like them all. Picked 'em out myself," Sam added proudly.

They reached the corral fence and the lanky youngster stooped his way between the bottom two rails. "Did you ask any of 'em if they wanted to make the trip?" he asked as he patted the rump of the nearest of the animals.

"Eh...well, no...I reckon I didn't. You think that should be a consideration, do you?"

The youngster glanced back over his shoulder. "Could be," he said simply. He then began meandering in amongst the animals for a closer look.

He spent the next few minutes wandering in and out between the animals, patting rumps, pulling up lips, checking front teeth and running a hand down a foreleg whenever the notion struck him. He would occasionally raise one to examine the condition of the business side of the hoof. On one occasion, he used a fingernail to pluck out a small stone that had been lodged.

A puzzled look came into Sam's eyes when the grading of the horses didn't stop there. The furrows deepened across his brow as he watched the kid talking softly to each of the animals in turn. Sam was too far away to hear exactly what he was saying but he was amazed to see each horse react in its own way. Some would bob their head, while others would shake theirs. Still others would wiggle an ear or maybe flutter their lips with a rush of air. Some would even paw at the ground. He was spellbound by what he was seeing and was feeling mighty stupid even considering what he was thinking.

Finally, the talking done, the youngster patted one last rump and climbed his way back between the rails. He then placed a booted foot on the bottom rail, and while continuing to look at the animals, said, "Good bunch of horseflesh you picked out."

"I already know that, but do they like you?"

"Some do. Some don't."

"Do enough of them like you to make up a team?"

"Yep, sure do. Reckon I'll take both of those two bays, the one over there with the blaze on her face," he pointed at the one he meant, "and that one with the stocking on her left front." He pointed that one out also. "That big chestnut, the good-sized sorrel and that other sorrel." He had continued to point out each of them as he spoke.

"That's only five," Sam reminded him.

"Yeah, I know. I'm still thinking on the last one."

Sam waited for the youngster to come up with his final pick. It was quick in coming.

"Okay…against my better judgment, I'll hitch up that gray mare over yonder." He indicated the mare with a jutting of his chin.

"Why are you thinking it's against your better judgment?"

"Well, I figure she's a real good mare…might even be the best of the lot, but she's in foal."

Sam had no idea the mare was in foal and was therefore taken completely by surprise. "What? How do you know that?"

"She just told me. But she peers like she has a genuine hankerin' to make the trip and I reckon that's good enough for me."

"So, you think she'll be able to make the trip okay?"

"Yeah, she'll do fine. She's still got a good ways to go before there's anything to worry about. She's strong an' will handle the trail alright enough."

"Okay. I reckon if you think she can do it, then I'm willing to go along."

"She'll make out," Darrel assured him with finality. With that, he turned and headed for the main house.

Sam was feeling more than just a little befuddled as he raised his hat by holding the brim between a thumb and index finger. After scratching his scalp with the three remaining fingers, he replaced the hat and watched the youngster as he continued to walk away.

Sam wondered at the boy's sincerity as he followed him. There was nothing to indicate that the youngster was trying to get his goat, but it was just a mite hard for a full grown man, with even so much as even a single speck of common sense about him, to buy into the fact that a fella could not only talk to horses, but would even want to.

Sam quickened his pace. "Those horses tell you anything else?" he asked, after catching up with him just short of the prairie schooner.

"Yep."

Sam wondered what that might have been while the youngster passed by the schooner and stopped at the Conestoga. He then took his sweet time checking over the wagon, being meticulous in his inspection of its condition.

⚘

The Conestoga wagon was first developed back in Pennsylvania as a freight hauler. It was especially suited for travel over bad roads and had a load capacity of up to six tons or so. The floor curved up slightly at each end to help prevent its contents from shifting around inside. It was an ideal selection for hauling the Bartlett's furniture.

⚘

"Looks to be in pretty good shape," Darrell said after completing his walk around by giving the final wheel a real good shaking. "Believe I'll take on the job if you're of a mind," he said, stating what Sam figured he already knew.

"Yeah, I'm of a mind. Now...what about wages?" Sam eyed the boy suspiciously, expecting the worst. "How much do you figure the trek's worth?"

"I figger we'll decide on that once we get to where it is we're going. I'm wanting to make the trip anyway, so I'm thinking you're doing me about as much of a favor as I'm doing for you. I ain't one to be robbing folks what are doing me a favor."

That made good sense to Sam and he stuck out his hand to seal the bargain. "Sounds like we have us a deal then," he said and smiled at his new driver. "So, what do you prefer folks call you?" Sam asked as the youngster accepted the offered hand.

"Well...I reckon most folks have kinda latched onto calling

me Stretch."

"Seems fittin' enough. You can call me Sam."

"Well now, who's this? I thought I heard you talking to someone out here."

Stretch quickly snatched the hat off his head and flushed a light shade of red as the sudden appearance of what was most likely Sam's missus had taken him by surprise.

"Oh...hello sweetheart." Sam extended a palm out toward Darrell. "This is Stretch. He's agreed to drive the Conestoga for us."

"Pleased to meet you, Mister...ahh...Stretch." She extended her hand and waited for the inexplicably nervous young man to accept it.

"I-I, ahh..." He timidly reached out and managed to make contact with her hand by barely touching the fingertips.

"Not much of a handshake if you ask me," she said and glanced Sam's way before returning her attention to Stretch.

"Best I can do, ma'am...under the circumstances," he responded and nervously worked the brim of the hat between the fingers of both hands as he cast his eyes toward the ground.

"And just what kind of circumstances might those be?"

Still keeping his gaze lowered, he continued to fidget with the hat before answering, "Well...eh...ma'am...it's just that...well...what with you being a female an' all—"

"That's what I thought." She looked at Sam. "Are you gentlemen just about finished with your business out here?"

"Yeah, pretty much."

"Good. Supper's real close to being put on the table and you, Stretch, are going to accept my invitation to stay and help us eat it."

"But, I—"

"But, nothing! You come along now and wash up!" She unexpectedly sided up to the terror-stricken youngster and hooked her left wrist around his right elbow. She lifted the front of her dress with her other hand so it just cleared the ground and repeated the command. "Come on now," she said and tugged gently on his arm.

It seemed to Sam that the poor kid was a prime candidate for heart failure. The terror that shown in his eyes was proof enough that he was being subjected to way more abuse than any fella should reasonably ever be asked to endure.

Sam remained behind and grinned as Jay towed Stretch toward the front of the house. They stopped by the door and she unhooked her wrist. Sam continued to look on as she pointed out the pitcher of water and washbasin that rested on the shelf next to the doorway. She then disappeared inside to finish preparing the meal.

Sam covered the distance to the washing shelf. He remained silent as he stood next to Stretch and washed his hands and face in the tepid water. After drying with the towel provided, he handed it to the boy and locked his gaze on the youngster's eyes. "You have a little trouble around women, do you?"

"You might say that. Never did have no call to be friendly with one of 'em, and—"

"Well...you might as well get used to it. In case you haven't already figured it out, Jay's a friendly sort and I can't imagine you being able to avoid her the entire trip."

Stretch plopped the towel onto the shelf and sighed heavily. "Yeah...I know. Reckon I might as well go get me another dose of her," he said, before pulling his hat and running a pitchfork of fingers through his tangled hair.

They entered the house where Stretch right away spotted little Tom with his arms wrapped around Jay's leg. "You didn't tell me you had a boy," he said, with a measure of delight that sent a genuine smile spreading across his face. "Now *boys* I ain't got a problem with." He hung his hat and coat on one of the wall-pegs that lined an area by the door, and squatted down to Tom's level.

Tom, being none too bashful around strangers, unlatched himself from Jay's leg and edged his way over to see who this new person was. As Sam looked on approvingly, and Jay went about completing the task of getting the meal laid out on the table, Stretch and Tom did their best to become friends. They seemed to hit it off real good. They talked and played with some of Tom's toys until Jay announced that supper was indeed ready.

"You two need to put those toys away. The food's on the table and it's time to eat it."

The toys were placed back into the box where they'd been packed away for the trip. Once that little chore was completed, Stretch reluctantly approached the table, his nervousness beginning to return.

Sam indicated the chair to his left with a pointing finger. "You sit there."

Stretch took the indicated seat and waited for the others to get settled in.

Jay put Tom in his usual spot and sat down opposite Sam.

"Lord..." Sam began.

Stretch quickly placed his hands in his lap and bowed his head.

"...tomorrow is a very special day for us as we set out in search of our new home in this vast land You've created. Father, I ask that You watch over us and protect us while we travel." Sam paused as Tom began banging his spoon on the tabletop.

Jay reached over, took it from him, and gently patted her son on the top of his head.

Sam continued with the grace, "And Lord, be merciful in Your dealings with us and help us to make the right choices and decisions. And finally, Father, I thank You for this food that You have provided and for the wife that fixed it. Oh yeah...and thanks for this skinny youngster You sent us to drive the Conestoga, and who, from the looks of him, surely needs to eat it…amen."

Stretch was obviously unsettled as he cleared his throat in nervous discomfort.

Sam took notice and asked, "You ain't much of a Christian are you?"

"Well…eh…no, I reckon I ain't," he replied, while shoveling a pretty good helping of mashed potatoes onto his plate.

"There's no reason to feel embarrassed about it. All it takes is a little desire to become one. Heck, who knows? It could happen when you least expect it." Sam glanced at Jay and caught her nearly imperceptible nod and accompanying slight grin. He returned his attention to Stretch who had wasted little time and had by then stuffed his mouth about as full of mashed potatoes as was humanly possible.

Stretch chewed the mixture with a necessary, exaggerated effort while he raised the spoon up in front of his face, and nodded. Finally, after managing to swallow just enough to leave room for a sensible response, said, "Might could, I reckon." He swallowed again. "But right about now I'd say it'd be a whole lot more sensible to say that I'm way more interested in doing justice to these here vittles. I reckon, if it's all the same to you," he gestured with the spoon, "I could use me some of that fried chicken what's stacked up on that plate over there."

❧Chapter 4❧

Sam reined his team to a halt right alongside the Conestoga. He stomped his boot against the brake handle, wrapped the bundle of reins into a half hitch around the same handle, waved a greeting to Stretch, and climbed down. "Morning, Stretch! How'd you sleep?"

"Slept just fine, thanks! Looks like it's gonna be a dandy of a day to hit the trail!" He inhaled deeply of the cool morning freshness. "I surely do appreciate me a fine morning," he added and tipped his hat to Jay. "Morning, Mrs. Bartlett. That young'un still sawin' 'em off?"

"Good morning, Stretch…and yes, Tom's still sleeping."

"I expect he'll be awake soon enough. In fact just about any time now, I'd say." He pointed. "Looks like Heck's coming."

Heck reined up a short distance from the pair of Bartlett wagons and quickly sent word out for all drivers to assemble for a short meeting. Sam passed the word on to the family in the wagon next to them and waited for the fella to pass it on to the folks in the next wagon. Sam then fell in step with him as the two of them, along with Stretch, headed for the spot that had been designated for the driver's meeting.

"Morning. My name's Sam...Sam Bartlett. This here's Darrell Henderson. We call him Stretch."

Pleased ta meet cha, Sam. Name's Kyle Hendricks." He nodded in Stretch's direction. "Howdy, Stretch. Me 'n the missus an' young'uns is happy ta make yer acquaintance...the both a ya in fact."

Sam wondered at the man's drawl. "You aren't from around here, are you?" he asked.

"Nope. Me an' mine hail from the Smoky Mountain hills a Tennessee. Been sittin' here nigh onta two weeks now just a lollygaggin' an' waitin' fer the next train ta form up. We been itchin' ta mosey, but just naturally figgered it'd be best ta wait for more folks ta join up with afore we lit out."

"That was most likely a smart decision on your part. I've been hearing stories about Mexican bandits robbing folks along the trail and would think a wagon out there on its own would be easy pickings."

"Yup. That's about the same way I had it figgered my ownself."

They arrived at the gathering and Sam made eye contact with the wagonmaster. He and Heck exchanged slight nods in greeting.

Presently, it seemed that just about everyone had arrived and Heck commenced to saying his piece, "I called all of you together before we get started to let you know what some of my rules are."

He waited for the murmuring to die down.

"I can see from the reaction that some a you ain't particular fond of rules."

Again the murmurs made the rounds. He held up a hand until things again quieted down.

"Well, fond of 'em or not ain't the issue here. I got more'n just a hatful of 'em and you're about to get 'em as well. So just keep yourselves simmered down and let me make 'em clear to the bunch of you before someone here goes off halfcocked."

He paused to suck in a needed helping of air before continuing, "I reckon it goes without sayin' that we got us a long an' hard trip facing us square, about five or six weeks, I'd say. There's most likely gonna be times when there'll be some dangers lurking around and about. And I'm of a mind that some of 'em will be of the mortal variety if we ain't mindful."

This time the murmuring lasted a good while but eventually died down on its own.

"When something unfavorable like that happens, I'll be ordering you to circle up. Course I know some a you ain't got the foggiest notion what that means, but you will shortly. Right after we get strung out on the trail, we'll be practicing making a circle. That way when we need to do it for real you'll have a pretty good idea about what's going on. Any questions?"

No one spoke up loud and a clear but Sam heard a couple of mumbles. He glanced around in an effort to see who might be the ones that could be of a hardheaded nature. However, despite those efforts, he was unable to put a finger on anyone in particular. He returned his attention to Heck.

"We'll also be circling up each time we stop for the night. The horses'll all be kept inside the perimeter...as well as the humans. If someone needs to leave the confines during the dark hours of the night, I'm issuing orders right here 'n now that that person will hafta let someone else know where he's headed and when he expects to make it back. Is that clear?"

A fella of about thirty or so stepped forward and hooked his thumbs into the top edge of his belt. "Does that mean that when a fella needs to go off and find a bush, he needs to be letting the whole world know about it?"

"That's exactly what it means, that or any other reason. An' that goes for every single man, woman, or young-un that's a member of this train. Don't none of you make the mistake of taking this none too lightly. We got chances of meeting up with them Mexican hombres what's been robbing folks out there, plus the fact that some of the Injuns has been getting riled lately because of all the white men what's been squattin' on their land."

He eyed the group of concerned faces before continuing, "Once we get far enough away from Independence and out into what I consider the wilds, we'll be posting guards every night when we stop. Each and ever' one of the men will be asked to take a turn now 'n then. That's all a part of being in a train and I'm saying right now that I ain't none too partial to hearing no grievin' about it, neither. If there's anyone here what isn't willing to do his fair share to protect the others..." he paused to look around at the circle of concerned faces, "then that fella better just call it quits right here 'n now and save himself a whole passel of trouble in the future. Is that making it clear enough to you?"

While Heck looked around, Sam did the same.

Sam's gaze settled on a group of three fellas who had scornful looks on their faces. He pulled his attention away from them as Heck continued.

"Okay, that's about all I gotta say for now. Just keep in mind that there can only be one man in charge of this whole shebang. I reckon it goes without sayin' that you folks hired me to be that man, so I'd appreciate it if I was to be given a free hand when it comes to doing what's necessary to give us the best chances of making a successful crossing."

After a short pause, he continued, "With that in mind, we're gonna string these wagons out now and I'm gonna be the one to assign positions in line. Now, I know that some of you may or may not cotton to who I put you next to while we're on the trail, but just trust me that I know what I'm doing. If you're patient enough, it'll come clear to you after we've been on the trail for a spell." He then took one last gander around the circle of faces. "Okay...as long as there ain't no other questions what needs answering, I'd say you all best be getting on back to your families and listen up for my instructions."

The group was anxious to get on the trail and dispersed quickly. After returning to their respective wagon, Sam and Stretch made a final check of their harnesses and climbed onto the seats to await Heck's orders.

"Sam," Jay said softly, as she placed a hand on his forearm.

He looked into her eyes. "Yeah."

"Pray for us, please."

"Sure."

Sam looked over and spied Stretch sitting aloft on the front seat of the Conestoga. "Stretch!" he called above the noises of the wagons that were now closing in all around them. "Come on over here for a second!"

"Yes, sir!" Stretch hollered back, and after securing the reins around the brake handle, climbed down. When he had reached the side of Sam's wagon, Sam looked down and said, "Jay here asked me to say a prayer before we get started. I figured you might want to be a part of that."

"Sure, why not. I reckon it couldn't hurt none...long as you ain't asking me to be the one doing the prayin'."

Sam grinned, figuring he'd be working on the youngster soon enough to get that way of thinking out of his head.

They all bowed their heads as they waited for Sam to begin. "Dear Father, before You sits three low-down sinners. We thank You for all You've done for us and pray that You'll watch over us as we start our journey into the vast unknown. Bless us, Lord, and keep Your protective hand on us. Help us to be better witnesses for You. And Father, I ask a special prayer for Stretch Henderson here." Sam took a sideways peek at the youngster and saw him fidget a mite. "Father, help him to drive that big old wagon like he had at least a speck of God-given good sense about him. In Jesus name I pray... amen."

Before Sam could say anything to him, Stretch had already

whirled on the balls of his feet and was headed back to the Conestoga. As Sam and Jay looked on, they saw him brush a sleeve across his eyes.

"He'll be under conviction real soon," Jay said softly.

"Yeah, I know," Sam replied. "Might already be. That boy's in for the surprise of his life once he realizes what he's been missing and accepts the Lord Jesus into his life."

Heck directed Sam and Stretch into line, positioning the Conestoga directly behind the schooner. They were near the middle of the formation, which suited Sam just fine.

Once everyone had been assigned their place in line, Heck made one last ride the length of the train and counted the number they were heading out with. Satisfied that all twenty-three wagons were present, he returned to the front, reined to a halt, and sat with his horse facing forward and his back to the formation. He sat there for a good moment or two before pulling his hat and bowing his head. It was plain to all that could see him that he was saying a prayer of his own. Once he had finished, he replaced the hat, and hipped around in the saddle. He took a moment or two to survey the sight behind him before raising his left arm high above his head.

Sam could clearly see Heck's figure a ways off in the distance and waited for the expected signal that would start the line of wagons snaking its way westward.

Finally, the arm came down in a forward motion, and at the same time the order was given, loud and clear, "Let's move 'em *owwuut!*"

As the lead wagons started rolling, the sounds of snapping reins and creaking wheels began filling the air as one by one the teams of horses were reined, coaxed, and whistled into motion.

Sam's own team was prancing and tossing their heads in anticipation of what was to come. Finally, the wagon in front of him pulled away and it was his turn. He turned to look into Jay's eyes and smiled as he said, with heartfelt tenderness, "I surely do love you, Mrs. Bartlett."

He lifted the reins above the backs of the team and quickly brought them down in a snapping motion. "Hup! Hup! Get up there!" he commanded and gave the team its head as the wagon lurched forward.

❧Chapter 5❧

Nearly all of the drivers had at least a passable understanding of how to handle a team. There were, however, a few who had little or no real familiarity with taking part in a wagon train. So, for the first few hours they found themselves engrossed in settling their teams into the proper pace, keeping the wagons in a respectable line, and in general just learning the tricks of the trade...so to speak.

The train had done its practice circle just as Heck had promised it would, and that had gone all right...well, sort of anyway. The enclosure hadn't been made near big enough with the result being three of the wagons were left outside the perimeter.

Heck, being a patient sort, had taken the opportunity to call the drivers together for a short meeting. He sat atop his horse in the center of the sorry excuse of what he had hoped for and surveyed the gathering around him. "Well, you fellas—"

A female voice sounded from the back of the gathering. "And ladies!"

"And ladies...excuse me, ma'am." He acknowledged the

female driver by touching an index finger against the folded up front of his hat before continuing, "You can all no doubt see we kinda missed the mark on our first try."

The mumbling and nodding started up and lasted until Heck raised a hand. Once he again had their attention, he continued, "But I'm of a mind that we done good...considerin'."

"Considerin' what?" The question came from the fella at Sam's immediate left. Sam looked his way and saw a grizzled oldtimer with a hawk-like nose and a sun-drenched leathery complexion. He was dressed in buckskin from head to toe. Well, leastways from neck to toe, the exception being his hat. It was fashioned from the hide of a raccoon with the tail still attached and hanging down the back. "Peers ta me..." He tongued the chaw over to the other side of his mouth. "Peers ta me we ain't near come close. Peers ta me..." he looked around at the faces, "we could use someone up front what knows what it takes ta make a respectable circle."

"You saying you're that person?" Heck asked the oldtimer.

"Yep," he replied simply.

Heck eyed the man. "Okay, eh...Mister C, is it?"

"Yep...that it is."

"That being the case, Mister C, you move your wagon on up to the front." Heck glanced around the gathering before continuing, "When we make our circle for the night, you all just do your best to follow the wagon directly in front a you. If it works out that we fall short again, like we just did, don't fret none about it. Just pull the leftover wagons along the outside and double up around the perimeter. Fact is, sometimes that's the best way anyways."

"Why's that?" came the same female voice.

"Cuz thataway the Injuns cain't get inside so easy," Mr. C said and spit into the buffalo grass at his feet.

"Ohh," she said softly, with a trace of uneasiness.

After the opinions concerning Mr. C's view of things had

died down, Heck continued with his instructions, "We'll be pulling out again real soon, but first I want to let you all know that we'll be stopping in a couple of hours for eating. If the terrain and trail allow it, we'll draw up three lines abreast instead of staying in one long one. That way we'll be a sight closer to one another an' will stand a way better chance of defending the train if something untoward shows itself. Anyone here passable with number figuring?" He twisted around in the saddle and began looking the group over.

Stretch raised his hand.

"Okay, Stretch. Clear yourself a spot in the dirt for figgerin' and pay attention real close." Heck turned back to the main group of faces while Stretch used a palm to smooth out the dirt in a bare spot. "We got us twenty-three wagons in this train. I want three lines bein' equal in length. How many does that put in each line?" Although he was looking around at the faces in the group, he was obviously addressing Stretch.

Stretch right away went to figuring. He started drawing some numbers in the smoothed out patch, but before he could come up with the exact proper answer, Sam whispered to him, "Eight, eight, and seven."

"Eight in the first line, eight in the second, and seven in the third!" Stretch announced proudly, and nodded his thanks to Sam.

"Alright then. Stretch...count me out which of the wagons will be leading each line and have them drivers stay here after the meeting. The rest of you will just follow the wagon what's directly in front of your own and that'll take care of things."

Stretch found out which of the wagons belonged to Mr. C and adjusted his count accordingly. He then put that wagon up to the front and skipped it in his count as he set about figuring out the other two lead wagons. After he had pointed out the number nine and number seventeen wagons, those two drivers were asked to remain behind while the rest of the drivers went back to the train and prepared to resume the journey.

Sam introduced himself to Mr. C as they were returning to their wagons, "My name's Sam Bartlett." He extended a hand and waited for a reply.

"Name's Cottonwood Charlie. Pleased ta make yer acquaintance." The oldtimer accepted the offered hand.

Sam liked the feel of the man's handshake, as well as the neighborly look in his eye. "You've been on these trains before, am I right?"

"Yep. Went on one up ta Or'gun once but didn't much like it. Came back last year and decided ta try the Santa Fe Trail. Kinda like me a dryer climate...if ya get my drift."

Sam nodded his understanding. He had heard stories about how wet and stormy it was up there in the northwest. "So, you figure on settling down at the end of this trail, or what?"

"Or what is all. I ain't completely decided yet, an' most likely won't know 'til I see what's at the other end." Charlie spit and adjusted the coonhide hat for a better fit. "Just depends," he added as an afterthought, and continued walking right on past once they had reached Sam's wagon.

"Who was that?" Jay asked, as she watched the bowlegged figure continue toward the front of the line.

"That, my dear, was Cottonwood Charlie," Sam said and climbed up onto the seat. He lifted young Tom onto his lap and cradled the boy to him.

"Is he as colorful as he looks?" she asked.

"That and then some I'd say," Sam replied as they watched the man continue on his way.

Stretch had remained behind in case Heck had a need for anymore number figuring. Once the meeting with the line leaders had broken up, he returned to the Conestoga and climbed aboard. He tossed a two-fingered salute and a smile to Sam in the process.

Sam returned the gesture and waited for things to get

underway again. It took another couple of minutes for everything to get settled, during which time Sam enjoyed the company of his son. Once the lead wagons started moving, he handed the boy to Jay, took up the reins, and weaved them through his fingers. When it was his turn, he snapped the reins along the horse's backs, urged them forward with a "Get up there!" and the wagon again lurched forward into the unknown.

☙

As the morning dragged on, Sam found himself faced with more than his fair share of problems keeping the team on task. Oh, they pulled the schooner all right, but he was forever having to prod and correct them. It was certainly a trying and tiring morning for him and it passed not without taking its toll on his disposition. Plain and simple, he was getting cranky.

With the blazing sun approaching straight up overhead, Heck came riding down the line and announced a short break for eating the noonday meal. Sam was understandably relieved that he would soon be getting a break from the strife of dealing with what was turning out to be a headstrong team.

The arrangements that had been made for the line leaders to lead each of their sections into a three-abreast formation went off without a hitch...so to speak. Sam and Stretch were in the second section, and Sam dutifully followed the wagon in front of him until they slowly reined to a halt. He kicked the brake handle forward and wrapped the handful of reins around it, again using the customary half hitch to secure the bundle of leather straps. He then sat calmly for a few seconds while he enjoyed the sudden contrast that was a welcomed and much needed respite.

"Tough morning?" Jay asked softly, and rested her hand on his forearm.

He sighed heavily. "Boy...that ain't the half of it. If I have to go through that day after day, I'm for turning back right now."

"Promise?" she asked, with a subtle glimmer of hope in her voice. She knew full well that he had no intention of turning back. So, instead of waiting for an answer, she gathered her dress and petticoats together in front of her and gave him a raised-eyebrow questioning look as if to say, "Well, are you going to help me down or what?"

"Oh...eh, yeah. Sorry, honey. Wait just a second and I'll help you down." He hurriedly got down and scurried around the rear of the wagon. Once he had reached the other side, he guided her feet as she made her way down onto safe ground.

"Why don't you go let down the tailgate and set out that box of lunch items?" she suggested, and after placing the flats of both hands against the small of her back, began to stretch out the kinks as best she could.

Tom had been asleep on the folded-over mattress they had arranged in the bottom of the wagon. He'd been jolted awake when the wagon stopped jostling him and was already peering around the front end of the canvas covering. "Wanna eat, mama," he said sleepily, and rubbed his eyes with both fists balled tightly.

"It's coming, son," she promised, as she unsuccessfully tried to smooth some loose strands of hair back into their rightful places.

Just then, Stretch approached the rear of the wagon. "Nice easy morning, wasn't it?" he said to Sam.

Sam bit his tongue and ignored the question while he proceeded to let down the tailgate. He slid the lunchbox back to the edge of the gate and held his arms out toward his son who had by then worked his way toward the rear of the wagon. "Come here, Tom."

The boy stumbled and fell over a few of the things that remained stacked in the way. After a concerted effort, he finally managed to make it to his pa's outstretched arms. Sam lifted him down, and after watching him go off to play with a stick he'd found lying at his feet, he turned to face Stretch. "If you had yourself an easy morning of it I'm real happy for you." He hooked his thumbs in the top edge of his belt and heaved a good-sized sigh. "My morning wasn't anywhere near enjoyable."

Stretch was genuinely concerned. "Why's that?"

"Well, to tell you the truth, I don't rightly know. There's just something about this team that makes it near impossible to get them to work together. It's like...well...like they aren't liking one another, or something. It's real hard to put a finger on, but I'm of a mind that something just isn't right."

"Mind if I have a look at what the problem might be?"

"No...go right ahead. Help yourself." He held an inviting palm face up out toward the team. "Might even be that they'll just come right out and tell you what the problem is," Sam suggested, with an obvious measure of sarcasm mixed in.

Stretch elected to ignore what he saw as skepticism. "Never can tell. They just might," he said from behind a broad grin, and headed off toward the team.

Sam busied himself with helping Jay rustle up some lunch. Once it had been portioned out, he took a plate for himself and one for Tom. Nearly exhausted, he gratefully slid down along the shaded side of the wagon with his back against a wheel. He coaxed the boy to him. "Come on over here, Tom...time to eat." Tom didn't need anymore prodding than that. He dropped the stick and scurried over to where his pa was. The two sat side by side in the grass and waited for Jay and Stretch to join them.

After Jay had lowered herself alongside Tom, Sam called out to Stretch, "You about ready to eat?"

"Yep. Fact is I am...I truly am," came the eager reply. Stretch left the team and finding his plate of food on the tailgate, snatched it up. He squatted beside Sam on the side opposite Mrs. Bartlett and eagerly grabbed up a piece of the cold leftover chicken from their supper the night before.

Sam purposely cleared his throat, "Ahhmmm!"

"Oh yeah, I forgot," Stretch admitted and let the drumstick fall onto the plate. He licked his fingers and removed his hat before placing the plate down in the grass beside him.

Sam said a grace that asked not only for a blessing on the food but an answer to the problem with the team as well. He also prayed for a better deposition so he would be able to remain calm when the horses tested his patience. After saying their amens, they dug into the chicken and biscuits the Lord had provided.

"You figure out what the problem is with those knotheads?" Sam asked, while gnawing on a wing.

"Yep." Stretch was busy with a mouthful of his own and didn't say anything more.

Sam eyed the youngster and could easily see that he wasn't anywhere near slowing down on his eating. "Well, what is it?"

Stretch motioned toward the team with the piece of chicken and swallowed hard, making room for some words. "Tell you in a minute or two...soon as I fill up the bottom of this empty spot I got in my belly." With that said, he chewed off another bite and followed it with nearly half a biscuit.

Sam decided it wouldn't do much good to hurry the youngster along so he ate in silence and waited for the news...good or bad. What was amazing to him was that Stretch could put away food the way he did and still be as skinny as a fencepost. "You always eat like that?" he asked, a teasing smile crossing his face.

"Yep...'specially when I'm hungry...like now." He turned slightly to face Jay. "Sure are a good cook, ma'am," he said, while punctuating the words by waving the chicken leg in the air between them.

"Why thank you, Stretch, but I think you'd be willing to eat anything right about now."

"Now that's a true fact," he said happily, and shoved in what remained of the biscuit.

Once things had slowed down, and it could safely be said that Stretch had finally gotten the bottom of that empty spot filled, Sam tried again, "So what did you figure out about that team?"

"It's really pretty simple." Stretch laid his plate in the grass and patted his stomach. "I think I'll live now," he said contentedly, and smiled his thanks to Jay. He then turned his full attention on Sam. "You were exactly right. The trouble's that the two you got leading ain't liking one another."

He paused to let that register while he lowered himself down onto one elbow. "My suggestion would be to leave the bay on the left front but move the sorrel to the left rear, switching her with the brown gelding. That way they'll be away from each other and not even able to see one another." He pulled a blade of grass and started to use it as a pick for his teeth. "That'll solve your problem," he said simply.

Sam was not entirely sure that the solution could be as simple as that. "That's it? Just rearrange those two?"

Stretch lay back in the grass and locked his fingers together behind his neck. "Yep. Wake me when it's time to head out."

Sam wasn't quite done with the problem solving, and felt the need to dig a little deeper. "So, how'd you figure out the answer...ask the horses?" he asked sarcastically.

"You don't wanna know."

Sam took care of rearranging the sorrel and the brown. Once he had finished, he found a comfortable spot against a rear wheel. The sun had passed straight up just enough to afford a sliver of shade along that side of the wagon. He propped his back against the wheel and stacked his forearms on his drawn up knees. He rested his forehead on his arms and let his eyelids fall for a bit of much-needed shuteye. About two seconds after they had blinked shut he was forced to deal with the realities of being on the trail.

"Okay! That's it! Time to hit the trail!"

Sam begrudgingly accepted his fate and rose. He readied

himself before resuming the confrontation with the bullheaded team by looking toward heaven and again asking the Lord to give him the needed strength to get through the rest of the day. He then hefted Tom up into the wagon and handed Jay up to her spot on the seat. Tom settled onto his spot on the mattress and Sam waved an acknowledgment to Stretch before climbing aboard.

The wagon ahead started rolling while Sam was unwinding the bundle of reins. He quickly wove them through his fingers and snapped them along the nearest pair of rumps. He was pleased to see the horses strain against the harness with no more than a "Git up now!" from him.

That turned out to be just the beginning of a very pleasant afternoon for Sam Bartlett. The team performed wonderfully and maintained their distance behind the wagon ahead with little or no prodding on his part.

"Seems to be going quite a bit better," Jay commented off-handedly.

"Yeah, yeah, I know. You don't need to say anything. I guess maybe that boy does know a thing or two about horses," he conceded.

Jay's grin indicated that she agreed with him completely.

The afternoon passed quickly. Jay spent the lion's share of the time in the bed of the wagon entertaining their son. Sam enjoyed listening to the sounds of their laughter and the turning of the wheels as he drove the team westward.

The clouds had turned from a grayish white to a mixture of brilliant orange and pink, and were just beginning to tinge purple when Heck called a halt. "Circle 'em up! Circle 'em up!" he hollered repeatedly, as he rode the length of the line while waving an arm high above his head in a circular motion.

The day's progress had ended and Sam was more than just a mite thankful. Even though the day had ended up being a whole lot more tolerable than it had begun, he remained nonetheless bone tired from their first day on the trail.

The circle was made, and none too soon to suit Sam. Cottonwood Charlie had known what he was talking about, and did a real good job of leading the forming of the enclosure. It turned out to be darned near perfect, and not a single wagon was relegated to the outside of the circle.

There were a few trees around and Sam and Stretch were able to collect enough dead wood to build a small cook fire. Sam tended to his team while Stretch got the fire going. After unhitching his own six-up, he busied himself with unhitching Stretch's team and was thankful when the youngster had completed his task and finally showed up to help.

"How'd it go with the team this afternoon?" Stretch asked and smiled a wry grin that most likely meant he already knew the answer.

"You really needing me to tell you, or are you just trying to rub it in?"

"Just rubbin' it in," he said, with a grin as he led the team away.

The evening meal was wonderful; Jay had outdone herself. Before they went to eating it, Sam asked the blessing and made it a special point to thank the Lord for the good day they'd had.

Shortly after most of the weary travelers had finished eating, a main bonfire was built near the center of the circle. Folks started gathering to discuss the day's progress and do some planning for the following day's journey. This was also the time when new folks were met and new friends were made.

As eager as Sam was to get over to the main fire, he instead shooed Stretch on over there and took the time to help Jay clean up after the meal and organize things in the wagon for the night's rest. Tom was plumb tuckered and hit the sack right after eating. It wasn't more than a minute or two before he'd dropped off and was sleeping soundly.

After Sam and Jay had finished their chores, and were

finally able to approach the circle of brightly lit faces, they saw that the conversation was indeed about the day's progress. Heck was talking and Sam sat down cross-legged next to Stretch, pulling Jay down beside him.

"I figure we done near fourteen mile today...give or take. Which ain't a record by any stretch, but it's surely a good ways."

"What cha figger we kin do on a average?" Sam looked in the direction of the question and saw the face of the fella from Tennessee that he'd met earlier that morning, but try as he might, he couldn't remember the fella's name.

"That all depends, Mister H," Heck said and spit toward the blaze.

The mention of the fella's initial sparked Sam's remembrance. *Hendricks...yeah, that's what it is,* he said to himself.

"On what?" Hendricks asked.

"On whether or not we get a rainstorm. On whether or not we get slowed by mud. On whether or not we get slowed by the heat. On whether or not we get slowed by the cold. What I'm sayin' is that there ain't no way of telling this time of year out here on the plains."

Heck looked around at the nodding heads before continuing, "You folks all need to realize that this time of year is a mite iffy along the Santa Fe. Why, one day could be just like it was today...all calm and peaceable like, then the next could blow up one of them twister fellas what can snatch a whole wagon clean up off the ground."

"That's a true enough fact right there," Cottonwood Charlie offered "I seen it afore with my own two eyes. Course I ain't never see'd a whole wagon picked up, but I see'd a cow go flyin' by once. And that's the God's truth, so help me Hannah."

No one disputed what was being said. Instead, the next fella tried his hand at telling an even bigger whopper.

And so went the evening. The yarn spinning and lie telling was some of the best Sam had ever heard. It went on for nearly an entire hour, until the fire was finally allowed to die down and folks said their goodnights before heading off to their respective wagons.

No guards were posted that night because of the wagon train's relatively close proximity to Independence. This however would be the only night for the remainder of the journey that guards would not be posted.

Sam and Jay said their goodnights to Stretch and left him sitting cross-legged in front of the fire's smoldering remains. They retired to the inside of the schooner where they undressed in the cool night air and hastily changed into their nightclothes.

Once they had gotten situated, and were nestled down for the night, Jay whispered to her husband, "Sam?"

"Yeah."

"I think I'm truly glad we decided to make this trip."

He smiled to himself. "Me, too."

She snuggled in as close as possible and laid an arm across his chest. He looked out through the opening to the rear and watched as a streak of light traced its way across the night sky. A gentle smile crossed his face, and he clasped her hand in his.

They both became lost in the togetherness of one another and the commitment needed to take on what they were facing.

They fell asleep with each of them wondering not only what the next day would bring, but also what would be in store for them once they finally reached the end of their journey.

❧Chapter 6❧

With the fourth day out from Independence being Sunday, and nearly three quarters of the travelers having a real need to trust in the Lord, they held a meeting that morning before hitting the trail. One of the men had given of himself and preached from the Bible on family living and loving thy neighbor. He had done a real good job, and folks were more than satisfied with his effort.

❧

The first week or so went well for the hardy souls in the wagons. There were the usual inconveniences: wheels needed greasing, horses needed shoeing, and children needed paddling. All in all, things were going along pretty much as expected.

The evening bonfires had already become a much-anticipated event to the members of the train. Of course, there were a few exceptions, but most folks looked forward to the enjoyment and fellowship of being around other families for that brief hour or so. On two separate occasions, the thunderstorms came and washed out the fire, sending everyone scurrying to the protection of their wagons. But overall, those get-togethers were a sought-after blessing.

Sam, Jay, and Stretch used the evenings of fellowship to get to know folks. There were the Appletons, George and Fay, from Virginia. They were a young newlywed couple who were heading for their first home. Then there was Harry and Agnes Carter, who had the wagon right in front of Sam's. They had a twelve-year-old son named Joshua who seemed to be more of a handful than a fella needed to have around him. Sam figured he was a good enough rascal, but just a little misguided was all.

In front of the Carters were Bill and Birdsong Hawkins. She was a full-blooded Comanche, and although folks had wondered about it, they hadn't asked Bill Hawkins how he'd ever come to marry an Indian. Bill was a fella that preferred wearing a buckskin shirt and britches. He also opted for moccasins on his feet rather than boots. He topped it all off with a floppy-brimmed buckskin hat with a feather trailing out the back on a short length of rawhide. He insisted that folks call him Wild Willie, as opposed to Bill.

Going back the other way in the train was a couple in the wagon right behind Stretch that were well into their forties. Mabel and Jacob Greenberg seemed to be happily married and had three teenage youngsters, two sons and a daughter. The boys were named Danny and Ronnie, ages fifteen and fourteen, respectively. The girl, Mary Jane, was the oldest and right about Stretch's age at seventeen. She was a pretty little filly and about as bashful as a seventeen-year-old could be, and that's saying something, considering how bashful Stretch was toward females.

What with her having been raised around two younger brothers you would think that she would have learned how to deal with the closeness of young men, but she hadn't.

Toward the end of the sixth day, the train halted at the banks of a tame-looking river that lay across their path. This being the first ford they would be making, Heck called a driver's meeting and went over the procedure for getting the wagons across safely. Once he felt confident that everyone was clear on the procedures he wanted to use, they returned to their wagons and prepared to make the crossing.

Although the waters of the slow-running river were barely high enough to tickle the underside of a tall horse's belly, Heck still insisted on having outriders on either side of Cottonwood Charlie's wagon with their ropes secured to the upriver side of the wagon for safety's sake.

Once Charlie had made the crossing without difficulty or mishap, and had driven his wagon up the far bank, a cheer went up amongst the remainder of the travelers and they began making the crossing, each in turn.

The fact that they were a ways back in the train gave Sam and Stretch ample time to check over their equipment and fill the water barrels that were lashed one on either side of the wagons.

Stretch eased the Conestoga down the bank and into the water just enough to facilitate easier filling of the barrels. He used a large cooking pot he had gotten from Jay as a dipping tool and had the job completed in about two shakes. Once he had finished, he tossed the pot into the back of the schooner and waded toward the front of the Conestoga.

Pausing to get a good handhold before pulling himself up, he glanced toward the bank and saw Mary Jane Greenberg standing with her back against a cottonwood watching his every move.

As soon as she saw that he had seen her, she blushed crimson, and hurried off toward her folk's wagon.

Stretch also turned a few shades of red and readjusted his hat to hide some of his discomfort. He then climbed aboard and waited his turn for the crossing. With his heart pounding heavily in his ears, he did, however, take the time to sneak a peek in the direction of the Greenberg wagon, but was disappointed when he didn't see her.

The outriders had latched onto Sam's wagon and were already steadying it across. Feeling braver than usual, Stretch twisted around in the seat and risked an all out look at the Greenberg wagon. This time he wasn't disappointed; Mary Jane was leaning out from her position in the back of their wagon and looking straight at him.

As soon as they spied one another, they both quickly jerked upright behind the protection the wagons afforded and looked straight ahead. Unbeknownst to the other, a broad smile was spread across each of their faces.

The outriders tied onto the Conestoga and Stretch told the horses that it was their turn to make the crossing. They responded favorably and crossed the river without any difficulties. Once up the far side he climbed down to watch the Greenbergs make the ford.

The two boys waded across, grateful for the opportunity to cool off in the stream. Mary Jane, on the other hand, elected to remain in the back of the wagon.

The crossing went well enough, but Stretch could tell by the body language of Mr. Greenberg's horses that there was a possible problem with the team. This became readily apparent when the right side lead mare reared up, displaying her displeasure with the whole thing. She settled back down after a few stern jerks on the rein from Mr. Greenberg, and the ford was completed without any further trouble.

Stretch watched as the team lunged their way up the steepest section of the bank. He decided to let Mr. Greenberg in on what he might do to fix his problem, so he approached the wagon as it came to a halt. "Ah…Mister Greenberg…sir?" Stretch pulled his hat and waited for the man to acknowledge him. At the same time, he was pleased to see Mary Jane stick her head around from the back of the wagon and look his way.

"Yeah, boy. What'dya want?"

"Well, sir, it's just that I wanted to tell you that I could see that coming a mile off."

"See what coming a mile off?"

"Why, that lead mare of yours, of course."

"What about her?"

"It's just that she doesn't have much of a hankerin' to be in the water and I'd switch her around so's she won't be able to rear up, if I was you."

"You saying you're some kinda expert when it comes to horses, are you?"

"No, sir, I'm not. It's just that—"

"Thanks for the advice, boy, but no thanks. That mare's been my favorite for a number of years now, and I'm thinking she'll do for a spell longer. Her rightful place is up front and that's where I'll be keeping her."

"Suit yourself. But I hope I don't get the chance to say I told you so when she causes you and yours some heartache." Stretch then tipped his hat to Mary Jane who had climbed out of the back of the wagon. "Ma'am," he said, as politely as he could in spite of the heated flush that had suddenly covered his cheeks. He then did the same to Mrs. Greenberg who was seated next to her husband. She smiled an acknowledgment and he turned and left for the Conestoga, thankful for the relief he was feeling as the flush on his face began to dissipate.

By the time the last of the wagons had made it across, it was late enough to circle for the night and Heck issued the orders. Guards were posted to walk the perimeter with instructions to remain just inside the circle's enclosure. The particulars of how the watches would be set up, as well as their duration, had been settled around the main fire after the first day's travel. Three men would be used at a time and were to keep watch for about two hours, when they would then be relieved by the next bunch, and so on until morning. Although this created a hardship for those who were called upon, it was something that needed doing and was generally accepted by everyone as part of their duties.

The only ones who seemed to have a problem with it were the same three that Sam had noticed with the scornful looks on their faces that first morning when Heck was dishing out his hatful of rules.

As it turned out, the three were a gent by the name of Noah Baxter, his oldest son, Wayman, and youngest, Rip. They were, it seemed, pretty much content to keep to themselves with little or no contact with the rest of the folks in the train. Oh, they'd speak whenever spoken to, but they were hardpressed to ever start up a conversation on their own.

Sam figured they just weren't the neighborly sort and decided to just leave them be.

A commotion had started up over in the vicinity of the Baxter wagon, which was right behind the Greenberg's. Sam and Stretch meandered over that way to see what the ruckus was all about. As they approached, it was easy to see that Noah appeared a mite upset about something.

"What'dya mean it's already my turn *again*? I just done a turn a couple of nights ago."

"Look, Mister B…" It was Heck doing the talking, and Sam could see he was doing his levelheaded best to keep from losing his temper with the man. "That was on our second night out from Independence, and since then every God-loving one of us has had a turn. Now we're startin' over again, and you're elected…and that's the end of it," he added with the fire starting to boil up behind his eyes.

"In the first place, Yellow…don't you be confusin' me with the likes of them Bible-thumpin' hypocrite friends a yourn. I ain't God-lovin' an' never will be. And that goes for my boys here, too." He gestured toward his sons with a wave. "And in the second place, it'll be the end of it when *I* say so." He struck a defiant pose by folding his arms across his chest and glaring scornfully into the eyes of the wagonmaster.

Heck stuck a finger in his ear and wiggled it vigorously. "Well, that being the case," he said as he removed the finger, looked at the end of it, and wiped it on his trousers leg. "That being the case, you'd best be deciding that this conversation is at an end, because about the next thing what's gonna happen is that I'm liable to forget that I'm a Christian and jump right in the middle of you."

"I figger that'd be a big mistake on your part, Yallow, because that'd rile my boys here and that'd give you a powerful lot to deal with." A confident smirk appeared on Baxter's face.

"That's not the way I see it," Sam said matter-of-factly. "No, sir, not at all. I figure I'm kinda partial to getting all the way to the end of this journey, and that means I'll be needing Heck here to do the leading. Keeping that in mind, I'll be taking his side in this, and I don't think I'll have any trouble at all whipping the daylights out of those two still-wet-behind-the-ears pups of yours."

As Noah started to reply, Sam raised a finger to his lips and said, "Shhh...I'm not quite finished yet. After sizing up these two boys of yours, I figure I could whip a whole corral full of fellas just like 'em and still manage to hold the gate closed with my other hand, if you know what I mean?" He then walked over next to Heck and looked straight into the now insecure expression that had invaded Baxter's face. "*Now* I'm finished. So, if you've got something else to say, say it. Or you can just go on and do what's expected of you and keep your trap shut."

Noah spun angrily on the balls of his feet and mumbled something unintelligible as he departed.

"Thanks, Mister B, but I coulda handled him my ownself," Heck said.

Sam remained silent. He was waiting for the two Baxter boys to decide if they wanted any part of him or not. Finally, they made the smart decision and followed after their pa. "That bunch could be trouble one of these days," he said softly, more to himself than anyone else.

❧Chapter 7❧

The next day marked the end of the first week on the trail. They had been averaging about fifteen miles a day and were right on schedule, as far as Heck was concerned. Water and good grass had been plentiful, and the animals remained in fine shape.

Late afternoon found the column approaching a river that was nowhere near as tame as the one they had forded the day before. This one was rain-swollen and running fast. After taking in the cloudless sky directly overhead, Heck figured there must have been a rainstorm somewhere upstream and the effects were just now reaching the part of the country where they were. He decided to call for a three-abreast formation so they could get together to think the situation over and decide on their next move.

Once the three lines of wagons had halted at the river's edge, Heck got all the members of the train together and patiently listened to suggestions and recommendations from anyone who wanted to have a say in the goings-on.

Right at first, the general feeling was to go ahead and try to ford across a wagon or two and see how it went. But the best alternative, at that point, was to wait a while to see if the swollen waters would subside. After a bit more discussion Sam came up with the idea of maybe sending out riders both north and south in search of a more passable crossing. He figured that with a little luck, they might find a place to ford that was of a shallower nature and therefore would surely be a bit more tolerable for the wagons to handle.

That seemed to be the most reasonable thing to try first, and it was decided on with just a couple of minor objections being voiced.

Heck asked for volunteers and settled on Wayman Baxter and another fella by the name of Jack Walker to do the scouting.

The pair quickly rode out.

Shortly after they had left, the circle was made and the camp settled down. The cooking fires were built up as they waited for the return of the two men.

After a couple of hours had passed, and just as the sun was giving it up for the day, Jack returned.

Sam motioned to Stretch and they followed him as he rode by, heading for the campfire Heck shared with Cottonwood Charlie.

They eased up to the conversation and squatted on their haunches as they listened to Walker's report. His assessment was that their chances weren't any better as far north as he had ridden, which was about two to two and a half miles, as best as he could figure.

Heck thanked Jack for his unselfish efforts and sent him off to get a bite to eat and rest up. The others stayed around the fire and talked about Jack's report while they waited for Wayman to return. It wasn't long before Noah showed up.

"That boy of mine get back yet?" he asked gruffly.

"No, he hasn't," Heck replied curtly.

"Well why not? That other fella come back already. Why ain't Wayman back yet?"

It was obvious to Sam that Heck was in no mood to listen to what this idiot Baxter had to say.

"Don't rightly know, Baxter. Maybe he's just sick and tired of hearing your mouth and decided to just keep right on a goin'."

"That ain't one bit funny, Yellow. I'm concerned about my boy, an' you ain't got no call to be belittlin' me because of it."

Heck softened noticeably. "Yeah, you're right. I'm just not in no mood for listening to you, is all. I've got problems of my own and am just as worried about your boy as you are. I don't know why he hasn't come back yet. But if it'll make you feel any better, you have my permission to head on out lookin' for him."

Noah nodded slowly, while giving the offer some thought. "Might just do that," he said pensively, and looked at the western sky. "There's about a half hour of daylight left. That'll be enough time for me an' Rip to progress a good ways. Yep, I believe that's just exactly what we'll do. Be back about a half hour or so after dark."

"Rip!" They heard him holler as he walked away.

ə

Wayman had ridden the better part of two miles without so much as a speck of good luck to speak of, as everywhere he tested was too deep and way too swift for just a horse and rider, let alone a whole passel of wagons. Not seeing any sense in going any farther, he had just made up his mind to head back to the wagons with the bad news and pulled his horse's head around. In doing so, he found himself face to face with four Indian braves sitting their ponies and blocking his way.

Where they'd come from he had no way of knowing, but that was the least of his worries. He knew enough about Indians to recognize these fellas as Comanche. He also knew he had no chance of outrunning them. That prompted him to take his next best option and he raised an open-palmed hand in a sign of peace.

"Howdy," he said.

The foursome was barely forty or fifty feet away and took only a few seconds to reach, then surround him. Amidst guttural sounds that were directed at one another, they began fingering his shirt, hat, saddle, saddle blanket, and just about anything else they had a mind to.

Wayman wasn't liking the way things were going and tried again to talk to them on the off chance that at least one of them spoke passable English. "I friend," he said and jabbed a thumb into his own chest. "Me come in peace. No want trouble." He surveyed the braves and realized that they had no guns that he could readily see. This gave him two options: either he could draw his pistol and try for all four of them, which wasn't likely to be successful, or he could make a run for the river at the first chance that came along.

"Shut face...White Eye!" one of the braves said bluntly. "You give horse to me." He indicated Wayman's mare with the business end of his tomahawk.

"But—"

"I tell you...*shut face!*"

The anger flared in the redskin's eyes and Wayman knew he'd best be doing what was being requested. He carefully eased from the back of the mare, keeping a wary eye on the fella all the while. Once on the ground he surveyed his chances and decided on a try for the river that was barely fifteen or twenty running paces away, and mostly downhill to boot.

His opportunity came right away as the Comanche angrily grabbed the bridle, which in turn caused the horse to rear.

Wayman bolted and took off in a dead run. He reached the river all in one piece and what with him being a real good swimmer, he didn't slow up none and dove headfirst into the swirling current. After sputtering his way to the surface, he started swimming as hard as he could.

The Comanches were just a split second behind him and waiting for him as soon as he surfaced. He rolled over onto his back for a look at his pursuers and almost immediately felt a searing pain hit him as a lance caught him in the fleshy part of his left thigh.

The pain was significant, but the current was indeed as swift as he had hoped and he was thankful for it as he remained on his back and clutched at the pain in his leg while he allowed the swirling torrent to carry him downstream. To his dismay, he saw that the Indians were riding along the edge of the bank, keeping pace with his movements. He forced the pain in his leg to the back of his consciousness, rolled over onto his belly and began swimming for the far side of the river.

Despite the agony it caused him, his efforts were soon rewarded and he approached the bank where he was eventually able to grab ahold of a tree branch that hovered out over the water's edge. He hung on with all the strength he had left in him and took a much-needed breather as he watched the Indians on the other side testing their intent by riding their ponies into the swiftly moving waters to about chest level on the animals before retreating up the bank. Finally, they gave up and rode up the bank one final time and out of sight.

Wayman figured he had his breath back well enough and released the branch. Instantly, he was again swept away. This time he was able to concentrate on making it all the way to the bank without worrying about anymore pursuing redskins.

The water was deep right up to the edge and he was unable to find the bottom with his feet. He could feel the current tugging at the lance that was still stuck in his leg. The water being as cold as it was rendered the leg numb. He was thankful for that because he felt very little pain to speak of as he bumped along the steep bank.

Finally, his feet made contact with solid ground and he grabbed onto a mesquite bush that leaned out over the water toward him. It scratched his face, but he was able to maintain his hold while he managed to work his exhausted body about halfway out of the river and onto the bank. He lay there for a couple of minutes and rested. Presently, he decided to deal with the injured leg and struggled the rest of the way out of the water and on up the bank. He rolled painfully onto his back and one-leggedly scooted backwards until he was able to prop himself against a handy tree trunk.

There was only a minimal amount of blood, but he knew that as soon as the cold effects of the river went away so would the numbness. That meant the pain would return and most likely the bleeding as well.

He continued to examine the wound and discovered that the tip of the lance was sticking clean through to the underside. That meant that it had missed the bone, and that meant there was a good possibility that he could pull it out. Of course, there was the option open to him of getting out his pocketknife and whittling the shaft off to a more manageable length, then try to make it back to the wagons, or…

The first option really didn't appeal to him much at all, but he figured it was the best way. He made up his mind, poked his index fingers between the edges of the hole in his trousers leg and pulled the tear even wider. He then took out his pocketknife and after a painful, concerted effort, managed to get the lance's shaft whittled off to where there was barely three or four inches sticking out. He then reached to the underside of his leg and took ahold of the business end of the lance with both hands. Not at all relishing what was to come, he paused to prepare himself.

Realizing that this was going to hurt more than just a mite, he figured he might not be able to maintain consciousness and could easily bleed to death if he fainted. He reached into his hip pocket, retrieved his handkerchief, and tied it as tightly as he could around the leg just above the wound. He then picked up a stout-looking stick, about an inch or so in diameter, and placed it securely between his teeth.

The beads of sweat popped out on his forehead as he again took ahold of the offending lance. He sucked in a deep breath and held it. He then made sure he had a good grasp on the shaft, clamped down on the stick, and yanked with all his might.

As the blackness closed in all around him, he fought to remain conscious while he continued to pull.

Finally, he felt the lance come free and fainted dead away.

Noah and Rip rode slowly along the river's edge. What daylight remained was fading fast, making it difficult to see the tracks. Noah was a good tracker, but was hardpressed to see the imprints. He hauled up, dismounted, and handed his rein to Rip. He walked slowly along the water's edge, allowing a closer inspection of the signs. Finally, the trail came to a spot where it seemed three or four other horses had approached.

He focused hard at this new development as he tried his best to recreate the scene, but had to admit that there just wasn't enough daylight left. He glanced around and spotted what he figured he needed. He walked over to some bushes and gathered a small bundle of sticks. He pulled his handkerchief and carefully wrapped it around one end of the bundle. He then reached into a pocket, found a match, and lit the crudely made torch.

The sticks were as dry as could be and because of that, the flame didn't last long. Nevertheless, even from just the brief illumination it had provided, Noah was able to piece together a good accounting of what had gone on here. While holding the torch close to the ground he studied the signs and was able to make out the prints of the unshod ponies as well as the boot marks where Wayman had dismounted and made a dash for the river.

The handkerchief quickly burned through and the

remnants fell to the ground. He tossed the smoldering sticks into the blackness of the swiftly moving current and stamped out the burning cloth at his feet. He made his way to the very edge of the river and quickly searched for any sign of Wayman's body. Finding nothing, he climbed the bank and accepted the rein from his son. "Looks like he made it to the river," he said to Rip, but more to himself.

Noah rested his gaze on the foreboding black expanse of water and realized the slimness of any chance of survival for anyone who might have tried to swim the raging torrent. He then mounted his mare and led the way as they resumed their slow-paced ride along the water's edge while calling softly into the descending night for any word from Wayman.

After about another quarter mile or so, they gave in to the futility of the circumstances and headed back to the wagons.

Little did either of them know that at the very point where they gave up the search Wayman was lying almost directly across the river, unconscious, but alive.

❧Chapter 8❧

Wayman awoke with a start. The pain in his leg was definitely less than he remembered it having been at any time during his waking moments all throughout the seemingly endless, miserable night.

The sky was a peaceful predawn gray, and there wasn't even so much as the hint of a morning breeze. A bullfrog sounded his unseen presence from a short distance away.

Wayman painfully propped himself up onto his left elbow and reached for the wound with his right hand, testing the tourniquet. He ran a finger under the handkerchief and was satisfied that it seemed to be just about the right tightness. The wound was wet with a minor amount of fresh blood, but nothing that caused him any undue concern.

He carefully worked himself up to a sitting position and tested the leg by trying to bend the knee. It was immediately apparent that that wasn't such a good idea. The knee refused to bend, and the pain intensified. He winced and fell back into the grass. Once the discomfort had subsided, he again struggled to a sitting position and propped his back against the base of the tree. He looked around and spotted the main part of the Comanche war lance laying a short distance away. He reached out and took ahold of it. The effort sent another pain shooting into the wound in his leg.

He knew that if he were to have any chance of making it back to the wagons, he'd best be figuring out a plan of action. With that in mind, he used the lance as a brace, and along with the sturdy assistance of the tree, slowly worked his way up the trunk to a standing position. He then gathered his courage and attempted a tentative step with the bad leg. It buckled and he collapsed in a heap. His head swirled as the blackness began to close in and threatened to consume him. Pain again shot through the leg. He gritted his teeth and whimpered helplessly.

Wayman knew he was in a bad way, but he also knew that he had to find a way to get back to the wagons. He glanced around and spied a spindly tree nearby that had branches suitable for fashioning one of those under arm crutches folks used when they were crippled. He slowly and with great effort began to drag himself toward it.

꙾

The dawning morning back at the circle of wagons remained filled with the same level of apprehension that had been a part of it the night before when Noah and Rip had returned. Noah had told them about finding the unshod pony tracks mixed in with those of Wayman's horse, and how it had looked as if he'd made a play for the river.

Heck decided that another trip to the spot was in order, so he, Noah, Rip, and Cottonwood Charlie headed out just before sunup.

As they rode along the riverbank, it was readily apparent that the waters had subsided significantly during the night. The level seemed to have lowered a good three feet or thereabouts. Heck felt a ford made later that morning was indeed possible, mainly because the swiftness of the current had also decreased proportionately, although, it was still far from what he would like to see for a guaranteed safe crossing.

The ride to the scene of the encounter was a relatively quick one because of not having to do any tracking. Once they arrived, Noah pointed out the different signs as he told the story of what he thought had gone on there.

Charlie, being a passable tracker himself and having more than just a time or two of past dealings with redskins, agreed with Noah's assessment. They mounted up and continued along the river's edge in hopes of finding any indications of where Wayman might have exited the water, if in fact he had managed to escape and was still alive.

They had traveled nearly another quarter of a mile when Heck spotted the figure on the opposite bank. "Well now," he said and drew rein. "Would you just look at that?" He pointed toward the lone figure hobbling along the opposite bank, leaning heavily on the forked stick he had propped under his armpit.

Wayman was relieved to see the rescuers and waved an appreciative greeting. He lowered himself to the grass and waited for them to figure a way across to his side of the river

୬

Heck rode into camp and let everyone know that they had managed to find Wayman and that although his leg was in a bad way, he would not die from the wound. He put them at ease by also letting them know that Noah, Rip, and Cottonwood Charlie were escorting him back along the opposite side of the river.

The apprehension disappeared as soon as Heck issued his orders, and the members of the train began packing up in preparation of making ready to begin the crossing.

Once the camp was broken and everything was packed away, the fires were extinguished and the teams hitched up to their respective wagons. There was no lack of volunteers to help with hitching up Charlie's and the Baxter teams.

Birdsong Hawkins would drive their wagon while Wild

Willie drove Charlie's rig. Jacob Greenberg took over the Baxter wagon, taking Mabel with him and turning his over to their son, Danny, who was quite capable. With all the wagons again manned, they proceeded to the river's edge, keeping the same order as before.

With the current still being a mite swifter than he would have liked, Heck instructed both outriders to be sure to stay to the upriver side of the wagons to better keep them on line against the force of the swiftly moving current.

Once they were in position, Wild Willie carefully drove Charlie's lead wagon down the embankment and into the water. As soon as the outriders had fastened their ropes, he whipped up the team and they headed across.

The going was slow but the wagon maintained good contact with the rocky river bottom.

There had been some well-founded concerns right at first that maybe the depth of the water would cause it to have a tendency to float, but to the relief of everyone looking on, that wasn't the case and Willie made it safely across. The usual cheer went up and the second wagon carefully made its way down to the water's edge.

That crossing also went well and soon it was Sam and then Stretch's turn. They both made the crossing without mishap. Stretch stood on the opposite bank and watched as Danny tried to coax his team into the water. The right side lead mare was definitely not wanting any part of the swift current and was showing her objections by refusing to enter the swirling torrent.

He looked on with concerned wrinkles creasing his brow as Danny pulled the whip from its holder and cracked its length above the mare's head. Mary Jane appeared from inside the wagon and took the seat between her brothers. It was plain to Stretch that she was not at all comfortable with what was going on.

"Use the whip, boy!" Mr. Greenberg hollered from just off

to Stretch's left.

Stretch looked his way, and their eyes met.

Greenberg again shouted his instructions to his son. "She'll do alright, boy! Use the whip like you mean it!"

Danny raised the whip and took charge of the situation. The mare responded and reluctantly waded into the water. The outriders tied up and they began the crossing.

Stretch glanced sideways at Mr. Greenberg and noted the arrogance on the face of the fool who was looking back at him. The smugness intensified as if to say, "Told ya I knew what I was talkin' about." Stretch bit his tongue but the word appeared in his mind, anyway... *Fool.*

Stretch then returned his full attention to the scene that was unfolding near the middle of the river.

The mare was not at all taking to the current as the rushing water beat against her side. She tossed her head and half reared as she protested the treatment she was being forced to endure.

Danny did his best and managed to keep her marginally under control with the use of the whip and a firm hand on the reins. Inevitably, the mare finally lost her footing and plunged into the swirling current.

The wagon had made it to just past the centerline of the crossing where the water was at its deepest. The mare thrashed helplessly, succeeding only in getting herself hopelessly tangled in the harness. This caused the remaining three horses to panic as the whole contraption was being pulled downriver, horses and all.

The wagon didn't stand a chance. As soon as it changed direction, the outriders were next to useless, but they gave it their best as they wrapped the ends of their ropes around their saddle horns and hauled back on their reins.

"Let it go!" Heck hollered.

They hastily unwound the ropes and flung them into the river, glad that their own horses hadn't been pulled off their feet.

The schooner began careening wildly until it finally went over center.

Mary Jane and her brothers jumped free just as the wagon started to tip onto its side.

"She can't swim!" Stretch heard Mr. Greenberg shout as the girl hit the water. "The boys'll do alright, but Mary Jane can't swim!"

Stretch was an excellent swimmer and had no second thoughts about what needed doing. He sat down on the bank and pulled off his boots. He rose, shucked out of his jacket, and while running headlong toward the river, grabbed the brim of his hat and tossed it just before he dove for the swirling water. He surfaced quickly and looked for Mary Jane. Unable to make out much of anything, he swam as hard as he could until he finally neared the overturned wagon. When he reached it, he also came face to face with Ronnie.

He had to yell to make himself heard above the sounds of the raging river and the screams of the terrified horses. "Where's Mary Jane? You see her after she hit the water?"

Despite his fear, Ronnie managed a teeth chattering, "Over th-th-that way." He pointed. "I see-seen her headin' over th-th-that way…just a little b-bit ago."

"Stay with the wagon!" Stretch yelled, and turning loose of the wagon, he let the current sweep him downriver. "God, please help me to find her." He didn't realize it but he'd said the prayer out loud. He raised himself as far up out of the water as he could and steadied his gaze ahead.

For just a darting instant, he caught a glimpse of her yellow hair, but was dismayed to see that she was still a good distance away.

He renewed his efforts and began swimming as hard as he knew how. In just a matter of moments he was rewarded by the sound of a gurgling, "Help!"

He again took the time to raise up and look ahead. This

time when he spied her, he knew she had seen him as well; she was extending a hand out toward him.

"Help me!" she shrieked. "I can't swim! Oh please help me, Stretch!"

He struck out again and reached her just as they passed under a tree branch that extended well out over the water's edge. He wrapped his arm around her just under her armpits.

Knowing she was now safe, he took the time to float in the swift current while they both enjoyed a much-needed respite before attempting to make shore. Leastways, he was enjoying it.

Mary Jane, on the other hand, was still a mite concerned and on the agitated side. "Am I gonna d—?" she asked. The water covered her mouth, obscuring the words.

"You'll be alright. I've got you now." He kept his voice calm and under control, not wanting her to get anymore upset than she already was. "I'm a real good swimmer," he assured her. "Good enough for the both of us, in fact. So you just lay back and enjoy the ride while I get us rested up before swimming our way over to the shore."

He could feel her shuddering and knew she was crying. Just then, Danny caught up to them. He rolled over onto his back and squirted a stream of water from between his teeth.

"Nice day for a swim...huh, sis?"

She didn't answer.

Danny could see that Stretch had things well under control and headed for the bank that was by now no more than ten feet away.

Stretch pulled Mary Jane the rest of the way to the shore and was grateful when Danny grabbed ahold and helped pull the both of them out onto the grassy bank. All three sprawled onto their backs, completely exhausted.

"Somebody gonna help me?" The plea came from the river. They all sat up and watched as Ronnie floated by, still holding onto the wagon. The mare had somehow managed to get untangled and had righted herself. In fact, all four of the horses seemed to be doing just fine. The wagon however, remained on its side.

Stretch and Danny looked at one another and grinned. "Might as well, I reckon," Stretch said.

"Yeah...I reckon," Danny agreed, albeit somewhat reluctantly.

They both headed for the water and jumped in. While Danny went after Ronnie, Stretch focused his attention on helping the men who were keeping pace along the bank. Grabbing onto the ropes they tossed out to him, he managed to avoid the thrashing hooves while he attached one around each of the two lead horse's necks. It was a simple process after that to get the wagon uprighted and back onto dry land where it was found to be none the worse for wear.

Stretch swam to shore and hastily headed back upstream. He was pleased to see that Mary Jane was right where he had left her.

She smiled when she saw him—it was the type of smile that could certainly get a fella's attention. "Thanks for what you did," she said softly, and wiped a wet dress sleeve under each eye.

"You're welcome. You know you could have been killed."

"You, too."

"Yeah, I reckon."

"I owe you my life."

She began to sob, so he lowered himself into the grass right next to her. He latched onto all the gumption he could scare up and took her in his arms. He pulled her to him and held her while she went about getting it all out. He liked the feel of her as she shuddered against his chest. Her hair smelled fresh and clean and he was secretly glad that she was crying so he could hold her. He lightly stroked the back of her hair.

She raised her gaze and looked into his eyes. "Your name is Stretch, isn't it?"

"Eh...yeah, it is. I-I been noticing you, too," he said and felt a tightening in his chest that was like nothing he had ever felt before. He gazed into her beautiful blue eyes as she shivered and sucked in a gasping breath. "You cold?" he asked and rubbed his hand up and down along her upper arm.

"Yeah, a little," she said as his eyes watched her lips form the words.

For the first time ever, he had a desire to kiss a girl, but successfully fought off the urge. "I...eh...we better get going. You're ma 'n pa'll be worried sick about you." He started to rise.

"Wait," she said and pulled him back down.

She placed a palm on each side of his face and gently pulled him toward her. Their lips met and he had a fleeting, guilt filled feeling that maybe he should pull away. However, the feeling was just that...a fleeting one. They both enjoyed the awkward kiss; it was the first ever for either one of them.

"Mary Jane!"

They hurriedly cut the kiss short and jumped to their feet. "Yes, Pa!" she answered as she tried desperately to smooth out the front of her dress. "Over here!"

It was obvious that Mr. Greenberg was happy and relieved that his little girl was safe. "Oh, honey," he said and threw his arms around her. "Thank God you're alright."

"You mean God and Stretch here," she said and touched him lightly on the arm. "He saved me, Pa. He saved my life."

"I'm beholding to you, son. I'll never forget what you did today. Thank you." He reached out and took ahold of Stretch's hand and went to pumping it vigorously while he continued, "I'll never be able to repay you for saving my Mary Jane here. But if there's anything I got that I can give you, or anything I can do...well, you just say the word."

"As a matter of fact, there is one thing. You can switch that lead mare like I told you."

"You'll not get anymore argument out of me. Not after what I just saw today. You were right all along."

"Oh...and there's just one other thing..."

Jacob squinted a suspicious eye at the youngster. "And just what might *that* be?" he asked pensively.

"With your permission...I'll be payin' my respects to Mary Jane from time to time...eh...sir."

He continued to eye the boy with a sternness that finally forced Stretch to swallow hard, sending his prominent Adam's apple on a trip up and down the front of his neck. A twitch jerked at the corner of Jacob Greenberg's mouth and he turned to face his daughter. "And just where do you stand in all this?"

She reached out and hooked her arm around the crook in Stretch's elbow. She spread a gleeful smile and moved in closer. She hugged the arm to her and said, "I'd say I'm standing right here next to my fella, that's where."

The rest of the wagons all made it across the river safely, with no further mishaps. Jacob had just finished switching the lead mare when the rescue party showed up with Wayman.

Most of the members of the wagon train held a meeting to discuss Wayman's confrontation with the Comanches and the problems facing the Greenbergs now that they had lost all of their food and belongings.

Birdsong Hawkins was distressed that it was the Comanches who were causing the trouble for the wagon train, but no one held the fact that she was a member of that tribe against her.

The discussion then centered on the precautions necessary to effectively protect the train. With that in mind, it was decided to double the number of men walking the perimeter at night.

As an added precaution, Heck decided that it was now time to institute the rule that no one would be allowed to wander from the train by himself, day or night. Some folks thought this was getting extreme, but it was a steadfast rule, laid out by the wagonmaster, and was therefore not open for discussion. It was also decided to have mounted outriders patrolling along the entire length of the train during each day's progress; they were to remain a ways off so there would be plenty of advanced warning if trouble were spotted.

Birdsong had more than just a little knowledge about healing herbs and such things and volunteered to look after Wayman. Wild Willie suggested he be laid out in their wagon so she could keep a close eye on him. Although Noah didn't much cotton to any heathen Injuns caring for his boy, he realized his shortcomings when it came to doctoring and reluctantly agreed to the arrangement. So a place was prepared for Wayman in the Hawkins wagon and Noah kept his mouth shut.

The Greenbergs found themselves inundated with offers of assistance. They were given not only food and clothing but they were also offered anything else they might have a need for. Jacob and Mabel were overwhelmed by the outright generosity of their fellow travelers and Jacob expressed their gratitude by saying a prayer of thanks and understanding that touched every heart present. After the amens had died down, a fella would have been hardpressed to find a dry eye anywhere around. That was probably because Noah wasn't there at the time.

Even though the majority of the folks in the wagon train weren't exactly born-again Christians, the helping thy neighbor way of thinking that had descended on the train was such that the whole thing had a bunch of them now leaning toward the belief that maybe there was a higher power up there after all.

Stretch and Mary Jane had a talk with her ma and pa about letting them share the Conestoga during each day's trek. With her riding with Stretch, it would help to alleviate the overcrowding in the Greenberg wagon. That made a whole lot of sense and Jacob agreed under the condition that they take Ronnie as well. Mabel smiled with perceptive understanding as she watched their daughter and her newfound beau head off toward the wagon with Ronnie tagging along close behind.

❧Chapter 9❧

The next week or so came and went without any more trouble to speak of. The outriders reported seeing an Indian or two every once in a while and that always caused more concern then it turned out to be worth. The redskins seemed to be keeping tabs on the train and just letting the white men know that they were around. There was never any indication that they had any intention of becoming hostile.

Birdsong let Heck know that the trailing Indians were not Comanche, but Arapahoe, and that some day very soon they would approach the wagons and let their intentions be known.

❧

The usual daily routine continued as the folks in the train went about their one-foot-in-front-of-the-other method of heading west toward their new homes. They worked their way across the mostly flat prairieland at a relatively good pace.

By the end of the thirteenth day, they had covered well over a hundred and fifty miles. Heck told everyone that as far as he could recollect, they were within two or three days of reaching the Arkansas River. Once there, they would follow it until it turned nearly due west. From there it would be a simple matter of just following it until folks found a spot that appealed to them and they left the train.

This news encouraged everyone and even gave a lot of them a false sense of security. One who was not fooled, however, was Birdsong Hawkins. She knew the Comanches would eventually return and cause trouble if they were of a mind to.

The nearly two weeks on the trail had brought the members of the wagon train closer together, and a good portion of them were fast-becoming good friends. There was a sense of togetherness developing that was not only a necessary way of doing things, but rewarding as well.

Stretch and Mary Jane were growing fonder of one another with each passing day. The biggest problem they were faced with was figuring out ways to get shed of Ronnie so they could steal those magic moments alone together. At times, that involved anything from fooling him into thinking that his pa wanted to see him, to letting him drive the team while they walked together hand in hand behind the wagon. Of course, that meant walking right in front of the Greenberg wagon with Mary Jane's pa watching them with an unobstructed view of the goings-on.

There was a time when Stretch forgot himself and slipped an arm around her waist, only to have that indiscretion met with the loud crack from Mr. Greenberg's whip. He quickly removed the arm, and twisting around, cordially tipped his hat to him.

Jacob returned the salute and suffered an abuse from his wife as she instructed him to: "Just leave them two young'uns be."

Sam and Jay had never been happier. He had taught her the finer points of driving the team and she eagerly accepted the challenge, which allowed him the freedom to spend time in the back of the wagon with their son. Of course, there were instances when the boy was sound asleep. Those were the times when he and Jay would sit atop the seat discussing what their plans would be once they arrived at their final destination. It was agreed that they would settle somewhere within easy distance of a populated area, rather than some far off, remote location where neighbors, as well as customers, would be a scarcity.

George and Fay Appleton were just about as happy as any two newlyweds could be. He was forever doing for her and her for him. Sam tried hard to remember if he and Jay had ever been as clingy as those two seemed to be, but just couldn't come up with a time. Jay said she thought it was wonderful that they felt the way they did about one another, but Sam was of a mind that it was bordering on unhealthy for two people to be that close all the time.

The Carters, who had the wagon right in front of Sam and Jay, were getting just about at their wit's end with their son, Joshua. Stretch saw this as an opportunity to occasionally get rid of Ronnie. He pushed hard each evening for Josh and Ronnie to become friends and maybe spend more time together. That panned out to enough of a degree to allow Stretch to steal a kiss from Mary Jane every now and then.

The Baxters, as well as the Hendricks', pretty much kept to themselves and didn't bother anybody. There were times when Sam would attempt to strike up a conversation with Noah, but the man just wasn't receptive.

Birdsong did a wonderful job of caring for Wayman's leg by keeping her concoctions of herb mudpacks changed on a regular basis. It wasn't long before they began doing the trick and the wound responded to the tune of healing much quicker than most folks in the train would have ever thought possible.

Wayman was not only grateful for the progress with his leg, but also the interest folks had seemed to take in his wellbeing. It was just a matter of time before he started opening up and became friendly with the folks around him. This wasn't setting too well with his pa, but Wayman didn't give a hang one way or another. He figured he was a grown man and could take on any kind of disposition he pleased.

The rainstorms appeared on a regular basis, coming about every other day or so. Everyone welcomed them as a respite from the stifling, hot afternoons. The morning that marked two weeks on the trail saw a low-level layer of fog hanging about fifteen or twenty feet off the ground. As the sun chinned itself on the eastern horizon, it bounced its early morning brilliance off the underside of the fog bank, casting a beautiful pale orange and pink glow over the landscape that was a sight to behold.

"Sure is a beautiful morning," Sam said as he and Jay were standing with an arm around each other's waist, taking in the elegant beauty that was God's creation.

She snuggled her head against his shoulder. "Um-hmm," she said contentedly. "I don't think I'll ever get tired of seeing sunrises. Each one is different from the last."

Before he could respond, the sounds of approaching horses reached their ears.

They looked up and were surprised to see a small band of Indians heading their way. "Go to the wagon," he said solemnly, and gave her a slight nudge with the hand he'd placed in the small of her back. He then rested the hand on the handle of his pistol as he watched the every move of the approaching riders.

They rode to within a few yards of him and pulled their ponies to a halt. In short order, he was relieved to feel the presence of other men from the train as they sided up to him.

"Do you speak English?" Heck asked after taking a step out in front of the others.

The Indians looked at one another until one of them began making guttural sounds while waving his hands.

Charlie recognized some of the signs and stepped forward to a positioning that put him right next to Heck. "Peers ta me that these here fellas is Arapahoe. He's tellin' us that they're here wantin' ta be our friends." Charlie watched some more, then translated again, "He's sayin' they ain't been able ta find any buffalo and are gettin' low on vittles." He paused and watched some more. "He's askin' if we got any food they can have that'll feed their women an' young'uns 'til they come across a herd."

"Tell him that we'll spare what we can. No, wait!" He turned to face the men who had gathered behind them. "Any of you fellas got a problem with sharing what we have in the way of food?"

"I ain't saying I'm likin' it, but by the same token I don't figger we got any choice," Noah said. "I reckon if we don't give 'em what they's askin' for, they'll most likely just attack the train and take what all they want anyway."

"That the way you see it, Charlie?" Heck asked.

"Reckon so, Heck. These fellas are seemin' to be peaceable enough right now, but don't let that fool ya none. They're just as treacherous as any other Injuns you can name...'specially if their squaws 'n papooses is hungry."

"Okay then...tell him we'll give 'em what little we can spare."

Charlie signaled the White Eye decision. The reaction was one of smiles and approving nods.

"Tell 'em to get down and come on over to the camp," Heck said and started for the train.

Charlie conveyed the message and the Indians dismounted. They assumed a meek demeanor as they led their ponies toward the wagons. Once they entered the circle, the sight of every man, woman, and child, who were able, pointing either a rifle or handgun their way, greeted them. The fella who had been doing the talking got Charlie's attention by placing a hand on his arm. He asked him to tell the people to put the firesticks down; they were not here to harm anyone.

"You folks all lower them guns. These here fellas are nervous that someone'll take a notion to commence ta shootin'. He says they ain't here to do no harm an' I'm of a mind to believe what he's sayin'." He watched as most of the guns were lowered. However, a few weren't. He raised his voice a notch or two and tried again, "I said...put them guns down. One shot outta any of you and we'll most likely be biting off more than we can chew. I'm figgerin' that these fellas are just an advance bunch that was sent in here to ask for food. I 'spect there's a whole passel of 'em just over one of them hills yonder." He gestured with a wave of his hand toward the north. "I 'spect they's just layin' out there listening for the sound of one of you pulling off a shot. Now put 'em down I said afore one of you fools gets us all kilt!"

This time all the guns were lowered. Birdsong was the last to lower hers. She was a Comanche and the Arapahoe were hated enemies of her people. She watched with hate-filled eyes as the smelly Arapahoe dogs passed by in front of her. A distasteful sneer curled her upper lip as her eyes met the gaze of the leader. He turned his head and glared at her over his shoulder as he continued on by.

Finally, she could stand to look at these Arapahoe no longer. She spun on the balls of her feet and headed for the solitude of her wagon.

Wild Willie watched as she hurried away. He quickly followed. He found her seated in the grass with her back propped against a wheel. "You havin' a problem with them Arapahoe?" he asked, already knowing the answer.

"Yes. I do not wish to see faces of these Arapahoe dogs," she said and angrily pulled a handful of grass and thrust it away. "They not fit to live." She jerked her head around to look straight into his eyes. "We will not give them our food!" she said and narrowed her eyes into an icy stare as she looked toward the center of the circle where the Arapahoe had gathered.

"Well, I reckon if that's the way ya feel about it, then that's how it'll be."

"Good." After saying that, she realized that he was on her side and the hate she felt began to ease from around her eyes. She closed them and the tears started as she remembered the time so long ago when her mother and brother had been killed in the cowardly Arapahoe attack on their village.

He knelt and took her in his arms. Willie knew the story of her family's slaughter at the hands of the Arapahoe and held her tightly against his chest. He stroked her hair while she dealt with her sorrow. Words were unnecessary.

The members of the train gathered what food they felt they could spare and brought it to the area at the center of the circle where the Indians waited patiently. Each time more food was added to the growing pile, the leader would nod his thanks. In anticipation of being successful in their attempt to get food from the White Eye, the Indians had brought along some buffalo robes to use for securing the items in before transporting them back to their people.

When the last of the food had been laid out, they spread the robes and placed the items in the centers. Bringing the corners together, they tied them securely with lengths of rawhide. After tying two bundles together with yet another short, but heavier strip of leather, they hefted them onto the backs of their ponies with a bundle hanging on either side. They thanked the White Eye with nods, smiles, and some hand signals, before swinging up onto the backs of the ponies and leaving the circle of wagons.

"Hope that's the last we'll be seeing of them fellas," Heck said as he and Sam stood together watching them go.

"Amen to that."

❧Chapter 10◈

The next day looked to be a bad weather day right from the start. The sky had clouded up overnight and the members of the train awoke to a cold, steady drizzle. There was a brief respite during the afternoon, but that was short-lived as the thunderheads billowed up and the storms swept across the open prairie one after another. Some of them were on the violent side with the rains coming down in horizontal sheets that blasted into the travelers, head on. The lightning bolts flashed incessantly as the seemingly endless choruses of cannonading thunder did their part in contributing to the severity of the storms.

The rain continued to beat down without let up. Sometimes it would transform into hail for a spell before changing back to rain. Finally, after having had enough, Heck called a halt and the wagons circled for the night, albeit about an hour earlier than was usual.

With the constant downpour being pushed by the driving winds, building fires was out of the question. The travelers then did the best they could under the circumstances and ate a cold supper. Sam dug out a good-sized piece of canvas from the Conestoga and he and Stretch built a makeshift lean-to that extended out from the side of the schooner. Once it was completed, Jay, Mary Jane, Tom, and Ronnie joined the two men, and they all settled down for cold biscuits and leftover beans. The canvas shelter did little in the way of keeping them dry, but it was marginally better than nothing at all.

Finally, just after sundown, the storms began easing and the swirling winds died down. Sam quickly noticed the change, and while there was still some daylight left, he dug out the dry bundle of firewood he kept in the wagon for just such occasions. He found a suitable high spot under the lean-to and built a fire on it. In no time at all the warmth of the small blaze did its job and the shivering and teeth chattering began to ease and eventually came to an end.

꙳

The next day was a whole lot better during the early hours, but by late afternoon the air had again grown heavy and sultry. Not a breath of a breeze stirred the prairie grasses. As the afternoon progressed, the clouds again boiled up in the southwest. What had started out as soft, puffy white clouds soon developed into dark, purple thunderheads. In the space of barely a few minutes, the winds kicked in and the sultry air was blown away to the east as the rain started falling and the thunder began to again have its say.

It was only mid-afternoon, but Heck wasn't about to put the folks through another day like the previous one. Despite the fact that the wagons had covered only about seven or eight miles to that point, he again called an early halt to the day's progress.

They circled the wagons on the lee side of a large but pleasant cottonwood grove that boasted of a small stream meandering through it. Although these storms didn't seem to pack the rain like those of the day before, the thunder, lightning, and winds more than made up for it. Folks huddled together and again dealt with the adversity as best they could.

Sam and Jay did their best to soothe Tom and keep him occupied. The sounds of the storms frightened him, and whenever a lightning strike was close enough for the flash to appear blue and the sound to emit a nerve-bending crackle, rather than the rolling rumble of a far off bolt, he would jerk with a start and begin to cry.

The storms continued throughout the rest of the afternoon as well as into the evening hours. They maintained their seemingly unrelenting fury as they flashed and splashed well past suppertime. Some of the canvas coverings on the wagons were unable to stand up to the heavy pounding and the occupants were forced to leave their wagons and belongings behind and double up with other families.

One such set of victims turned out to be the Hendricks family.

"Sam…Sam Bartlett!"

Sam worked his way to the rear of the wagon and peered out. "Yeah!" he hollered, while managing to keep his hat on his head by clamping a forearm across the top of it. The nearly horizontal hailstones painfully pelted his face. He used the other arm to shield his eyes from the onslaught. Finally, he spied Mr. and Mrs. Hendricks and their two young'uns. He didn't hesitate. "Get in here! Get them young'uns out of that storm and in here under cover!" He reached out, took hold of the girl, and lifted her into the wagon while the boy waited his turn. Once the two children were safely inside, Mrs. Hendricks climbed aboard, followed by Kyle.

"Oouu-wee," Kyle said, as he pulled his hat and hugged his wife who was already hugging the children. "That storm's near tore our wagon ta pieces. Thanks fer yer hospitality. Surely do hope our wagon makes out well enough ta be drivable tomarrah." He then stuck his head out through the opening and took a gander. "Nosiree, just don't seem ta be lettin' up none out there," he said once he had pulled his head back in.

"Are you alright?" Jay asked, looking at the children.

Both youngsters nodded, and Mrs. Hendricks spoke, "We sure are beholdin' to ya fer helpin' us. Ain't partial ta bein' a burden ta our neighbors, but—"

"You're not being a burden," Jay assured her. "Not at all. I would expect you to do the same for us if the shoe were on the other foot, ahh...Mrs. Hendricks. By the way, what is your name? We've been traveling this train together for nearly three weeks now and I still don't know your given name."

"Mainly that's cuz I ain't used ta bein' friendly with folks 'til I knowed 'em fer a spell, but seein's how we're gettin' cozy tagether...I reckon it's alright. My name's Ethelda Mae." She extended her hand.

Jay took it and looked into her eyes. "My name's Judith, but those who're my friends call me Jay. And I'd like it very much if you'd call me that."

A smile crossed Ethelda Mae's face. "Alright...Jay. I'm right pleased ta make yer acquaintance," she said with her smile continuing to grow wider. "These here young'uns is Kyle Junior and Charlette."

Jay nodded and smiled at the two shivering children. She found a blanket and passed it to Ethelda Mae. "Here, put this around them before they catch their death."

The nest building was interrupted as a panic-filled voice could be heard jabbering something from somewhere outside.

"What's that all about?" Sam wondered aloud as he made his way past Kyle to the rear of the wagon. He peered out through the opening and gasped. "Oh my God! It's a *twister*!"

"What's a twister?" Kyle Junior asked.

"Come here and look for yourself."

The boy leaned out the back end of the wagon. His eyes grew to nearly twice their normal size. "Golly!" he said in pure amazement. "I ain't never see'd nutin' like that afore. Gosh 'n golly!"

"C'mon, everybody out!" Sam said and pushed back the flap. "We need to find us a low spot to lie down in! If that twister decides to head this way, we'll be in for one heck of a time!"

"What'dya mean?" Ethelda Mae asked. "What'll it do ta us?"

Sam had already climbed out and had started lowering kids down to ground level. "If it gets near enough to these wagons, it'll pick 'em up like pieces of paper and toss them wherever it takes the notion to! And it'll do the same with people, too! Now come on!" He took a quick glance over his shoulder. "It looks like it's figuring on heading straight for us! Come on! Hurry! I'll go get Stretch and the others! You all head over by the stream and lay down flat in a low spot! Get in the water if you have to!" With that, he turned, leaned into the wind, and headed for the Conestoga.

"Stretch...Stretch...get out of there!" he hollered as he reached the wagon. "There's a twister coming this way! Head for the stream!"

Stretch emerged and climbed down the back of the wagon. "Where is it?"

"Right behind you!"

Stretch jerked his head around to look. "Oh my God! Mary Jane! Ronnie! Get out of there and fast! It's *here*!"

As Mary Jane showed herself, he grabbed her around her middle and none too gently pulled her out the rear of the wagon. Sam did the same with Ronnie and they all ran as fast as they could toward the small stream.

As soon as they reached it, they slid down the slight embankment and watched the fury of the tornado as it approached. It was now within a hundred yards of the wagons and it was looking like all Hades was about to break loose.

The trees were twisting and swaying savagely. Suddenly, a huge cottonwood, just on the far side of the circle of wagons, exploded into what seemed to Sam to be about a thousand pieces as a bolt of ear-splitting lightening tore into it. The remains of the tree briefly erupted in flames, but the fire was quickly extinguished as the driving torrents of rain made short work of the emerging flames. The wagons were rocking violently as a result of the tornado tearing into them, sending at least two of them high into the air. Sam ducked his head under a protective arm as the nearly intolerable, deafening sound suddenly increased in intensity to a level that blocked out everything except a man's thoughts...and prayers.

Sam was sure that more than one person up and down the line was praying as hard as they could so he joined in. He spoke the prayer aloud, but no one but God could hear him, not even himself. "Dear God, help us to survive this storm. Be merciful in Your dealings with us and spare us from Your wrath." He took the time to glance at Stretch and Mary Jane.

Stretch had his arm across her back and was pulling her into the protection of his own body.

Sam did the same to his son and beloved wife before continuing, "Father, at least spare these youngsters. None of 'em's had much of a chance to know what life's all about. Spare them, Father. I ask this in Your precious Son's name...amen."

Once he had finished, he cast a gaze at Jay and saw that she was looking into his eyes. The expression in her eyes was one of fear, yet she had found the strength to show him a grim smile. He returned it halfheartedly. Neither of them knew if this would be their last moments together on this earth.

Just as quickly as the funnel had lowered itself from the heavens, it left the ground and disappeared into the clouds. The winds immediately died down and the deafening noise subsided.

Sam raised his gaze, as did the others. "Well I'll be," he said softly, at the timing of the end of the tornado. He then rose onto his knees. He looked toward the heavens and mouthed simply, *Thank You*.

The inhabitants of the train appeared from their places of hiding, somewhat reluctantly, and went about the task of sizing up the situation. The twister had left the majority of the wagons in tatters. Nearly every canvas top was either torn, shredded, or missing all together. Sideboards had been worked loose on a few of the older wagons, and more than one wheel had been broken. The two wagons that had suffered direct hits were lying nearly fifty yards away from the main body of the train. At first glance, they appeared to be total losses. A good portion of the stock had panicked and ran off, but by the grace of God, none of the travelers had been killed or even seriously injured.

With the condition of the train being what it was, Heck decided to lay over for as long as was necessary to repair what needed fixing in preparation to getting the entire train back in traveling shape.

The travelers pitched in and did what they could with what little light remained, but they were soon forced to call off their efforts and spend a nearly sleepless night wondering what the following day would bring.

❧Chapter 11❧

The dawn broke under clear skies and a general feeling of despair as folks went about the grim task of putting their lives back together. Not a single soul had come through the storm unscathed. However, some had been more fortunate than others, yet they worked just as hard as those who hadn't been so lucky. All available extra pieces of canvas were dug out and stacked in a community pile for use by anyone with a need.

Wayman Baxter, bad leg and all, did his part by doing the cutting for the women as they sewed replacement wagon tops for the ones that had been destroyed. The rest of the women were given the tasks of running herd on the children and tending the meals. The men were kept busy with rounding up the stock and repairing the wagons.

Sam hoisted a wheel onto the freshly greased rear axle of the Hendricks wagon. He twisted, turned and shoved against the heavy wheel until he felt it bottom out against the stop. Ronnie stood on the far end of a tree limb they had lain over a rock and were using to lever the corner of the wagon off the ground. He was holding onto a handy sapling for balance while Stretch stood nearby with retaining washer and nut in hand.

A noise drew Stretch's attention and he looked up to see an approaching wagon. "Lookee there," he said, with a jutting chin thrust in the direction of the wagon.

Sam glanced over his shoulder. "Get that washer on here and let's fasten this wheel down. Then we'll go see who the visitor is."

Stretch slid the washer into place and followed it with the nut. After screwing it down hand tight, he picked up the wrench and hastily snugged it before giving a final tug for good measure. He looked up at Ronnie. "Okay, I reckon that'll do it for this one."

The youngster jumped off the limb, allowing the wagon to come crashing down with a vengeance, but it and the wheel held together.

Sam took ahold of the top of the wheel and gave it a good shake. "Yep, that'll do," he said and went about wiping the grease from his hands with the piece of cloth he had pulled from his hip pocket. He tossed it to Stretch. "C'mon, let's go," he said.

They arrived just as most of the other folks were getting there as well.

Heck greeted the driver, "Howdy, stranger. What brings you out here all by your lonesome?"

"Is this Hector Yallow's train?"

"You're lookin' straight at him."

"My name's Harold Jenks...*Pastor* Harold Jenks. Mind if we get down?" he asked and began climbing down.

A woman's face appeared from inside the wagon and she made her way to the edge as well. He assisted her to the ground. Next came four boys. They formed a line, obviously in order by age, from oldest to youngest. "This is my family," the pastor said proudly. "Maggie here's my wife." He placed a hand on her shoulder and she smiled dutifully. "Her real name's Margaret, but Maggie's what she prefers. And these are my boys." He went around behind them and placed an open palm atop each of their heads as he spoke their names respectively, "Matthew...Mark...Luke...and John."

"What brings you folks all the way out here, Pastor?" Sam asked. "This isn't real hospitable country, especially when a wagon's out on its own."

"We were meaning to join this train before it left Independence, but were delayed in arriving. Then when we finally did get there, we were dismayed to find out that you folks had already left. We started out almost three days behind. It took us this long to catch up."

"Well..." Heck dug an index finger into the inside of his cheek, pulled out the chaw and let it fall into the grass. "I reckon..." he paused while he gnawed off a fresh chaw from the plug he'd fished from his vest pocket. "I reckon you caught up now, so I reckon you're welcome to pull in line and ride along the rest of the way if it suits ya."

The pastor patted John's shoulder. "Thank you, Mister Yallow."

"You just go on and pull your rig in line right at the tail end."

"Whatever you say, Mister Yallow."

"The name's Heck. And I'd appreciate it if you was to call me that. Mister Yallow was my daddy's name." Heck turned to face the others. "Let's get on back to getting this train in shape to roll," he said.

"You folks have trouble?" Pastor Jenks asked with genuine concern.

"Yeah," Heck replied over his shoulder. "Had us a near disaster with a tornado yesterday evening."

"Anyone hurt?"

Heck turned to face him. "A few bumps an' bruises is all. Mostly it was the wagons what suffered the most."

Pastor Jenks pulled his hat and quickly scanned the gathering of faces. "You folks mind if I ask the Lord's blessing on this train?" Without waiting for a reply, he began saying a prayer for the safety of the folks in the train. He then went on to include the sturdiness of the wagons, the well being of the children, the continued health of the horses, and just about anything else he could think of that might pertain to getting the train back on the trail and safely on its way to its intended destination.

After he had finished, and the amens had died down, Sam and Jay were making their way back toward the wagons. "Mite on the windy side, wouldn't you say?" he asked matter-of-factly.

"What'dya mean?" she answered, while looking around but not noticing any breeze to speak of.

"Kind of a longwinded prayer...not that I mind what a pastor's got to say."

She smiled up at him, and taking his hand in hers, circled his arm around her shoulders. "Well, good thing I'd say, because good pastors are supposed to be longwinded."

The remainder of the day was spent finishing the repairs and reconditioning of the wagons.

Pastor Jenks and his wife made the rounds, meeting every member of the train and getting to know each ones standing with the Lord. Overall, he was pleasantly surprised at the favorable number of those who were truly Christian and had been saved by God's grace. However, he was particularly distressed when he tried to discuss salvation with Noah Baxter.

"I ain't partial to hearin' no preachin', Preacher. So, just go on about your business and just leave me 'n mine be."

"But don't you want to know without a doubt that when you die you'll go to heaven?"

"Now that'd be a real good question, Preacher. Mainly because I ain't even sure there is a heaven...or a hell either, for that matter."

"If you were to read your Bible you'd have that question

answered for you. And a whole lot more besides."

"Well now...right there we got us two more problems. First off, I ain't got no Bible. And second off, I ain't never learnt ta read. So it wouldn't do me no good even if I did have one."

"There's other ways of learning about the Lord. I'd say your best bet would be to attend my services once we get settled in."

"Yeah, Preacher, I'll be sure an' do that," Noah said and rolled his eyes as he turned and hastily walked away.

The pastor sighed. "Sure is set in his ways, Ma. I'd say that's a project that needs my personal attention."

"I'd say so, Pa," she said, looking up at him.

He smiled down at her. "In the meantime...what say we finish meeting the rest of these fine folks?"

It was late in the day when the last of the repairs had finally been tended to. Exhausted and hungry, everyone sat down to the best hot meal they'd had in a while. After supper, the main fire was kindled and things were pretty much back to normal. Heck informed everyone that they would be reaching the Arkansas sometime the following morning. This was good news to the beleaguered group of travelers and spirits picked up considerably.

The talk around the bonfire eventually centered on the threat of future trouble from the Comanches. All during the time that the repairs were being made, nobody had seen hide nor hair of any Indians, hostile or otherwise. However, that didn't mean there weren't any around. Birdsong assured them that the Comanches would show themselves when it suited them and not before.

એ

The next morning arrived in all its glory. The sky was crystal clear and there was not even the slightest hint of a breeze; it was promising to be a hot one. Breakfasts were made and eaten and the dishes were dealt with while the teams were being hitched up. Everyone was anxious to resume the journey. That way of thinking was soon to change.

It was shortly after the wagons had resumed their westward trek that, to everyone's chagrin, the Comanches again made their presence known. They appeared almost ghostly atop small rises, from behind small clusters of trees, and even boldly right out in the open. They would disappear just as quickly as they had appeared; the tactics served to keep everyone on edge.

The game of cat and mouse continued well into the late morning until word was finally sent down the length of the train that the Arkansas had been spotted just ahead. A cheer went up and the threat of the stalking band of Comanches was temporarily pushed toward the backs of their minds as the drivers urged their teams to a faster pace.

Arriving at the river's edge, the wagons were halted along the shore in the three abreast formation. Although it was barely late morning, the decision was then made to have an early midday meal. A few extra men were positioned to keep a wary eye on the Indians while small cooking fires were built and the womenfolk went about the task of preparing the vittles. The remainder of the men gathered around Heck for a briefing on what lay ahead.

Heck gnawed off a fresh chaw and slipped the plug back into his vest pocket. "I been right in this same exact spot before," he said and pointed down at the spot where he stood. He then spit and wiped his mouth with the back of his hand. "There's about a day's push to the northwest along the river. Then she cuts a mite to the west for a spell until she makes a real big bend to the south before heading out to the southwest. It'll be takin' the better part of a whole day just making it around that bend. Once we do get around it, we got us a decision to make an' stick to that might just as well be made right now."

"What kind of decision?" Sam asked.

"Well, we can either head out across country kinda west-southwest, or we can stay right alongside the river."

"What difference does it make which way we go?" Harry Carter wanted to know.

"Well...if we was to head out across country, there's no guarantee about what the waterin' situation would be like, and—"

"How far is it across the open?" Sam asked.

"Anywhere from five to eight days, depending."

"On what?"

"On how fast we can go, of course."

"What about keepin' to the river route?" Noah asked. "What's that do for us?"

By staying along the river's edge we can figure on adding maybe a day or two onto the trip. But the good side is that we know we'll have water all the way, and not to mention the fact that we'd most likely be a whole lot safer if we was to have the protection of the river along one side of us." Heck paused to let the options sink in.

"But, that ain't necessarily no guarantee," Cottonwood Charlie said. "It's a true enough fact that the river bein' on one side would be of a help, but it's a mighty shallow river in most spots and them murderin' redskins could pretty much wade their ponies across about anytime they took the notion." After finishing his say, Charlie looked around the circle of concerned faces.

There was no doubt that he had certainly just given them food for thought.

Heck allowed the murmurings and what-ifs to circulate and finally die down. "Okay, what'll it be? You fellas wanna stick with the river, or head out across country?"

Sam held up his hand for silence. "It appears to me that the most sensible thing to do would be to remain with the river. An extra day or two isn't going to make that much of a difference." Sam's opinion right away got the murmurings and what-ifs to going again and he joined in, trying to make his position understood to Kyle Hendricks.

Heck took charge. "Hold it down now!" When that didn't seem to do much good, he shouted, "I said...shut up!" Faces turned his way and grew silent. "I know all you folks is in an all-fired hurry to get where it is you're going, but I'm here to tell you that I've been both ways before and am kinda partial to sticking by the river just like Mister B said. It could work out that we'd run into plenty of water the other way, too. But I'm reasonin' that a sure thing is better'n a jab in the eye with a sharp stick. I reckon I could just say which way we was going an' be done with it, but I'd druther let you folks decide on your own. There's advantages to both ways and there's disadvantages to both ways. I'm fixing to take a vote here and whichever way it goes I'll go along with. Does ever'one else agree to do the same?" He looked around.

Again, a few murmurs could be heard that turned out to be short-lived.

"Okay, good. Is everyone of the wagons represented here?" He waited, and when it appeared that each of the wagons were indeed represented, he went on, "I'll be allowing just one vote per wagon, so you folks got about a minute to decide which way your wagon is votin'...so get on with it."

After giving them their minute, and then some, he continued, "Stretch, you do the counting."

Stretch moved away from the group and sided up to Heck. He raised a hand to eye level and extended the index finger. Casting a sideways look at Heck, he nodded as if to say... "Well, go ahead...I got my countin' finger ready."

"All those who are of a mind that it'd be best to head out the shorter way and risk getting scarce on water...raise your hand."

Stretch carefully counted the upraised hands. When he'd decided on the total, he announced the findings, "Twelve!"

The show of hands went down.

Heck nodded. "Alright. Now...them that favor the river way...raise 'em up."

Again Stretch made his count, starting with himself. Once he'd finished, he assumed a quizzical expression. "Raise 'em up real high!" he said and counted again. After completing the count for the second time, he turned to Heck. "I got twelve for that way too, same as the first. That makes it a tie for both ways."

That was the signal for the arguing to start up in earnest. It was clear that there was a real problem going on here. Finally, Heck raised both arms high above his head and got everyone's attention by again shouting for them to shut up.

"Well, you can't say that I didn't try to let you folks decide on your own, but seein's how I didn't vote yet on one way or the other, that'll be leaving it up to me to do the deciding after all."

"So what'll it be, Heck? Do we stick by the river, or do we head out across the prairie?" George Appleton asked.

Heck stroked thoughtfully at the stubble of gray beard. He then lifted his hat and scratched his head. "I'm thinking I'll wait 'til after we make it around the big bend. Then I'll look at all aspects and decide which way is which." With all the yapping having started up again, he ended the meeting. "That's it for now! Let's go eat some of them vittles what's starting to smell so good."

Jay had invited Mary Jane to share the meal with them. As soon as the men returned from the meeting, they made short work of the food that the two women had prepared. Jay made sure that Stretch knew that Mary Jane had helped with preparing it.

"You sure are a good cook, Mary Jane," he said and smiled his thanks.

"Thank you, Stretch, but I —"

Anything else she'd had a mind to say was interrupted by the dull THUD! of an arrow smacking into the side of the wagon just above Stretch's head.

He looked up. "What the — ?"

Jay was immediately afraid." Oh Sam," she moaned and reached out to her son. She cradled him to her bosom and looked toward her husband with pleading eyes.

"Get under the wagon!" he shouted. "Now!"

As everyone scrambled to reach the relative safety of the underside of the wagon, a blood curdling "AIEEE!" sounded from somewhere along the river's edge.

❧Chapter 12❧

It was immediately apparent that the attackers were hitting the wagons from two sides. Sam fired at a running figure over by the river. His aim was good and the Indian threw up his arms, sending his weapons flying. He hit the ground, somersaulted once, and skidded to a stop.

"Stretch!" Sam hollered, "There's another pistol in the front of the wagon…on the floorboard just under the seat!" He squeezed off another shot, but this time to no avail.

Stretch waved his thanks and scooted out from under the wagon. He headed for the front and climbed aboard as Sam watched his feet disappear above the bottom edge. After just a few seconds, he reappeared with the pistol in his hand and a wide grin on his face. He ducked back under the wagon and forced Mary Jane down as close to the ground as he could get her. He held her there with a hand placed strategically in the middle of her back. He then took aim at a particularly aggressive brave. He squeezed the trigger and watched as the warrior was spun around from the force of the bullet.

"Nice shot," Sam said, nodding his approval.

Stretch acknowledged him with a thin, determined smile

and a slight nod of his own. It wasn't long before some of the other men had joined them. It didn't take much after that for the attackers to break off and pull back to a safe distance.

Things quickly settled down after that, and an eerie silence filled the air around them. Sam reached out to his family and pulled them to him. He was a compassionate sort of man and the tears welled up as he hugged them. Stretch, too, was holding Mary Jane, but his tears of relief remained on the inside.

Jacob came running right about then. "Mary Jane, are you okay?"

"Yes, Pa. I'm fine," she said, then added in a soft whisper as she looked up into Stretch's eyes, "Thanks to my fella here." She craned upward and kissed him softly on the cheek.

"Now that's just about enough of that sort of nonsense!" Jacob instructed from behind a threatening finger. "You get yourself out from under that wagon! Why, I outta tan your hide!"

"Why...because I just kissed the fella that saved my life? I'll just bet that if you'd a seen him pluggin' that heathen that was fixing to get my scalp, I expect you'd be kissing him your ownself."

"That right boy" You save my Mary Jane's life?"

"Well, I—"

"Yeah, that's right," Sam offered. "He darned sure did. Why, that girl of yours is lucky to be alive. That Indian was barreling down on her and old Stretch here, just as calm as a cucumber, took a bead on the savage and plugged him dead center. Yes, sir, I'd say he saved her life alright."

A thankful smile appeared across Jacob's face and he immediately turned it loose on his daughter. "Well now...that being the case, give him a kiss for me, too."

Mary Jane didn't need to be told twice. Sam grinned as she threw her arms around Stretch's neck and planted a kiss right smack dab on his lips. Sam judged that it wasn't no, "Nice-to-see-you-again-Aunt-Nellie." kind of kiss, neither. No, sir. It was most likely more of a, "I'm-truly-thankful-to-you-for-saving-my-life." kind of kiss. But if that wasn't true enough, he imagined that if a fella was to be on the inside of Mary Jane's brain right about then, he'd have found out that there was probably even way more to the smooch than that. He figured it was probably her intention to convey the fact that it was really a, "I-sure-do-have-a-hankering- to-be-your-missus-someday." kind of kiss.

When she finally unhooked her arms from around his neck and pulled away, Stretch was more than just a mite on the pinkish side. Fact is, there most likely wasn't a single redskin around that could have held a candle to him if it came right down to deciding who was the redder.

"I...eh..." He flushed an even deeper shade. "Just doing what I could," he managed to say and crawled out from under the wagon, pulling Mary Jane along behind him.

As they stood in front of her pa with an arm around one another, Jacob gazed down into his daughter's eyes. "Now I'd say that's showing some gratitude alright enough," he said while rubbing a palm against the side of his chin and spreading a suspicious smile. He looked at Stretch. "Fact is...me knowing my Mary Jane the way I think I do, I'd say that there was a sight more to that then just a—"

"Don't you nevermind now," she cut in. "I'll be the one letting Stretch here know how I truly feel about him without you leading the way. You just satisfy yourself that I'm safe 'n sound and let it go at that while you head on back to the wagon."

Jacob started the chin rubbing again and allowed the hand to find its way around to the back of his neck where he let it do some serious rubbing back there as well. The grin widened "Well, alright then," he said simply, turned on his heel, and headed back to his own wagon.

She threw her other arm around the front of Stretch's waist

and hugged him tighter while snuggling the side of her face against his chest.

"Well now," Jay offered, "it would appear that your father approves of Stretch here…although I can't for the life of me understand why."

Right about then, word came down that Heck figured they were sitting ducks where they were and he wanted the train to get under way. The midday meal things were hastily packed away and the fires were hurriedly doused. Heck then gathered everyone together for a short meeting, during which time he announced that from now on they would not stop without forming a circle. The discussion quickly deteriorated to a level of calling the Comanches vile names and accusing them of being heartless heathens with little to no regard for human life.

Noah was by far the worst of the lot. "Those yellow cowards even stuck a lance in my boy's leg and stole his horse. And not to mention the fact that they left him out there overnight to die from his leg wound."

Birdsong had heard more then she cared to. "You do not know the Comanche!" she fired at Noah. "You cannot say these things!" She fought to hold back the tears.

"All I know is what I seen with my own two eyes. And as far as I'm concerned, they ain't worth the powder it'd take to blow 'em straight ta kingdom come." He was pleased to see a few nodding heads of the folks who were agreeing with him. He waved a dismissive hand in the general direction of the area away from the wagons. "And she ain't much better'n them what's out there," he added, feeling some safety in numbers.

"You best watch yer mouth!" Wild Willie said as he came to his wife's defense. "How can you say that when she took care of yer kin and nursed him back?"

"Just statin' a fact, is all," Noah said, with a triumphant smirk. "An Injun is an Injun is an Injun…plain 'n simple."

Birdsong jerked away from her husband's hold and lunged at Noah. She managed one glancing openhanded blow off the side of his face before anyone was able to catch up and restrain her.

Noah pointed accusingly at her. "See! See what I mean! They're all heathens!"

She struggled to break free, but Jack Walker had a good hold on her and wasn't about to let go. "Just simmer down now!" he said, tightening his grip.

"Yeah...and I'd say that goes for you, too, Pa."

Everyone turned to see Wayman standing with a crutch braced under his armpit and the weight of his bad side resting heavily on it.

"You need to apologize to this lady here. She gave of herself and her time to see that I pulled through this mess alright, and I figure that makes her one heck of a good friend of mine." He hobbled forward until he was directly in front of his pa. They stood face to face for a few moments with everyone else keeping quiet and just watching to see what would happen next.

Birdsong again tried in vain to twist free.

"I ain't apologizing to no heathen redskin! And that's the end of it! If any of you decides to trust that Comanche woman, you ain't got the good sense God give a rock! Now —"

"Does that mean you've started believing in the Lord, Noah?" Pastor Jenks asked.

The veins were bulging in Noah's neck as he glared at the pastor. He spun on his heel and headed for his wagon.

With the confrontation now at an end, Birdsong began to simmer down and Jack was able to loosen his hold on her. Heck then broke things up and everyone headed for their respective wagons. Although the air was filled with disgust and abhorrence for the way one of their own had treated Birdsong, they were all relieved to be leaving the site of the ambush.

Heck had no desire to be caught off guard again, so every man who had access to a horse, and was not needed to drive a team, was used as an outrider. Wild Willie turned their team over to Birdsong. Joshua Carter, even though he was just twelve, was big for his age, and his pa, Harry, had taught him to handle the team while they were back in Independence. So the task was turned over to the boy and Harry joined the outriders. Danny and Ronnie borrowed a couple of horses and helped out. Despite his injury, Wayman was able to handle his pa's team and did so. That freed up Noah, who also enlisted Rip. Those driver changes upped the number of outriders to a very comfortable twelve...including Heck.

Heck assigned permanent positions to each of them. There would be five on one side and six on the other. That left him to remain free to wander from one side to the other as he saw fit. He instructed them that if they spotted anything that even resembled a redskin, they were to shoot first and ask questions afterward.

As the train continued to make its way along the edge of the river, an uneasiness hung over it that was thick enough to whip up a mess a biscuits out of. The smiles were gone from the faces, children were no longer allowed outside the wagons to walk alongside as had been usual, and every single wagon kept a rifle on the seat where it was easily accessible to the driver, whether they be man or woman.

Conversations were kept to a minimum as the day wore on. The tension that rode with the members of the wagon train served to keep the travelers vigilant to their surroundings.

Jay was seated next to Sam and was doing her best to keep Tom entertained, but he was being uncooperative, and it tested the limits of her patience to finally wear him down to the point where she was able to rock him to sleep in her arms. She continued to hold him the rest of the afternoon and into the early evening.

Ever since the attack, Sam had been aware of her

reluctance to put the boy down. He remained concerned for her state of mind. He had mentioned it to Heck and was relieved when Heck told him to drive his wagon instead of taking up the job of outrider.

"Why don't you lay him back there on the mattress?" he suggested, tilting his head toward the area behind them.

She stopped her rocking motion and the humming as well. She smiled weakly. "I think I'm of a mind to just keep him right here in my arms. What if the Indians came and took him away? What would I do then?"

"Nothing will happen to him, Jay," he said softly, then added, "I promise."

"Are you sure?" she asked from under pleading eyes.

"Yes, honey." He switched the cluster of reins to his left hand and placed his right arm around her shoulders. "I'm sure," he said sincerely, and drew her closer to him. He decided right then that she was in need and inwardly vowed to ask Pastor Jenks to intervene on her behalf.

The wagons reached the beginning of the big bend in the river, right about on schedule. Heck called a halt and the drivers made short work of getting circled and making camp for the night. The evening meals were cooked over extremely small fires, because it was felt that any large sources of light would only invite the Comanches to shoot arrows in that direction. The travelers dispensed with the main bonfire that evening and everyone except for the perimeter guards retired early.

§

"Sam? Wake up."

Despite being dead tired, he managed to open his eyes. "Yeah, what is it?"

"Time ta get up an' take yer turn a watchin'," Kyle said and lowered himself down off the step at the back of the wagon.

"I'll be right there. Just give me a couple of minutes to get my boots on and grab my rifle." He could hear the soft rustle of footsteps in the grass as Kyle walked away. Sam pulled his trouser-clad legs out from under the covers—all the men had taken to sleeping with their pants on just in case the Comanches took the notion to attack in the middle of the night. Although Birdsong had assured them that they only attacked at night on rare occasion—something about their spirits not being able to find their way in the dark if they were to get killed—they elected to do it anyway.

"Wha...what is it?" Jay asked, after rolling over. "Is Tom alright?" she asked, with a startled realization that something might have happened to her baby. She popped bolt upright, and with the help of the rays of silvery moonlight that filtered through the opening in the canvas, was able to make him out down by her feet, fast asleep.

"He's just fine," Sam assured her while he was pulling his boots on. "I'm just getting up to go take my turn at standing guard."

"Will you bring him up here to me?"

He was puzzled by the request, but did as she requested. He vowed again to get the pastor to have a talk with her as soon as possible and maybe help out with getting her a measure of reassurance and comfort from the Lord.

Once the boy had been settled in next to her, he kissed each of them on the forehead, and while touching a hand to her cheek, whispered, "I love you."

She grabbed ahold of his arm as he reached for his Sharps. "You be careful, Sam Bartlett. Don't take any unnecessary chances," she cautioned. "I ain't ready to get shed of you just yet."

He leaned over and this time kissed her full on the lips. "Count on it," he said softly, and climbed over the tailgate.

"Kyle? Where are you?" Sam asked, as he was pushing the buttons through the proper holes down the front of his coat.

"Over here." Came the soft reply from beside the wagon

just ahead.

Sam looked in that direction and could easily make out the figure in the bright moonlight. He hefted the Sharps from where he had propped it against the wagon wheel and covered the distance quickly. "Let's get away from here so we can talk," he whispered.

Kyle nodded and they moved away from the wagon with its sleeping occupants inside. Once they were at a safe distance, Sam asked, "How'd everything go? You see or hear anything suspicious?"

"There was a time, just a little while ago, when I was hearin' some mighty peculiar coyote howlin'."

"What'dya mean, peculiar?"

"Dunno. Just seemed a mite peculiar is all. It'd be one a comin' from one place, then one a comin' from another place, then one from another place. I dunno, just seemed peculiar that there never was any two of 'em howlin' at the same time. What would you make of sumpthin' like that?"

Suddenly a coyote howled mournfully, and not too far away from the sounds of it. "See, there it is right there," Kyle said as the two of them had turned to face the sound. "Now you just wait a few seconds and I'll bet six bits up against a bent up horseshoe nail that there'll be another one a soundin' from a different direction."

He'd no sooner gotten the words out when sure enough the answering howl came just as predicted.

Sam crouched slightly. "Looks like you win that bet," he whispered. "Sounds to me like those aren't coyotes. But just to be sure, let's go wake up Birdsong and see what she thinks about all this. Ain't no sense in anyone going off halfcocked."

They made their way ahead two more wagons, and as they approached the Hawkins wagon, she came sliding silently over the top of the tailgate.

"Good that you are here," she said as they came face to face. "I want to tell someone those are not coyotes. That is

Comanches telling other Comanches they will attack very soon. Is good idea to make the people to be awake so they not be surprised when they come to kill us when we sleep."

"Can you tell which way they'll come from?" Sam asked.

"Yes. The signals say the attack will first come from over there." She pointed to the north. "Next they will come from that way." She pointed again. "Then that way." She indicated yet a third direction.

"Thanks, Birdsong," Sam said with genuine sincerity. "Okay, Kyle...you go round up the rest of the guards while we warn the folks in the wagons. Let them in on what's going on and have 'em all congregate over along the north side in case the Comanches decide not to wait. We'll get some of the other men to cover the other two directions. Make it quick. We don't have any idea for sure just how much time we have."

Kyle nodded and quickly set out with a parting, "Gotcha."

Sam and Birdsong didn't waste any time, either. He went one way and she the other. In just a matter of a few short minutes, the encampment was wide-awake, completely warned, and ready for just about anything. With about two hours left until dawn, they waited with rifles in hand for what they now knew to be an imminent attack.

❧Chapter 13❧

From his scant protection behind the wagon tongue, Sam peered intently into the dull gray early morning. Remembering Jay's words about her not being ready to get shed of him just yet, he figured he could do better and scooted over behind the wheel. No sooner had he settled in, then he caught a flicker of movement out of the corner of his eye. He smiled knowingly as he hunkered down and rested the barrel of the Sharps between the spokes. He took careful aim and waited for the bush to move again. When it did, he squeezed the trigger. An instant after the rifle discharged the clump gave a yelp and tipped over, coming to rest on its side.

"Good shot," Stretch said from his position about an arm's reach away.

"Thanks." Sam pulled the breech open and used a fingernail to dig out the spent shell. He snatched a fresh one from the supply he had lined out on the step, pushed it into the receiver and slammed the breech closed.

The potshotting had been going on now for the better part of a half hour. As far as Sam could tell, no one in the train had been injured. However, the Comanches were losing warriors at a pretty good clip. Another shot rang out from over along the north side. Sam didn't take the time to look. Instead, he intensified his scrutiny of the small area he was responsible for.

The Indians had started this hide and seek game just before sunup. Charlie had said that it was their way of unnerving the white men to the point where they would get jumpy and frazzled. When the heathens figured the time was right, they'd attack in force. Then and only then would the wagon train know for sure what it was up against.

Birdsong had agreed with his assessment, saying, "What Charlie say is true. Comanche will first make the white men nervous. Then it will be easy for them to come and take whatever they want. Sometimes it takes a long time for this to happen. But the Comanche will always win," she assured them.

The game of nerves continued for the better part of the morning. Shortly after nine or so, the Indians disappeared and the area assumed an eerie quiet. After a few minutes, during which no shots had been fired, Heck and Charlie made the rounds, asking each lookout if they had seen anything in a while. The answer was the same from each of them; no one had seen hide nor hair. Heck decided to find out from the authority on the subject just what was going on, so he and Charlie made their way to the Hawkins wagon.

"What's this all about?" Heck asked as he looked into Birdsong's dark eyes.

She folded her arms in stoic reflection. "I think the Comanche are gone. I think too many are killed. I think they will wait for another time to come back."

"So you're sayin' that it's most likely safe ta skedaddle outta here?" Charlie asked, and pushing his fingers up under the back of his hat, scratched the bald spot toward the rear of his head.

She unfolded her arms and gestured with a one-handed,

sweeping motion. "I am say...the Comanche are no longer here, but is never safe for the white man in this country. If you want to make some tracks, then I think now is a good time." She again folded her arms and waited.

"What'dya think Charlie? Should we give it a try?"

"'Peers ta me she ought to know enough about her own people ta have a handle on how they'd act. Yeah...I figger this's about as good a time as any."

"Sounds fair enough to me. Let's get 'em hitched up and get on out of here then." Heck turned toward Birdsong and touched an index finger to the folded up front side of his hat. "Thanks, Birdsong. I'm beholdin' to ya."

She nodded once while maintaining her stoic demeanor.

Heck and Charlie spread the word that they were moving out. Folks worked feverishly and the train was ready to roll in near record time. The outriders were sent out with the usual orders to shoot to kill anything that moved. Charlie whipped up the lead team and the train began snaking its way around the big bend in the river.

✍

By late afternoon they had completed that part of the journey and Heck called a halt. They were now faced with the moment of truth; it was time to decide on a course of action. They hastily pulled the wagons into a circle of sorts and the drivers met inside the scant safety of the confines where Heck again spelled out their options. After a bit of discussion, it was decided that it made a whole lot of sense to leave the river and head out across country. That way they would not only be able to cut a couple of days off their journey, but they would be away from the river, which the Indians seemed to favor as a hiding place from where to launch their attacks. He reckoned that the cut across the prairie would amount to about a hundred to a hundred and ten miles, give or take. Of course, there was no way of knowing what their chances would be of coming across water along the way, so he ordered everyone to replenish their supply before they got underway.

The atmosphere was a solemn one as the outriders rode guard while the water barrels were being filled to overflowing. As each wagon finished stocking up on the life-sustaining liquid, it was pulled in line away from the river. Pastor Jenks was the last to reposition his wagon, mainly because he'd taken the time to say one of his longwinded prayers.

Once it was clear that everyone was ready, Heck waved his arm and shouted, "Let's head 'em west! And may God go with us!"

Those within earshot said a hearty "Amen." and the outriders fanned out. Charlie laid his whip out above the backs of his team and snapped it just above the ears of the left side lead. The team strained against the harness and the wagon lurched forward. One by one, the others followed and they headed into the unknown dangers of the vast expanse of open prairie that stretched away from what had once been the security of the river.

Jay sat next to her husband on the wagon seat. Her back was ramrod straight as she held her son in her lap and hugged him to her. Her mouth was set with grim defiance. She glanced down at the rifle on the floorboard. *Lord, forgive me, but I'll kill anyone who tries to take my baby*, she vowed inwardly, and felt immediately ashamed for even thinking such a thing. She then pulled her son even closer to her bosom.

Sam noticed the extra attention she was again giving to Tom. "Why don't you just let him lay down in the wagon?" he asked.

She shifted uncomfortably. "He's doing just fine," she assured him without looking his way.

He decided to let it go for now and after saying, "Suit yourself," returned his attention to handling the team and watching out for heathen Comanches.

The day's journey finally came to an end and the circle was made as compact as possible. Household items were stacked in the gaps between the wagons and sentinels were posted behind each of the fortifications. The fires were again kept small and the evening meal was eaten with a minimum of conversation. Those who stood guard had their food brought to them and ate in silent, cold discomfort.

The strain of not knowing what the Indians would do next had taken a prodigious toll on the members of the train. Husbands and wives had begun bickering with one another and children were becoming more unruly than usual from the effects of being cooped up.

After supper, Sam decided that now was as good a time as any to have his talk with the pastor. "I'm going to take a walk," he said and pushed his way up from the warmth of the fire.

"You want company?" Stretch asked.

"Naw...I just wanna stretch my legs," he lied. "I won't be gone long, honey," he said to Jay. He leaned down and gave her a peck on the cheek. She showed no reaction, so he turned and headed for the pastor's wagon.

"Howdy, Pastor...Mrs. Jenks," he said as he approached the Jenks' fire.

"Hello, Sam...out for a little stroll I see."

"Yeah, you might say that...but...well...I was really needing to have a talk with you just as soon as your supper's finished," Sam said as he watched the pastor push the remnants of a biscuit into his mouth.

"Well then..." Pastor Jenks said around the mouthful, "I'd say your timing is just about perfect, because that, sir, was the very last bite of my supper." He pushed a hand against his knee and grunted his way up from the rock. He glanced behind him, and placing both hands against his backside, tried to get the circulation going again with a slight rubbing motion. "Not the most comfortable piece of dining room furniture I've ever had the misfortune of sitting on." He stopped rubbing his backside and added, "But I would think that the good Lord has His reasons for sending me and mine out here. I reckon that it's His will and I'll just have to do the best I can with what He gives me." He looked down at Maggie. "Thank you for the meal, Ma. It was wonderful, as usual."

"You're welcome, Pa," she said and smiled appreciatively. "Now, whose turn is it to help with the cleaning up?" she asked the semicircle of youthful faces seated around the fire.

"It's mine and Mark's," John said and reached for the stack of dirty dishes.

"Go easy on the water, boys," the pastor reminded them.

"Yes, sir. C'mon, Mark, let's get 'er done." Mark scooped up the ones that his ma and pa had used and the two boys went off to tend to their chore.

The pastor placed a gentle hand on Sam's shoulder. "Now Sam, what seems to be on your mind?"

"Let's walk," Sam countered.

Once they were away from the fire, he began explaining his suspicions about the way Jay had been acting lately. The pastor listened intently as Sam told him how he had talked her into leaving her family and the high society way of life she'd been accustomed to in New York, and how he had then carted her off to Independence. He then told about how he'd been called by the Lord to leave Independence and make the trip west to supply horses to wagon trains and anyone else with a need. A tear welled up when he told about how he had promised Jay faithfully that he'd take care of her and Tom if she would agree to make the move with him.

When Sam had finished, the pastor stopped walking and turned to face him. "You know, Sam? I think you're feeling some guilt because of placing your family in what has turned out to be harm's way." Sam opened his mouth to protest, but the pastor raised a hand between them and continued,

"There's nothing wrong with feeling that way. I'm not real fond of having my family out here dodging arrows either. But the undeniable fact remains that we *are* here, and are now faced with finding a way to deal with that unfortunate circumstance." He looked at Sam's downcast eyes. "Do you understand what I'm saying, Sam? We all have to keep the faith."

Sam sighed heavily. "My wife and son are the two most important things in my life...next to God, that is," he added, remembering who he was talking to. "They're counting on me to bring them safely through this mess, and that's just what I intend to do. But in the meantime I'm thinking Jay could use some comforting from the Lord."

"Say no more. I understand fully and you can rest assured that you're not the only one that's concerned about the condition of folks' faith around here. I've been noticing all the bickering that's been going on between some of the husbands and their wives, and not to mention the shortness of tempers toward the children. Tomorrow being the Lord's Day, I think I'll be taking a few minutes to see if I can help get these folks back on the right track."

Sam extended a hand and the pastor clasped it warmly. "Thanks, Pastor. I hope you can do something to help all of us before it's too late."

The pastor placed his other hand on Sam's shoulder and said softly, "I'll do my best, Sam."

⁊

The next morning was just about an exact copy of the one before, except without the Indians harassing them. The sky was clear and without a speck of cloud to be found anywhere.

Sam had just finished hitching the team and had walked over to see if Stretch was in need of help. "How you doing, Stretch? You just about got it done?" he asked as he approached the Conestoga.

"Yeah, purtnear," Stretch replied and tugged a strap

through the buckle until it was as tight as it needed to be. Reaching for yet another strap, he hesitated, then forgetting the task at hand, turned to face Sam. "Sam, I ain't one to be nosy, but..."

"But what, Stretch? You can feel free to talk with me. Fact is you're darned near family."

"Yeah, I feel that way, too, but...well...what's eating on Jay anyway?"

"Oh, that," Sam said wistfully. "That's something that's in need of attention alright. I think she's afraid for young Tom and is having a hard time dealing with those fears."

"So what're we gonna do about it? We can't just let it keep on the way it is. I don't know if you noticed the difference or not, but that breakfast she fixed this morning weren't fit for a—"

"Yeah, I know. I had me a talk with Pastor Jenks last night, and he says most all the folks in the train are getting intense about things. He says he's gonna try his levelheaded best to give them a sermon this morning that'll maybe get 'em back on the right track."

"Boy, I sure hope so. Many more meals like the one we just had and I'll be needing to marry up with Mary Jane just so I can get enough vittles in me to keep from drying up and blowin' away."

Sam chuckled. "Hopefully we can get things straightened out before it gets to that point. But to look at you, I'd say you're in a whole lot better shape right now then you were a few weeks ago when we first started this trip."

"That's exactly what I'm talking about." He patted his stomach. "These few pounds I've put on are settin' real good with me and I'm figgerin' on hanging onto them."

They both chuckled this time and returned to the business of completing the task of harnessing the team.

As each group completed the things necessary to prepare for the day's journey, they brought their Bibles and collected in the center of the circle. Guards were left posted on all four sides of the encampment with a request that the pastor preach loud enough for them to hear as well. Noah had no desire to listen to any hypocrite preaching and volunteered to be one of the guards, saying he didn't much care if the preaching was loud, soft, or not at all.

Once everyone with an interest was present, which included a goodly number that was more than half the folks in the train, Pastor Jenks stood quietly at the head of the congregation and scanned the faces before him. He was in no hurry and took the time to gaze into the eyes of each one present. He lingered for an especially long time on those of Judith Bartlett. Once he had everyone fidgeting and wondering what was going on, he said, "Let us pray."

Folks bowed their heads and again waited for the pastor to continue.

Finally, the words came. "Dear Lord, before You stands a flock of frightened children...Your children. As You can see, they are in need of encouragement and understanding as to why You sent them out here in the face of these dangers."

Sam tightened his arm around Jay's waist and was pleased to feel a slight response from her.

Pastor Jenks continued, "There are times in our lives, Lord, when we feel as though You've forsaken us...but..." he paused and raised his gaze. "Everyone look up here at me," he said.

They all did as instructed.

"But that time is not now. Does each and every one of you accept that?"

Jay started to speak, but decided against it and instead let the tears begin to flow.

"Because if you don't, then you might just as well admit that you have no faith in what God is about. He is all powerful, Almighty and all seeing. He knows you're here and He also knows you are His children. If you don't accept that, then you might just as well renounce your Christianity."

The only sound Sam could hear was that of a bothersome fly buzzing around his left ear. He brushed at it.

The pastor bowed his head, and the rest followed his example. He waited a good while then said, "Yea, though I walk through the valley of the shadow of death, I will fear no evil: for thou art with me; thy rod and thy staff they comfort me." He paused as those wonderful words of encouragement from the Twenty-third Psalm gripped every heart present. "Amen," he said softly, and raised his gaze.

Jay let Tom down to the ground and Sam felt an elbow nudge into his side. He looked in that direction and came face to face with the grin on Stretch's face. Stretch patted his stomach, and the grin intensified.

Sam was thankful that the Lord had sent this man of God to join their train. He felt that even though the pastor's opening was uncharacteristically brief, it stood a passable chance of being effective. He felt even more thankful as Jay slid her arm around his waist. He looked down at her and thumbed a tear from her cheek as he mouthed the words, "I love you."

Pastor Jenks then resumed the meeting by preaching a sermon on the joys of being fulfilled through believing in Jesus Christ and that all things are possible when a person is a child of God. He stressed that peace of mind came only through understanding that God does not give His children a task or a situation that is too big or too intense for them to handle.

After listening to the blessing that the pastor had bestowed on them, Sam and Jay returned to their wagon with an arm wrapped around each other's waist and little Tom tagging along on his own two feet.

It wasn't long after that that the wagons resumed their journey into the unknown, but this time Sam felt a reassurance that he was no longer fighting this battle on his own; his beloved wife was again at his side.

The day proved to be a long one for the travelers. There was no stopping for the midday meal. Whatever eating needed to be done, was done while the wheels continued to roll westward.

When dusk finally did come to the prairie, the weary travelers had made almost twenty-one miles despite their late start. Folks ate their evening meal in relative silence, and after the guard situation had been laid out for the night, everyone else turned in. Sam was dead tired and almost immediately dropped off into a deep sleep.

❧Chapter 14☙

Sam heard a faint scratching coming from somewhere beneath the wagon and figured it was a prairie mouse looking for his breakfast. He shivered against the early morning chill and pulled the covers up under his chin. A coyote sounded its woeful call from somewhere off in the distance. He smiled at the realization that, near as he could tell, it was indeed a real coyote this time.

He lowered the blanket, swung his legs out from under it, and despite having his trousers on, again shivered against the effects of the early morning chill. He looked over at Jay, pleased to see that she was sleeping soundly. He pulled aside the rear flap and took in the hint of gray along the eastern horizon.

He glanced at the Conestoga as a shuffling from within reached his ears. He located his boots, pulled them on, and found his shirt. He quickly put it on, covered it with his coat, grabbed his hat, and carefully made his way to the rear of the wagon. He quietly worked his way over the tailgate and lowered himself to the ground. Tom twisted, squirmed, and finally turned over as Sam let the flap close behind him. He waited a few seconds to see if the boy would awaken. When he was sure that Tom had continued his sleep, he headed for the fire pit and went about the business of kindling the morning fire.

By the time Stretch had emerged from the Conestoga and joined him, the fire was good-sized and licking at the morning crispness. Stretch reached out to the flames. "Mornin'. Bit on the cool side this fine morning," he said cheerfully. "Might be a tolerable day for a wagon ride."

"Mornin', Stretch. You seem to not have any cares this morning."

"Just an Injun or two trying to take my scalp is all. Other than that..." He turned around and bent over, giving his backside all the opportunity it needed to get the beneficial aspects afforded by the flames. Satisfied that he was fast approaching toasty, he straightened up, and while rubbing in the warmth, turned to face Sam. It was then that he realized that Sam was preoccupied with something other than the heat from the fire. "You see something out there?"

"Dunno just yet...might be," Sam replied. He took a couple of tentative steps toward his wagon and then stopped and squinted into the dawn. "Might wanna go get your rifle," he suggested softly.

Without a word, Stretch headed for the Conestoga while Sam quickly made his way to the front of the schooner. He reached under the front seat and pulled the Sharps from its usual spot. He grabbed a handful of shells from the small box on the floorboards and stuffed them into his coat pocket. He reached for another handful just as a muffled moan reached his ears. He turned toward the sound and in the gray dawning light was able to make out the vague outline of a figure as it crumpled to the ground about twenty or thirty yards ahead. An uneasy shiver ran up his spine.

"Jay, wake up!" he hissed into the wagon, then crouched behind the wheel for whatever little cover it afforded.

"Wha…what is it?" she asked sleepily.

"I think the Comanches are back. Keep your head down and watch out for Tom. Stay inside until I find out what's going on," he whispered hoarsely.

"Please be careful."

He remained bent over in a crouch while he made his way toward where he had seen the guard go down. As he drew near, he saw the figure attempt to rise and then fall back with a groan. "Stay down," he warned. He swallowed the lump in his throat as he continued to ease forward.

Suddenly, a slight movement caught his eye. He froze and peered intently until he saw the movement again. Just behind the front wheel of a nearby wagon was another figure lying in the grass. He raised the Sharps and pulled the trigger.

The Comanche grunted and rolled over as the slug ended his days of raiding wagon trains.

"Forgive me Lord," Sam said as he dug out the spent shell. He hastily loaded in another casing and made his way to the downed guard while the rest of the camp sprang to life. He knelt beside the figure and saw that it was Wild Willie. There was an arrow protruding from his midsection.

"Danged redskin got me when I weren't lookin'," Willie said. He winced as a pain hit the wounded area. "Prop me up against that wheel over yonder and git on about yer bizness. I might be able ta pluck off one or two of 'em whilst I still got some pluckin' abilities left in me."

Sam felt sorry for his friend, but didn't argue. He got a good hold under Willie's arms and dragged him to the nearby wheel where he sat him upright facing the center of the circle.

Willie smiled through the pain and tipped his hat with the barrel of his pistol. He pulled his knife and rested it across his thighs. "Go give 'em what fer," he said and shuddered his way through another spasm. He coughed and a red trickle appeared at the corner of his mouth.

"May God bless you, Bill Hawkins," Sam offered softly,

and turned away.

He hadn't noticed until now, and was surprised to realize, that the camp was full of the sounds of yelling, screaming Indians mixed in with sporadic gunfire. He heard a scream and instantly picked it out as belonging to Jay. He whirled and caught a glimpse of a figure disappearing into the front of their wagon. Panic stricken, he sprinted to the schooner, jumped onto the hub, and scrambled onto the seat. He pulled his knife and jerked aside the flap. Right in front of him was the naked back of a Comanche brave. Without a second thought, he plunged the blade in as far as it would go.

The Indian started to slump forward, but Jay raised a bare foot to his chest and pushed with all her might. As Sam shuffled to get out of the way, the Comanche somersaulted backward over the seat and continued to the ground, banging his head against the wagon tongue for good measure.

"You and Tom alright?"

"Yeah," she replied and brushed a fallen lock from in front of her eyes. "Where's your pistol?" she asked.

"Right here under the seat." He reached down and retrieved it. "Here, keep it handy. I'll be back just as soon as I can. In the meantime...stay put." He stayed just long enough to see her check the load. He felt genuinely thankful that he'd taken the time to instruct her in its use.

In his haste, he fell off the wagon, but managed to regain his balance when he reached the ground. He glanced at the prone Comanche before looking to the outer side of the circle where he spotted a naked figure hunkered down and coming in. He raised the Sharps and squeezed off a shot. The attacker progressively crouched lower until he just kinda tipped over and lay still. Sam reached down and pulled his knife from the Comanche's back. He then wiped both sides of the blade against the Indians bare shoulder and slipped it into the sheath at his waist.

In the meantime, Stretch was having troubles of his own.

"Stretch! Help me...Stretch!" Mary Jane hollered hysterically as a Comanche brave wrapped his arms around the upper part of her legs and hefted her up onto his shoulder. "Help me, Stretch!" she hollered again as she beat on the brave's back with her tiny fists.

"Mary Jane!" Stretch yelled and headed toward where he figured the plea was coming from. "Mary Jane! Where are you?" His heart raced as he rounded the corner of a wagon. His worst fears were realized when he spied a Comanche brave running away from the circle with his beloved Mary Jane draped over his shoulder. "Mary Ja—"

Blackness enveloped him as the tip of a Comanche arrow gouged his scalp, knocking him out cold.

Sam had seen the Indian capture Mary Jane, heft her onto his shoulder, and disappear between the wagons. He saw Stretch run to her aid, and feeling as though everything was under control, had spun around, returning his attention to the fight at hand. He took out another attacker just as the Indian was about to grab up one of the Hendricks children.

The battle raged for only about five or six minutes, yet it seemed more like hours. Finally, things eased up as the Comanches retreated and finally disappeared behind a rise in the prairie floor. A lingering report could be heard as someone mistakenly figured he could make good on a long range shot.

Once the gunfire had ceased all together, the moaning and wailing for the dead and injured took over.

Sam helped Jay and Tom down from their place of safety inside the wagon and hugged them to him, thankful that they were unharmed. "You two okay?" he asked.

Concern filled her eyes. "We're fine. Let's go see where we can be of help," she replied solemnly.

They went to where Sam had left Willie. As they approached, Jay shielded Tom's eyes from the gruesome sight.

Sam was distressed to see two more arrows sticking out of Willie's chest. He was slumped over, almost lying on his side.

Four Indian braves were sprawled in front of him. One was lying across his legs with the knife stuck in his chest and Willie's blood-soaked hand still holding onto it. Sam checked the load in Willie's pistol that lay in the grass beside him...it was empty. It was plain to see that he had given a good account of himself before giving up the ghost.

Sam brushed a thumb and index finger downward across the unseeing eyes, closing off the sightless stare of death. "Rest easy, my friend," he said morosely.

They turned away from Willie's remains and crossed the circle toward the Greenberg wagon. They were disheartened by the sight of the dead and wounded as they passed them by. Jack Walker lay in a pool of blood, a tomahawk lodged savagely in his scalp. Wayman Baxter's wounded leg had busted open and was bleeding profusely. Heck had taken an arrow in the upper portion of his left arm, but was handling it well enough. He had broken it off to no more than just a stub and was doing his best to comfort those who had been less fortunate. The arm dangled uselessly at his side with the crimson blood dripping off his fingertips.

Birdsong was just about the closest thing the train had to a doctor, and she was doing her level best to patch up those who needed her most. Sam slowed as they approached her. She was applying a flat, square compress to a gushing head wound on the side of Harry Carter's head.

"You will push tight against this," she told Harry while placing the flat of his hand against the bandage. She picked up a strip of cloth and carefully tied it around the wounded head, being careful not to cause him any more discomfort than he was already being subjected to. "You will not move. You will sit here," she told him and pointed at the ground. Harry nodded but didn't speak. She rose, turned, and came face to face with Sam.

"Birdsong, I...Willie's..."

"Where is my man?" she asked, reading the remorse in his

eyes. "Where is…?"

Sam pointed. "He's over there," he said softly, and placed a gentle hand on her arm.

She looked up at him as a cloud of foreboding shrouded her eyes.

"He's gone," Sam said with heartfelt tenderness.

She closed her eyes and stood quietly, allowing the full impact of the simple statement to enter into her being. She swayed slightly and mumbled some words in her native tongue. A small blue and gray bird lit on the very tiptop of a nearby clump of brush and rattled off its song of life. Once she heard the delightful song, her spirit was at ease with the tragedy and she allowed her eyes to open. "Did he die bravely?" she asked and looked into his eyes for the truth.

"Yeah, he sure did. You'll see that when you go over there."

Satisfied that he had spoken truthfully, she said simply, "Today I will make him pretty. Tomorrow I will light him on fire." She turned and slowly walked away toward the grisly scene that awaited her.

Sam put his arms around his wife and son as they stood together and watched her go. "She sure is a strong woman," he said and pulled them closer.

Pastor and Mrs. Jenks were also doing their best to comfort those who needed it, which was just about everyone. A true accounting of the extent of the damage would be some time in coming. The main thing now was to figure out how many of the children had been taken.

They reached the Greenberg wagon just as Mabel finished wrapping Jacob's right arm in the near-white strip of cloth she had torn from her petticoat. "You alright?" Sam asked.

"Yeah, I'll get by." He glanced around. "Where's Mary Jane…and Stretch?"

"Last I seen 'em one of the heathens was hauling her off and Stretch was hot after him…over there between those two wagons." Sam pointed.

Hank was instantly apprehensive. "Are you saying he never came back?" he asked.

Sam was immediately fearful of the possibility that Stretch may have been killed and Mary Jane was gone. "You stay here," he said to Jay. "I'll go see what I can find out."

He expected the worst as he proceeded to the area where he had last seen Stretch. He breathed a sigh of relief when he turned the corner between the two wagons and spied the boy sitting up in the grass holding a hand to his head. "You alright?" Sam asked as he knelt beside his friend.

Stretch looked around with a dazed, confused expression. "I dunno. What happened?"

"That's a good question. Last I seen, you were hightailing it after a Comanche that had Mary Jane slung over his—"

"Mary Jane!" Stretch jerked his head around in a frantic attempt to look in every direction at once. "Mary Jane!" he said again and struggled to get up. The effort sent a sharp pain shooting through his wounded scalp and he fell back to earth. "Owww. What happened to my head?" His hand found the wounded area and he explored it with tentative fingertips. He pulled the hand away and inspected it. Blood shown on his fingers. He looked up at Sam. "Am I hurt bad?"

Sam bent over and inspected the gash. "Don't look too bad. It'll need some bandaging, though, but I think you'll live. C'mon, I'll help you to your feet."

As Sam assisted him to his feet, the youngster's concern again centered on Mary Jane, "Where's Mary Jane anyways?"

"Near as I can figure she got hauled off by the Comanches."

"But that can't be. It just can't be. Why…" He grabbed Sam by his shoulders and continued the plea, "Sam…we gotta go after her. We can't just let her go." He crumpled back to the prairie grass and sobbed his anguish. "It's all my fault. I should have been there when she was in need. I let her down." He raised his tear streaked face to the heavens and prayed in earnest for the first time in his entire life, "God, watch over her and keep her alive 'til I can find her."

He lowered his gaze, pulled his shirttail from out of the tops of his trousers, and used the end of it to wipe the tears. "I'll find her, Sam. With or without your help, I'm gonna find her," he vowed.

Sam was nearly overcome by the genuine sincerity in the boy as he said, "It'll be with my help, Stretch,' Sam assured him. "I promise I'll help you get her back. But in the meantime we need to deal with what went on here." He waved toward the interior of the circle.

He then proceeded to tell Stretch about the severity of the attack and about those that he knew of who had been either killed or wounded. His voice quivered as he told of Wild Willie and his gallant fight to the very end.

"How are the Greenbergs dealing with Mary Jane's being gone?" Stretch asked.

"I don't think they know yet."

Stretch closed his eyes briefly, while he went about heaving a heavy sigh. "Well then, I reckon I got a duty to go let 'em know," he vowed resolutely.

"I think that'd be a good idea. In the meantime, I'm going to go see if I can help get some of these folks back on their feet. I imagine that after things settle down, we'll be having a meeting to go over our options and decide how we're gonna handle things from here on out."

"I'll come look you up after I deal with Mary Jane's ma 'n pa, but I don't need any meeting to tell me what I'll be doing."

Sam nodded his understanding.

The toll on the wagon train had been significant, but Sam had already seen the worst of it. There were numerous bumps and bruises and a few more cuts and scrapes, but the only two fatalities had been Willie and Jack Walker. Although many were wounded, none of the injuries was thought to be life threatening, except maybe Harry Carter's head wound. It all depended on how well they could keep it from becoming infected.

After the wounded had been bandaged and Jack was laid to rest in a shallow grave, Heck called the expected meeting. Folks had tried to talk Birdsong into letting them bury Willie right along with Jack but she had already set her sights on cremating him.

The meeting got under way with everyone present except for the two men who were posted to stand watch against the general direction the Comanches had taken when they'd pulled back.

Blood shown through the sling that cradled Heck's arm as he started to speak, "Looks like we got us a passel of trouble lookin' us straight in the eye. We got two dead, a sight more than just a few folks wounded, and four young'uns what got carted off; Mary Jane Greenberg, Charlette Hendricks, Josh Carter and the pastor's youngest, John, and ain't none of that to be taken lightly."

"So, what're we gonna do about getting our children back?" Jacob asked.

Heck exhaled heavily. "I wish I could say we're just going to ride right out there and fetch 'em back, but that would not only be foolish, but most likely life-ending, as well. In the first place, we don't even know if they're still around and are going to attack the wagons again, or if they done hightailed it out of here and are miles away by now. Those Injuns is on their home grounds and that, all by itself, gives 'em a real big advantage over us."

The meeting broke down temporarily as small groups of dissenting voices grew prominent and each group tried in its own way to solve the mystery of what the Comanches were doing at that very moment.

"So when do you reckon we'll be knowing if they're still around or not and when will we be going after Mary Jane and the others?" The question came from Stretch and everyone agreed with it openly.

Heck pondered his options for a few moments as folks waited for his answer. "Now that's most likely the easiest question I've been asked in a coon's age, Stretch. The answer is a plain 'n simple...I don't know."

"What'dya mean, you don't know?" Jacob asked, the agitation he felt was evident in his expression as well as the words. "That's my little girl out there. She ain't done nothing to deserve being hauled off by them savages. Why...there ain't no telling what kind of abuse she'll be put through. She's—"

"Yers ain't the onlyest young'un out there, Jacob!" Kyle Hendricks interrupted. It was easy to see that he was more than just a mite agitated. "In case you didn't hear the report, there's some others of us what's got a stake in this, same as you! My baby young'un's right there alongside a your girl!" His tone lessened in intensity as he continued, "That means I'll be lookin' fer answers my ownself, but givin' Heck a hard time about it ain't a gonna git it done." He looked around and his expression conveyed the despair that was in his heart. "I imagine the pastor and poor old Harry, with his cut up head, is lookin' fer answers they ownselves. I reckon about all we kin do right now would be ta trust in the Almighty and see what kinda hand He deals us."

There was a general chorus of agreement.

After things had settled down a bit it was Pastor Jenks' turn to have his say, "My son John is a good Christian boy, just as I'm sure the others who were taken are good Christians, as well. They all know enough to trust in the Lord and put their faith in His hands. He will care for them until such time as we're able to launch a reasonably thought out attempt to find and rescue them. In the meantime, we have no choice but to do as Brother Hendricks says and trust in the Lord to watch over them. If we run out chasing after them in a halfcocked manner...well, chances are we'll be food for the scavengers before the day is done. With that in mind, does anyone think they have a more reasonable way of approaching the problem?"

"They are safe." The words were spoken softly and reassuringly. As everyone looked toward the sound of the voice, Birdsong stepped out into the inner part of the circle. "They will not be harmed," she repeated.

"How can you say that?" Noah asked and rose from his haunches. "Far as I'm concerned you ain't no better'n them what just kilt some of our folks. Seems to me—"

Birdsong fired an icy stare at the White Eye as she cut him off, "Some of our folks was my man. Some of our folks was my husband. These Comanche are not my people. My people are Comanche, too, but are of the northern tribe." She waved an arm in a sweeping motion that encompassed just about everything other than the south. "My people live in peace beside the Lakota Sioux. These Comanche are Penateka and live to the south. My people do not steal women and children. My people are not cowards who sneak in the night and kill without warning." She paused and bowed her head before continuing with an obviously heavyhearted remorse, "My man is gone. I now have no more reason to continue this journey. I will help to find the children. If I die, I do not care. My man is gone. But you must understand I am not of the Penateka, but I know of their ways. These children will be kept in good health and will not suffer beatings. They are for buying things from other tribes. If a child is not kept unharmed, they will be worth very little in a trade."

The silence that followed was deafening.

Jay pushed between the two men in front of her. "I would think there's been enough accusations piled on this woman. She has just lost her husband, who, by the way, died protecting each and every one of you. Now if you, Noah Baxter," she pointed an accusing finger at him, "had any semblance of a brain in that thick skull of yours, you would realize that there's only been one perfect human being on this earth, and that was the Lord Jesus Christ. Just because a person has red skin, black skin, or brown skin, doesn't give you the right to lump that person into a pot with all the others you don't like...for whatever reason."

Noah shifted his weight from one foot to the other and darted his eyes from one face to the next, looking for a sympathetic eye. He wasn't able to identify even a single one. Not even from either of his own sons.

Jay smiled as she addressed what she saw, "Peers to me that you might be having some second thoughts about being an all out bigot, that right? The best way you have of redeeming yourself is to understand that this young woman is ready to sacrifice herself for those that she considers her friends." She looked at Birdsong, reached out to her, and brushed a lock of black hair back off her face. "She's willing to give of herself the same as Jesus did when He died for all us sinners. And you know something else, Noah Baxter? I'll just bet that if one of your boys had been taken in the raid, she'd be just as willing to help rescue him as well, although I can't for the life of me imagine why."

No one spoke as the truth in her words touched everyone present...even Noah. Every face was on his as he rested his gaze on Birdsong. "I'm sorry...I guess I just—"

His apology was suddenly cut short by the sound of a rifle shot.

"Here they come again!" one of the sentries hollered.

❧Chapter 15❧

This time around, as the men engrossed themselves in defending the train, they had a new motivation; their children were the main targets of the Indians and that just didn't set any too well with them or their wives. The women remained right beside their husbands and kept the extra guns loaded so they could keep up a steady fire.

A couple of the wagons had been pulled well inside the circle, away from the others, so the younger children could be hidden away. At the very height of the battle, Tom had decided to stick his head out through the rear flap to see what was going on. A particularly aggressive Comanche had made it through the perimeter defenses, and seeing the boy peeking out, immediately headed for the sought-after prize.

Stretch was down on one knee behind the Conestoga with Ronnie doing the reloading for him. He pulled off a shot and was disappointed to see that he had missed. He cursed under his breath and reached for a freshly loaded rifle. As he turned his head to locate it, his peripheral vision picked up the movement of a figure running away from the center of the circle.

The fleeing Indian held a kicking, screaming child in his arms. Visions of Mary Jane being whisked away appeared in his mind's eye. He jumped up, dropped the rifle, snatched the pistol from his waistband, and began running as fast as he could. He covered the ground quickly, gaining on the culprit with each stride. The Indian halted, dropped his prize, and turned to face the oncoming threat.

Stretch didn't slow any and barreled full force into the Comanche. The few extra pounds he'd put on as of late, served him well and his momentum sent the both of them tumbling. Although still dazed, he recovered enough to work his way onto one knee while he shook his head in an attempt to right things and clear the cobwebs. As his senses began to settle into a more tolerable way of thinking, he also saw that his opponent was pulling a knife from the sheath at his waist.

The Indian glared with icy hatred, screamed, and lunged.

Stretch instantly collected himself and dove to the side, narrowly missing being cut. He rolled in the grass, and just as the Indian had gathered himself to pounce, Stretch remembered the pistol he had managed to keep ahold of. He pointed it and pulled the trigger three times in rapid succession. The Comanche collapsed not more than three feet away. Stretch grinned his relief as he watched the wounded Comanche wither in pain in the blood-flecked grass.

The youngster had begun to cry. Stretch glanced at him and saw that it was Tom who had nearly been taken. This enraged him all over again, and he glared with renewed hatred as he stuck the barrel of the pistol up the Indian's left nostril and eased back the hammer.

"Don't do it," Jay said from behind him. "He's already done for and Tom's alright…thanks to you."

"If I'd have known it was Tom he was making off with, I'd have kilt him about three times over by now."

"Thankfully, that won't be necessary. You best get on back to the main fight. I'll watch this heathen until this whole mess is over and done with."

Stretch still had the barrel of the pistol shoved up the Indian's nose. He gave it a final push and watched the unwavering defiance in the fella's eyes. He figured that he wasn't going to get him to cow down and that Jay was right. He eased the hammer down, let the tension drain, and rocked back on his haunches.

"Now, give me that pistol and go help Sam," she said softly, and reached out for it.

"Yes, ma'am," he said meekly. He then handed it to her and rose.

The fighting hadn't slowed much, so he headed off at a run. He slid to a stop on his knees beside Sam, picked up the rifle that was lying in the grass, and yanked open the breech. "I'll load...you do the shootin'," he said, and after pushing in a fresh shell, slammed the breech down and handed the rifle to Sam.

Sam put it to his shoulder and drew a bead. "Nice job you did back there."

"Yeah, but I wish I'd a done the same for Mary Jane this morning."

Sam squeezed the trigger.

"Nice shot," Stretch said as he accepted the spent breechloader and handed Sam another freshly loaded one. "Where's Ronnie?" he asked, looking around.

"Don't know," Sam replied. "I expect that after you left, he went off to help his pa...leastways that's the way he headed." Sam squeezed off another shot and squinted his dismay at having missed.

The fighting lasted for a total of only about six or seven minutes—about the same as before—but this time around, the folks in the train had been prepared and suffered only minor injuries. The gray mare that had been a member of Stretch's team, and in foul, took an arrow in the neck and had to be put down; Sam was unable to save the colt. The newlywed, Fay

Appleton, took an arrow in the folds of her petticoats. The women had a time locating and dislodging it, but once they did, other than having a small tear in the front of her dress, she turned out to be none the worse for wear.

The warrior that Stretch had taken down turned out to be a real ornery cuss. Even though Stretch had pulled off three shots at the man, there was just a single hole in the upper part of the heathen's right leg. Whenever someone tried to have a look at it, he would get belligerent and refuse to cooperate. Finally, they called for Birdsong to come and see what she could do.

As the brave saw her approaching out of the corner of his eye, his expression grew puzzled. She set her basket in the buffalo grass and loomed over him with her hands on her hips. She looked down with an expression of disgust. Seeing her attitude toward him infuriated him to the point of attempting to rise and put her in her place. She pointed at him, and while looking at George Appleton—who had been assigned to guard the prisoner—said forcefully, "You will make him to sit!"

George grabbed ahold of the rising Indian and pulled him back down and none too gently either. The fella glared at him and snarled something in Comanche. George just smiled back and tipped his hat while he waited for Birdsong to take charge.

She then spoke in Comanche. "You will sit and be quiet."

"Squaws do not tell a warrior what to do!" he snarled back at her.

"This one does. You will do as I tell you, or I will let you die from your wound."

He did not respond to this unexpected reply and remained silent as she knelt and began to examine his leg. He winced as she touched the wounded area.

"It is good that it hurts. You steal children...it is good that you pay for this with much pain."

"Why do the White Eye not let me die? Why do they send a Comanche woman to care for my wound?"

"I do not know," she said simply, and busied herself with the contents of the basket.

He watched as she deftly applied some healing leaves. Once that had been completed, she then wrapped a cloth around the thigh.

"Why does a Comanche woman live with these White Eye?" he asked when she had completed her task.

"My man was a White Eye."

"Where is your man?"

"He was killed in the attack this morning," she said solemnly, as the grief she felt for Willie again saddened her. She then rose, turned, and without another word, walked away, taking the basket of medicine with her.

The rest of that day was spent watching and waiting: watching for any signs of movement outside the circle of wagons and waiting for yet another attack. Toward evening, a lone rider appeared on the northern horizon, just beyond what would be considered effective rifle range. He sat motionless on the back of his pony, with a feather festooned war lance propped atop his thigh and pointing straight up toward the evening sky. He remained even after his image had faded from view in the falling darkness.

%

Birdsong had spent the afternoon dressing her man in his finest buckskins in preparation to sending his spirit skyward the following morning. She finished with the ritual just after the sentinel had appeared to the north.

Sam arrived at her wagon as she was putting the finishing touches on Willie. "He sure looks pretty," he said, while looking at Willie's neatly parted, slicked down hair. He had remembered that she'd said she would make him pretty today and light him on fire tomorrow, so he just naturally figured that "pretty" was what she wanted to hear.

"Yes," she said softly. "He is pretty and is now ready to go home to be with his ancestors. He will start the journey as the sun rises. He will rise with the smoke and travel with the sun as it makes its journey across the sky." She had traced a hand across the sky as she'd spoken the words with heartfelt emotion.

Sam waited patiently while she lightly traced the lines on her man's face with a gentle fingertip. He felt that she was reliving some good times spent with him. Finally, she returned to the present with a slight jarring.

"You loved him, didn't you?" Sam asked softly.

"Yes, he was a good man."

"I will help you in the morning to send him on his journey."

"Thank you. Is good. He was your friend and because of that I will let you."

He felt a need to change the subject, and asked, "You see that Indian fella sitting his pony over there?" He pointed toward the sentinel.

"Yes, I see."

"Do you have any idea what he's doing out there?"

"Yes, I know."

Sam didn't push her. Instead, he waited for her to straighten Willie's collar. Finally, she rose. "Come," she said. "I will tell you."

They strolled slowly with no particular destination in mind. She seemed melancholy, and rightfully so, Sam decided.

"This brave," she indicated the rider to the north, "is looking to see the spirit of someone."

"What'dya mean?"

"When someone is lost who is a very important member of the tribal council, another someone who is very close to his family must watch the place where he became lost. He must watch until he sees his spirit rise or he finds the lost one's body."

"You mean like a chief or something?"

She nodded. "It could be a mighty chief, a lesser chief or even a tribal healing one, but someone will remain there and continue the watch until the wagons have gone and the body is found."

"Does that mean they won't attack again?"

"No. They will continue to attack until they have what they want."

"And just what might that be?"

"I think they want more of the children, but I am not sure. Maybe I can find this answer from the captured one."

Sam nodded. "Might not be such a bad idea to try."

She glanced toward his wagon. "You will go now to be with your family. I go to my wagon to be with my man and prepare some food for the captured one." She turned and was gone.

Sam returned to his wagon. Jay had fixed a hurried meal and it was eaten just as hurriedly. Neither he nor Stretch wanted to be caught unawares, and accepted the meager meal of cold biscuits and warmed over beans as part of the price they had to pay. They polished off the meal and wasted no time as they returned to their lookout positions.

Birdsong gathered some jerky that had been made from the body of a deer, as well as a generous amount of dried cornmeal cakes, which she placed in a small basket. She also put in some bandages. Satisfied, she went back to where the prisoner was being held.

By the time she arrived, the darkness was nearly complete, but she was still able to make out the guard standing nearby. "Would you please find some sticks to burn in a fire?" she asked. "I have bandages for his wound, some food for us to eat, and some words to speak to this prisoner. I have need of the warmth and light from a small fire."

Danny had taken over for George. "You figger this skunk's

worth building a fire for?" he asked. "His lowdown thievin' friends took my sister and most likely ain't letting her have the warmth of a fire tonight. Why...they most likely ain't even feeding her, neither."

"She will be treated well," Birdsong assured him softly. "They will not harm her."

She waited patiently while he decided whether to believe her.

"Yeah, I'll just bet," he said sarcastically, and stomped off to find some firewood.

She watched him go and then turned her attention to the Penateka warrior. "How is your wound?" she asked, placing the basket in the grass near his side.

"Ummm," he grunted and glanced at the basket.

His slight interest confirmed that he was indeed hungry. "I have brought food," she informed him.

He eyed her. "I will eat," he said simply.

"We will wait for the fire to be made and then I will share your meal," she said and looked in the direction Danny had taken. She changed the subject, "Was a chief lost today?"

"Yes," he replied quickly, then added, "Me."

"You are this chief?"

Now it was his turn to change the subject, "What band are your people?" he asked knowing a true Comanche would never turn down an opportunity to brag about his or her village.

"I am of the northern tribe," she said. "My people are —"

"This is about all I could come up with," Danny said and lowered his arms, letting the scant collection of sticks roll off.

৯

It was getting late and the light of day was fading rapidly. Mary Jane watched through the slit made by the partially open entrance flap to the lodge. She saw a fat Indian woman approaching. She appeared to be carrying what looked to be some long awaited and much hoped for food.

She quickly drew back from the opening and settled into a spot on the far side of the enclosure just as the flap flew open and the woman entered with a flurry. She extended the flat pieces of bark and uttered something that none of the children could make out, but the meaning was plain enough.

Mary Jane accepted the two crude plates and passed one to the boys. The other she kept for her and Charlette to share. With barely enough light to see by, they all began to eat hungrily as the Indian woman left, pulling the flap closed behind her which made it all that much harder to see inside the lodge.

"This here stuff ain't half bad," Josh said around a mouthful of dried bread. "Better'n what my ma makes sometimes." He gnawed off a chunk of the meat. "Why...I'll just bet—"

"That ain't no way ta be a talkin' about chur ma," Charlette drawled through misty eyes. "You'd most likely be sayin' different if'n you was ta lose her forever." The misty eyes changed to tear filled ones. She sobbed noisily, as the two boys kept right on stuffing their faces.

"There, there now," Mary Jane said as she placed a consoling arm around Charlette's shoulders. She then tenderly pulled her to her. "You'll be back with your folks as soon as the men of the train come and rescue us."

"Do ya reckon?" The question was more of a woeful plea than anything else. "I don't know what my kin would do if I was ta be kilt by Injuns. Boy...that no-account brother of mine would surely be sorry that he always called me his snot nosed, heathen brat sister. Bet he'd never call me that ever again." She wiped the palms of her hands across her cheeks and sighed her despair.

"Course not...because by then you'd be his *dead*, snot nosed, heathen brat sister," Josh said and tried his best to elbow a grin out of John. But John was busy filling the inside of his neck with grub and didn't respond the way Josh would've liked. No, sir, just one little twitch at the corner of his mouth turned out to be about all there was.

"I'd say that's just about enough out of you, Mister Ignoramus," Mary Jane scolded. "Can't you see that she's scared near half to death an' misses her ma 'n pa?"

John looked at Josh, and said, "And not to mention that it's just plain unchristian to make fun of her, just because she loves her ma 'n pa an' you don't."

"Now, that ain't true! I love my ma 'n pa same as anyone. I just don't see no reason to cry over spilt milk. We got us a predicament here that cryin' ain't gonna fix. It'll take more of a—"

"Shhh!" Mary Jane warned. "Someone's coming."

Fear surrounded them as the flap abruptly flew open and an Indian man ducked inside. In his hand he carried several lengths of rawhide. He centered his gaze on Josh and grunted something in an impatient manner that made it sound like an order. He grabbed Josh by the arm, spun him around, and shoved him roughly to the dirt floor.

Josh began to cry.

The Indian pulled the boy's hands together behind his back and bound the wrists tightly. Next, he pulled his legs together and tied the ankles. While Josh continued his blubbering, the Indian tied the three remaining captives, hand and foot. Once he had finished, he inspected his handiwork with a tug here and there and grunted his satisfaction at each favorable inspection. He then made his way to the entrance, and after casting a backward glance, snorted with contempt, and ducked through.

Once the crunching footsteps had died away, an acute awareness of their situation overcame any composure that might have remained. John and Charlette lost it and began to cry. Mary Jane, too, wanted to cry as the hopelessness of their plight threatened to engulf her. The tears welled up. She fought to keep them in, but finally lost the battle as they overflowed and ran down her cheeks. She closed her eyes, and thought of her family…and Stretch.

ஓ•Chapter 16•ஓ

The sticks were dry and caught hold quickly. While Danny piled on more kindling, Birdsong rummaged through the basket and began removing the food she had brought. Once the fire was going real good and the food had been laid out, she held a piece of hardtack out to Danny. He was hungry and smiled his appreciation before accepting it.

"I have food for the prisoner as well," she said. "Will you untie his hands?"

"You reckon that's a good idea?"

"Yes, it is a good idea. He must eat. His feet will remain tied to the wheel. He leg is also badly wounded and he cannot run away."

Danny nodded and clamped the biscuit between his teeth. He reached around behind the prisoner and loosened the bindings. He then squatted beside the blazing fire and went back to eating the biscuit.

Running Antelope was thankful for the partial removal of his bindings. They had been tied very tightly, but he had not complained; that would be a sign of weakness. He rubbed his wrists, slowly returning the feeling into his hands. Once he felt satisfied that the circulation was sufficient, he looked at the woman and said simply, "I will eat now."

She smiled and picked up a piece of the hardtack as well as some jerky. She offered them to the Comanche chief. She was not at all averse to looking into the eyes of this man. He had a strong face and muscular body. She imagined that he was probably a fierce warrior. She glanced at Danny. He was busy eating his meal. She nibbled on a piece of the jerky and decided to try to find out more about this Penateka. "What is your name?" she asked.

"I am called Running Antelope," he said and took another bite. "What are you called?"

"I am Birdsong. As I have said before...I am of the northern people."

"Are you a mighty chief or a sub chief?" she asked.

"I am the adopted son of the mighty chief, One Eye. I am a war chief with many coup. I have counted coup on the Arapahoe, Kiowa and Cheyenne." His chest puffed out slightly as he told her of his accomplishments.

"I can easily see that you are indeed a great warrior, but why are you adopted? Were your mother and father killed?"

"I do not know that for sure. I was taken from them when I was but a boy. The Penateka came to my village and raided our people. I, too, was of the northern people."

She felt immediate surprise.

A trace of sadness crept into the sound of his words as he continued to tell the story of his capture, "They stole many horses and took many children, as well. I have not returned to my people since that day."

She listened intently as he continued. She asked questions and was pleased to discover that he was from the same hills and valleys where she had spent much of her life. Their villages had been very close to one another. The excitement warmed her heart as she listened to him speak the names of tribal members that she recalled playing with as a child. She watched closely as he spoke and noticed a hint of sorrow darken his eyes whenever he spoke of his childhood days with his northern family. She could see that he was not very happy with his life and saw an opportunity to maybe gain his help.

"I am happy that we are of the same people." She spoke just above a whisper. "I see in your eyes that you were very happy as a child. I also see in your eyes that although you are a sub chief, you are not as happy with the Penateka."

"You have no right to say this!" he blurted angrily.

"I am sorry if I have offended you. Please forgive me." She bowed her head submissively.

The awkward moment was mercifully interrupted as Danny rose and retrieved some more sticks for the fire. They watched in silence as he tossed them into the dying flames.

"I'm gonna tie him up," Danny announced and retrieved the length of rope he had removed earlier.

She told Running Antelope of the White Eye man's intention. He did not complain as the rope was pulled tight around his wrists. He was appreciative that it was not tied nearly as tightly as before.

Once the task was completed, Danny turned to Birdsong. "I'm gonna go get my bedroll. Heck wants me to sleep the night where I can keep an eye on this fella." She nodded and watched as he left the light of the fire and disappeared into the surrounding darkness. Once they were alone, she asked Running Antelope, "Are you tied too tightly?"

"No...I will be okay. Why are you worried about me? My people killed your man. My people have taken the children from your friends. My people have—"

"No!" The single word from her demanded his attention.

His gaze followed her as she rose and came around the fire to where he remained bound to the wheel. She lowered herself to the grass in front of him and gazed tenderly into his eyes.

She spoke softly, "The Penateka are not your true people.

Your people are of the northern tribe. You have chosen to remain with the Penateka, and this is as it should be. But your people are my people. You are my tribal brother."

They remained seated in the grass, looking into one another's eyes. He knew that what she had just spoken was true.

"Now I will again help to heal your wound." She smiled pleasantly, and reached into the basket for the bandages.

∽

Mary Jane awoke to the sound of a dog barking. Her body ached from the position that being bound hand and foot had forced her into during the long night. She had gotten only short snatches of sleep and was exhausted from the ordeal. Her mind was fuzzy as she looked around at the surroundings in the dim, gray light of dawn. The children were asleep. Charlette whimpered and squirmed in her discomfort. Josh was doing well enough, but jerked convulsively as he was no doubt experiencing a dream of some sort. John was calm and sleeping peacefully. She envied the boy as she watched his serenity.

She painstakingly worked her way up to a kneeling position and attempted to arch the kink out of her back, but to no avail. She lowered herself onto her side and despite the biting pain the effort caused to her lower back, she wormed her way over to the entrance flap. She looked out through the slit and saw a pair of legs standing right in front of her. Startled, she quickly drew back. She reasoned that it had to be a guard. After regaining her nerve, she cautiously returned to the slit and again peeked out. The legs moved to the left and she was afforded a somewhat restricted view of the immediate area.

She saw a few lodges, a smoldering fire pit, and a contraption made of sticks that had what looked to her to be strips of meat laid out across the top of it.

Returning to her thin sleeping mat, she lay back down and

stared at the wall of her prison.

୬

Birdsong looked up as Sam and Stretch approached. She nodded a greeting and rose from her position of grieving beside her man. She turned to face them squarely. "He is ready to go to be with his ancestors," she said pleasantly.

"What do you want us to do?" Sam asked.

"I have gathered the wood."

He nodded solemnly.

"He is to be placed on the wood and the fire started. His spirit will rise into the sky with the smoke." She looked at Willie. "He has told me this thing. He told me before that once the flames have devoured his body, the spirit will have already left and he will be in a place he called...ahh..."

"Heaven?" Sam asked.

"Yes...heaven," she said. A smile crossed her face. "He has told me of this place where he will go. He spoke well of it. I think someday I would like to go there, too."

Sam smiled and vowed inwardly to someday have a talk with her about the Lord Jesus and salvation.

"I will miss my man, but..." A single tear spilled over the bottom edge of her left eye and she quickly wiped it away.

"Birdsong, it is alright to weep for a lost one," Sam said, and reaching out, gently pulled her to him. When she did not resist, he held her tenderly as she shuddered her grief against his chest.

Stretch stood by and felt grief of his own as he wondered about Mary Jane. He wanted to join Birdsong in her sorrow, but he fought the urge. With the tips of his fingers, he wiped away the wetness that had collected at the corners of his own eyes. *Oh Mary Jane...where are you?*

୬

As Mary Jane opened her eyes, she could tell from the sounds outside the lodge that the camp was coming to life. The other captives were also beginning to stir. She was amazed that she'd managed to sleep as soundly as she had. She shifted her positioning and wound up on her other side, relieving some of the numbness in her hip.

"Are you awake, Mary Jane?"

"Yes, Joshua...I'm awake."

"What'dya think they'll do with us?"

"Oh...probably nothing," she lied.

"Mary Jane?"

"Yeah."

"Would you say another prayer?"

She smiled inwardly. She had been praying all through the night. Each time she had awaken, she'd prayed herself back to sleep. "Yes, Joshua, I'd be proud to," she said affectionately, and paused to gather her thoughts. When she felt at ease, she began, "Our Father...strengthen us in this, our time of need. Help Joshua here to remain strong and understand that Your love will carry him through this. Amen."

"Thanks, Mary Jane...and Mary Jane?"

"Yes."

"I'm real sorry for makin' fun of Charlette last night."

"Might not be such a bad idea if you was to tell her that when you get the chance."

"Yeah...I believe I will."

As if on cue, Charlette awoke with a start. "Wha...what's that?" she asked and popped up to a sitting position. She looked around, and as soon as she realized where she was, she began to cry.

"It's okay, Charlette," Josh said. "We're all in this together and I won't let nothin' happen to you."

She shuddered and forced a smile despite the tears.

"And I'm sorry about making fun of you last night."

Unable to speak, she nodded instead.

John, too, had awakened and now sat up. He saw her tears and asked, "You okay, Charlette? Is this heathen still being tough on you?"

"I ain't no heathen. I'll have you know that—"

"That's just about all I care to hear out of the both of you," Mary Jane said forcefully. "Now shut your faces and listen to what I've got to say." She fired an angry glare at each of them. "In case you two haven't already realized it, the only way we'll most likely stand a snowball's chance of getting through this is to stick together and trust in the Lord." She softened a bit. "Of course...I ain't your ma, but I'm just about the closest thing to one you've all got right about now." She noticed the almost imperceptible nod from Joshua. "So stop bickering with each other and see if we can pull together and love one another the same way Jesus loves us."

No one spoke; they all knew she was right.

Josh felt ashamed. "I-I'm sorry," he said meekly. "It's just that—"

No one had heard the approaching footsteps and they were startled as the entrance flap opened unexpectedly. The morning sunlight burst onto Josh's face.

The harsh glare hurt his eyes and he turned away from the stark intrusion. "What the...?" he protested.

The same man who had tied them up the night before entered. A wide grin spread across his face at seeing the boy's discomfort. He said something unintelligible and chuckled lightly. He knelt and pulled a knife from his belt. Scowling into the defiant face of Mary Jane, he growled and then chuckled again.

His breath smelled terrible as a blast of it hit her full in the face. She drew back from the putrid stench and turned her head away from him while she fought to keep the tears from appearing.

Once he had finished cutting their bindings, he gathered up the pieces of rawhide and left through the flap, leaving it open this time.

Mary Jane breathed a sigh of relief. "See how that works?" she said cheerfully. "That's what we need to do; stick together and try our best to not show fear. The Lord will protect us from whatever comes our way."

Shortly, the same woman as before brought more food. They eagerly accepted it and she left without a word. This time Mary Jane remembered to say grace over the meager meal and they ate in silence while each of them wondered what would happen next.

After they had eaten, the young captives took turns peeking out through the entrance at the activities of the camp. There was a definite gathering of horses and assembling of people. As Mary Jane watched, they streaked stripes of bright colors on their faces and bodies. They even decorated the horses. She was fascinated as they drew circles, painted zigzags, and even patted handprints onto the sides, necks, and rumps of the animals.

Suddenly, the goings-on were forgotten as a particularly important looking man appeared from a nearby lodge. He was dressed in buckskin pants and wore rows and rows of beautiful colorful beads across his chest. On his head was a magnificent feathered headdress that hung all the way to the ground. He stretched both arms above his head and chanted something that got everyone to raising a ruckus. They whooped and hollered until he gestured with the hatchet looking thing in his hand.

That must have been some kind of a prearranged signal, because all of a sudden the entire group climbed onto the backs of the horses. They continued to whoop and yell until he also mounted and led them out of the camp.

అ

"Did you sleep well, my brother?" Birdsong asked Running Antelope as she, Sam, Heck, and Stretch stood in front of the prisoner.

He elected to not answer. Instead, he chose to glare at his enemies. He was relieved, however, when one of the White Eye reached behind him and released the bindings that had confined him throughout the night. He was further pleased when they untied his ankles and he was allowed to rise. His wound was painful, but by using the sturdy wagon behind him as a means of support, he managed to straighten himself to a standing position. He was pleased that no one attempted to help him, even though his feet felt as if they were being continually pierced by many tiny knives.

"Your leg is good?" Birdsong asked, watching his progress.

"It has seen better times," he replied, continuing to eye the White Eye warriors. "What do they want?" he asked while gesturing with a slight tilting of his head. He continued to hold securely onto the side of the wagon with both hands.

"They want to know why the Penateka take the children. They want to know *where* the Penateka take the children." His grip slipped and he nearly went down. She'd seen it coming and was there in an instant with a helping hand and a supporting shoulder for him to lean on. "You will sit now," she said looking into his eyes.

"I will stand," he corrected her.

"My northern Comanche brother will sit...please," she added softly, while conveying a genuine concern in her tone as well as her eyes.

"As you say," he conceded and allowed her to assist him back to the grass.

She pulled the basket of bandages close beside her and started to unwind the bloodstained cloth from around his wounded leg. "Will you tell my friends where the White Eye children are being held captive?" she asked softly, as she continued to unwrap the wound without looking up.

He winced as the pain became significant. "The Penateka...I mean...my people." She smiled but remained silent as he continued, "My people will sell the White Eye captives to the Mexicans. They will be taken to the south for a long time and made to do the work of many."

"When will they do this thing?"

"I think maybe two or three suns will pass before the Mexicans will come to our village."

"Will you say where the village is that holds the captives?"

"I cannot. That would betray those who have accepted me. It would place them in grave danger."

"These White Eye have taken good care of you and will set you free if you will tell them where the children are being held. They do not wish you harm or to see you die. They are here only to ask for your help in return for your freedom."

Suddenly, any further conversation was impossible as the entire eastern horizon erupted in war whoops and yelling. Running Antelope's face broke into a wide grin. The Penateka had returned to again attack the wagons.

The three White Eye warriors scrambled away from him and hurried to meet the threat. Birdsong looked into his eyes; a feeling of sorrow came into his heart as he saw the look of dismay cover her face.

"You must never forget that you are my brother," she said and was gone.

He watched her leave and pushed his pain aside as he slowly worked his way to a standing position. With great difficulty, he made his way toward the sentinel that awaited him to the north.

❧Chapter 17☙

Birdsong was close behind as Sam and Stretch ran to their rifles. Heck had disappeared off somewhere unseen to do his own fighting. She took one last glance over her shoulder shortly after she had arrived at Stretch's side. She saw Running Antelope making his way out past the circle of wagons. Her thoughts went to him as she watched his escape. *May the gods go with you, my brother.* Her mind returned to the task at hand.

The children were quickly herded to the wagons near the center of the circle and hastily stuffed inside. Danny and another young man were assigned to guard them. Each took up a position under the protection of the wagon with rifles pointing out through the wheel spokes.

The members of the train had done all they could to prepare themselves, and had now reduced their efforts to waiting and watching for the impending attack to begin. With every eye behind the fortifications trained on the line of Comanche horsemen, the wait stretched to nearly five grueling minutes.

Jay glanced at the wagon where her son had disappeared

from her view a few minutes before. She then reached for Sam's hand, found it, and gave it a gentle squeeze. They smiled into one another's eyes.

Suddenly, a cheer of sorts went up from the line of Indians. The figures sat on their ponies and pumped their weapons high above their heads as a lone pony approached them in a wide arc from around the eastern side of the wagons.

Birdsong watched as the pony arrived at the area toward the middle of the line of warriors. The chief sat on his pony with his headdress extending to below its belly. It showed that he was indeed a mighty chief. She remembered his name and knew that One Eye had regained his lost son, but she also felt that she had lost her brother. She watched as the two clasped forearms in greeting.

The tension grew thicker as the members of the train gripped their rifles in anticipation of the impending attack.

Finally, One Eye raised his feathered war lance, pulled his pony's head around and disappeared into the mist of the throngs of his people. The line of horsemen also turned and quickly disappeared behind the crest of the hill.

"What's going on?" Stretch asked Birdsong as a cheer went up from behind the barricades.

"They are returning to their village," she said with a smile. "The chief's dead son has reappeared from the spirit world and they go home to rejoice."

"You mean that fella we had captured was the chief's son?"

"Yes. He is the adopted son of Chief One Eye."

Sam sided up to them while Jay scurried off to find Tom. "Birdsong, what'dya think our chances would be of following them Indians to see where their camp is? Should be easy enough to track 'em."

She nodded slowly. "I think it would be easy to find the village, but not so easy to get the little ones away from them."

"Yeah," Stretch breathed, "but at least we could trail 'em

and find out where Mary Jane is," he added.

"Let's go have us a talk with Heck and see what his thoughts are on the subject," Sam suggested.

The trio quickly located the wagonmaster as he stood talking with Charlie. Sam then laid out his idea while Cottonwood Charlie and the others listened in.

Heck was not too fond of the idea, but Charlie was. What with him knowing a mite about Injuns, he was able to convince Heck that the redskins would not be expecting the whites to follow, and that made their chances of being successful about as good as they were apt to get.

Birdsong agreed and it was settled.

Preparations were made and they didn't waste any time determining who would be a part of heading out after the Comanches.

Charlie was the best tracker, so it figured he'd be the one to head up the bunch. Birdsong, knowing the Comanche ways, was a logical choice to tag along. Now Sam and Stretch were a different story altogether. Neither one of them had any good reason to be out there chasing down a bunch of thieving Comanches. Stretch was there just because no one was able to stop him from going after Mary Jane. Sam, on the other hand, just plain and simple didn't have any better sense.

They rode out with Charlie leading the way with Birdsong, Sam, and Stretch close behind.

&

As predicted, they had no trouble following the signs left by the Indians. The tracks led pretty much due south, with only a slight variation to the east. After about a half hour of steady riding, they topped a small hill and Charlie raised a hand. He dismounted and motioned for the others to keep low. He then led his horse back to just below the crest of the hill where he tied the gelding securely to a handy bush. The rest of them also dismounted and tied up. They lowered themselves onto their stomachs and squirmed forward until they were able to barely see over the crest.

Portions of the Comanche lodges were obscured by a good-sized stand of cottonwoods with some willows mixed in. Although they couldn't see any, the presence of so many trees was an indication that there was water running through the entire area. There was also ample grass throughout that afforded good graze for the Indians' ponies.

"Not a bad place ta set up housekeepin'," Charlie commented as he removed his coonhide cap. He wiped the sweat from his balding head with the filthy neckerchief he'd pulled from a hip pocket.

"Ummm...yes. This is a good place," Birdsong said, as she too had noticed the favorable attributes of the site. However, that's not all she'd noticed; in an area at the edge of the trees was a gathering of Penateka who were holding a celebration of sorts for the return of Running Antelope.

"I can't see any sign of Mary Jane," Stretch commented.

"I don't reckon they'd be lettin' them captives have the run of the place," Charlie said, with a slight hint of sarcasm to his tone.

"Yeah, I reckon you're right. I was just hoping—"

"Well, I'm afraid hoping isn't going to get it done, not by a longshot," Sam said and sighed a deep sigh that indicated he might have been feeling a little on the hopeless side right along with Stretch. "As far as I can make out, there's no way to approach that camp from any direction without being seen. I would expect—"

"I know a way," Birdsong said.

They all looked her way.

"And just what might that be?" Sam asked.

"After the sun goes to sleep and the darkness returns, I will walk in the village and learn where the little ones are being held."

"You don't think that's a bit risky?" Charlie asked.

"What is risky for a Comanche woman to walk in a

Comanche village?" she reasoned.

"Well now...I'd say that's a real good point you got there," Charlie conceded. "But the simple fact remains that you ain't a member of *that* particular Comanche village." He pointed a stubby finger at the camp. "If one of them was ta figger out that you was a stranger...why...who knows how big a ruckus they'd raise over that?"

"You are right, but when it is dark and I do not go near the fires, they will see only another Comanche woman."

Charlie rubbed the stubble on his chin. "Hmmm. Ya know...she might just be able to pull it off at that," he said and allowed a slight grin to appear. "Yep. Just might do the trick," he decided. "In the meantime, how about we back off a ways and wait for dark. Wouldn't do for us to get spotted out here in the open, like we are."

৵

The children huddled around the entrance as the sounds of running horses reached their ears. There was more than just a little bit of laughing and frivolity going on as the returning Indians pulled their ponies to a halt and slid down amidst the swirls of dust that had caught up to them. As far as Mary Jane could tell, the main focus of all the carrying on seemed to be a man who had a bandage tied around his leg. He was helped down and assisted to a place in front of one of the lodges, where he was lowered onto a colorful blanket.

"Sure do wish I could understand Indian lingo," Josh said as he peeked around Mary Jane at the scene outside.

"I wanna see," John whined from behind Mary Jane.

"Okay, but just for a little while," she said and moved aside slightly, allowing him to squeeze in beside Josh.

Charlette was not to be left out. "Me too," she begged.

"Just wait a minute," Josh said as he continued to look out at the Indians, while at the same time trying to shoo her away with a waving hand behind his back.

Food was brought to the man, and using his fingers, he ate

hungrily. He would nod periodically and talk sparingly around the food in his mouth as questions were asked of him.

Charlette tried again. "Can I see now?"

"Oh…alright. But just for a little while." He drew back and reluctantly surrendered his watching spot to Charlette. A wide grin spread across her face as she edged forward and peered out.

Mary Jane drew back from the entrance and tried to reason her way through what was going on. The fact that the Indian was wearing a bandage meant that he had been hurt. That would indicate contact with the wagon train. Had he in fact been wounded, captured, and tended to after the attack on the wagons? If so…?

The questions rattled around inside of her head, but she was unable to come up with any reasonable answers. It just didn't make any sense for him to be captured and then set free while they remained prisoners in this smelly lodge waiting for God only knew what to happen to them. She needed to watch some more.

"That's enough, John. I need to see what I can to maybe help me understand what's going on out there."

"Aw…Mary Jane. Just a little while longer…*please.*"

"Move it now, I said."

He moved aside and crawled to his sleeping mat, where he sat facing the other three. "Don't never get to have no fun," he mumbled from behind a pouting lower lip. He then picked up an innocent pebble and flung it angrily against the side of the lodge.

As Mary Jane watched the Indian with the wounded leg, he turned his gaze toward her and smiled while nodding slowly. Another brave was seated next to him and was doing a powerful lot of talking and gesturing. It seemed to her that the animated conversation was pretty much directed at the enclosure where she and the children were being held. It was as if the wounded Indian had just been told of the captives and was enjoying their plight.

"Okay, that's enough looking, Charlette," Mary Jane said and gently nudged the girl away from the entrance. "Let's all just stay back and see what happens next."

❧Chapter 18❧

Heck and Kyle peered into the water barrel that was lashed securely to the side of Kyle's wagon.

"What'dya figger, Heck? We gonna have enuf ta make it to the Arkinsaw? Ain't much more'n about two...maybe three days worth is all what's left in there." Kyle then peered again into the depths of the more than three quarters empty barrel.

"Don't know for sure, Mister H, but one thing I do know...if we don't start taking it easy on it, we ain't gonna have anymore than about a sip or two left over by the time we do get there. And that's only if we was to get out of here purty durn quick. My way of thinking is that the longer we put off getting back on the trail, the more of it the horses will be drinking up without us even making a lick of headway." Heck looked up into the cloudless sky. "Sure wouldn't hurt none if the good Lord was to bless us with a real good Texas frog floater."

"Amen ta that," Kyle said. "But judgin' from the looks of it..." he too gazed into the expansive blue sky, "I'd say that ain't likely, leastways not right off anyways."

Heck pulled his hat and wiped his brow against the sleeve

of his good arm. "Yeah, I'm afraid you're right about that." He sighed, replaced the hat, and glanced at his tied-up arm. "Sure would be feeling a whole sight better if I hadn't a took that arrow the other day." He gingerly rubbed the wound before continuing, "We need to spread the word for folks to start skimpin' on what little bit of water they got left. Tell 'em that drinking has to be kept to the bare bones minimum and that the stock and the children got dibs over the rest of us. And also tell 'em to use the prairie grass to clean their dishes with..if they ain't already doing it."

"They ain't gonna necessarily appreciate givin' most of the water ta their horses," Kyle said, shaking his head slowly.

"You're probably right about that, but I figger most of these folks is smart enough to realize that without the horses being alive to pull the wagons...well...amen. Just tell 'em what I said and if any one of 'em's got a problem with that, tell 'em to come see me about it."

"Whatever ya say, but in the meantime, maybe we could send out a scout or two to look for some. Ain't no tellin' how long we'll be holed up here waitin' fer either the Comanches ta finish us off or our children to get found so we can get on with getting on down the trail."

Heck rubbed his chin thoughtfully while he went about pondering the suggestion. "That might not be such a bad idea at that. I reckon if Charlie and those other fellas ain't snatched them young'uns and got back here by sometime tomorrow morning, I believe I'll do just that."

જ

As dusk laid itself out across the prairie, the foursome rode slowly toward the Comanche village. A plan had been decided on that would enable Birdsong to sneak into the camp. They had taken note of a convenient finger of cottonwoods that extended a ways along the southwestern edge of the village and looked to be connected to yet another stand of trees a couple of hundred yards even farther to the south.

It was decided that she and Sam would circle around and approach from the west side of the furthest trees. He would then wait there for her return while she used the cover to sneak in and see if she could in fact find out where the children were being held. Once that was established, she was to make her way back out of the village and they would decide if a plan could be thought out that would get the children out safely.

In the meantime, Stretch and Charlie would remain hidden in the scrub oak on the hill to the north until if and when they might be needed.

As the foursome drew to within a quarter mile of where they remembered the village to be, Sam and Birdsong split off. They rode steadily, giving the general area a wide berth. They remained diligent but took their sweet time.

It took the better part of a half hour, but they were finally able to locate the small finger of Cottonwoods in the silvery moonlight. Once inside the protection of the trees, they reined up and dismounted.

They spoke in hushed tones.

"This is good place for you to stay," she said and handed him her rein.

"How long you figure you'll be gone?"

"I do not know. I will come back as quickly as I am able."

"You be careful. If you get caught—"

"Yes, I know." She smiled a smile that in the silvery moonlight seemed to him to hold very little confidence. She turned and was gone.

He tied their reins to a couple of branches that extended nearly to the ground. He then seated himself with his back resting against the trunk of a suitable tree and closed his eyes. He was not in the least bit sleepy or tired, and instead had chosen the opportunity to have himself a serious talk with the fella who was in charge of all of this.

৯৯

Birdsong quickly made her way through the small stand of trees until she arrived at an open area that extended out for about twenty-five or thirty yards. She paused to scan the open expanse. Not at all sure, but somewhat satisfied that it was safe, she continued across the opening, while using a bent over bouncing gait that ate up ground quickly. She arrived undetected at the far side of the clearing and paused on bended knee, this time to catch her breath. Once she felt rested, she continued at what was a much slower and more deliberate pace.

She had gone only a short distance before encountering the first of the Penateka lodges. She again knelt in the moonlight and carefully surveyed the area. There seemed to be a minimal amount of activity on this side of the village. The majority of the people appeared to be gathered toward the other side around a large fire.

She knew that if she tried to wander through the village in her half Comanche half White Eye clothing, she would stand little or no chance of getting past the first person she met. She quickly glanced around and spotted a blanket lying by the entrance to one of the nearby lodges.

She was extra cautious as she moved forward until she was finally able to duck behind the protection of the lodge. She circled around until she was within easy reach of the sought after prize. She retrieved it and threw it around her shoulders, leaving sufficient excess around her neck in case she found the need to use it to shelter her face.

Once she had prepared herself, she cocked an ear in the general direction of the fire and was able to faintly make out little clips of conversation. The discussion was mainly centering on the return of Running Antelope and the capturing of the children. She pulled the blanket up slightly so it covered her ears. She pinched it together in front of her nose and mouth, held it securely in place, and boldly walked out into the open.

As she neared the gathering, a woman turned from the area and headed straight for her. "This is a nice night to walk," she commented lightly, as she drew near Birdsong.

"Yes, I am pleased to enjoy the moonlight," Birdsong said in passing, and lowered her face away from the woman. She glanced furtively over a shoulder and was pleased to see the woman continuing on her way in the opposite direction.

Birdsong stopped next to one of the lodges and breathed a sigh of relief. She was still a safe distance from the circle of Penateka, but near enough to clearly hear what was being said. She listened intently and learned that the children were indeed being held in the village. It was expected that the Mexicans would come sometime within the next two days. Once they arrived, the children would be sold for clothing and blankets. The people felt that with winter fast approaching, this would be a good trade. She was also able to discover which lodge they were being held in. She looked in the direction of the spoken of lodge, and with the help of the light that was being cast from the fire, was rewarded to see a pink face peering out through the opening.

She remained a short while longer so that she might look some more on the face of Running Antelope. He was indeed a very important sub chief and seemed to be well respected by everyone. She had a fleeting thought that she wished she had met him when they were both young and still up north with their own people. She had loved Wild Willie, but she also knew that she would have been happy had this adopted Penateka been her husband and protector.

She realized that she had acquired enough of the needed information and it was time to leave. She turned away from the fire. Her intentions were then abruptly interrupted as she bumped into the returning woman she had passed earlier. She had been caught with the blanket away from her face and immediately lowered her gaze while attempting to push past her.

"What is your hurry, little one?" the woman asked suspiciously, as she hooked Birdsong's arm with her hand.

"I have to make water. Please let me go before I wet myself." Birdsong knew the excuse was flimsy, but it was the best she could do on such short notice.

"Which lodge are you from?"

"I...ahh..."

"I think you are someone I have not seen before. Let me look into your face."

Birdsong slowly brought the blanket down. "I am a friend of Running Antelope," she said hopefully.

"Then come, we will go to see him."

"That is a good idea, but first I must make water."

"I think you are not what you seem to be. I think you do not know Running Antelope, and I think you do not need to make water." She then took Birdsong by the elbow and gently guided her toward the fire.

Birdsong resigned herself to the fate that awaited her and let the blanket fall from her shoulders as they walked slowly toward the gathering. The woman ushered her through the crowd and straight to a position in front of Running Antelope.

As the rest of the Penateka began to notice them, the talking dwindled until finally the near silence was broken only by the sound of the fire's licking flames.

Running Antelope looked up into Birdsong's frightened eyes.

"She says she is your friend. Do you know this woman?"

❧Chapter 19❧

The moonlight's silvery sheen lit up the prairie well enough for a fella to make out individual blades of grass. Charlie pulled one and stuck it in his mouth. He glanced at Stretch's prone figure a short distance away and wondered how the youngster could sleep at a time like this. He was balanced onto one side, using a forearm as a makeshift pillow. Charlie shook his head in mild wonderment and returned his attention to the Comanche village below.

The drone of voices had remained steady ever since they'd taken up their position shortly after separating from Sam and Birdsong. It was plain to see that the fella with the bandaged up leg was still the center of attention.

Stretch snorted and rolled over. He then sat bolt upright and began spitting repeatedly while pawing at his mouth. "What the heck?"

"What's ailin' ya, boy?"

"Some kinda critter..." He spit again. "A bug or something crawled right into my mouth." The spitting continued long enough for the bug to be long gone and then some.

Charlie hadn't realized just why Stretch's episode with the

bug had seemed so loud to him, but then it dawned on him...the noise from the Injun camp had lessened considerably. "Might not be such a bad idea for you ta pipe down a mite. You're makin' about enough of a ruckus to wake the dead." He turned his full attention toward the camp and was distressed to make out Birdsong in the firelight. He squinted his chagrin. "Dang...peers like Birdsong's done been found out."

The bug forgotten, Stretch crawled over beside Charlie and made his own assessment. "Yep. Sure nuf. Now what?"

"Let's keep an eye peeled until Sam shows up. Then we'll decide on our next move."

"Don't see no other way," Stretch said. "Maybe they'll decide not to kill her, I mean what with her bein' a Comanche and all. Maybe we'll even get lucky and see where they decide to hold her."

"Don't know if she's a Christian gal or not, but I reckon she needs to be doin' a powerful lot of prayin' right about now," Charlie offered.

"Amen to that."

Birdsong focused a strong, unwavering gaze on that of Running Antelope.

The woman who had brought her nudged her closer to the firelight. "She has said she is your friend. Is this true?" she asked again.

"Yes. She is my friend," Running Antelope replied. "Her name is Birdsong. She is of the northern people. She was the one who cared for me when I was wounded and held captive by the White Eye."

A murmur spread throughout the gathering as each one present voiced their opinion about what she had done for Running Antelope.

"Why are you here?" The words came from the old man seated to the immediate left of Running Antelope.

Birdsong looked into his face. She knew instantly that this was the mighty chief, One Eye. Where his left eye should have been was nothing more than a dark cavity. "I have come to find the captive children," she said.

"You are a brave woman. Did you come alone?"

"No...I came with some White Eye friends." She noticed a slight indication of alarm wrinkle his forehead and decided to attempt to put him at ease. "My friends do not come to make trouble for the Penateka Honeyeaters. Their only interest is to locate the captives and try to find a way to take them back to their families. They would prefer to do this without harm to the Comanches who now hold them prisoner." She paused and lowered her gaze, waiting for his reaction.

"Why do you not lie when I ask you these questions? A lesser person would not admit the true reason for being here. Maybe I will decide to kill you because you dared to venture into my village."

"A lesser person would not understand that telling a lie to a mighty Comanche chief will bring certain death. I have no reason to tell a lie. My friends are safe in the night while they watch your village. They have already seen that I have been taken and will soon return to their own people."

Although the revelation that they were being watched by White Eye intruders was of a concern to the Comanches, it was not a matter that worried them. They were strong and fierce fighters and were not afraid of a few White Eye who would send a Comanche woman to do what they were not brave enough to do themselves.

Running Antelope leaned over and conferred with his adopted father. Their conversation was kept low and confidential, even though she could see those who were near attempt to listen in by leaning slightly closer. Finally, a decision was made and everyone straightened up.

"Running Antelope has said that you are a woman with a good heart. He says he will take you into his family...as his worker. He says that you have knowledge of the healing plants and wishes you to continue to care for his wounded leg." He looked at his son. "Is this your wish?"

"It is."

"So be it. This woman now belongs to Running Antelope."

Birdsong was relieved that she was not to be killed for venturing into the Penateka village. She bowed her head in submission to the chief, accepting his decision without question. She then raised her gaze and looked into the eyes of Running Antelope. She liked what she saw. He was not showing any signs of domination over her, nor any indication that would suggest anything other than what the chief had ordered. She liked the face she looked into. It showed a strong character that pleased her.

She felt safe because she now belonged to Running Antelope.

෴

The serenity of the night had gotten the better of Sam and he had dozed off while waiting for Birdsong's return. He awoke with a start as an owl sounded its eerie call from the branches of a nearby tree. He rubbed the sleep from his eyes and wondered how long he had been asleep. He looked at the position of the moon and decided that he had been out for the better part of an hour or so. *Wonder what's holding her up?* he wondered. *Woulda thought she'd have returned by now.*

He stretched, yawned, and slowly got to his feet while two-handedly brushing the leaves from the seat of his britches. He then gazed toward the direction she had taken and wondered again at her tardiness. He decided to go have a look, pulled his pistol, and checked the load. He replaced it in his holster and cautiously headed off through the trees.

He remained vigilant as he made his way through the sparse cover provided by the cottonwoods. When he arrived at the clearing that separated the two groves, he stopped and knelt behind the protection of the final tree. He surveyed the clearing and decided it was safe. He hurriedly crossed to the other side and again knelt. Satisfied that he remained alone, he rose and continued into the grove.

He quickly arrived at the outskirts of the village and ducked under the protection of the hanging branches of a particularly expansive willow. He used the next couple of minutes to peer from the branches at the activity in the camp. It seemed to him that the majority of the Comanches were turning in for the night, but there was no sign of Birdsong. *Where in tarnation is she?* He'd almost said it out loud, but had somehow managed to keep it to himself.

Being somewhat restricted in his ability to see enough of the camp to make heads or tails out of its layout, he moved back and forth under the willow and looked out in different directions. This tactic worked pretty well and with the aid of the bright moonlight, was able to come up with a fairly complete picture of what he figured he was up against.

There was what appeared to be a thick stand of trees to the east that extended out beyond the edge of the camp. He figured that if he could backtrack a ways and head off in that direction, he would have good cover for just about the entire distance to the northern end where it seemed most of the lodges were set up. He took one last gander at the camp and let the branches of the willow fall together. He then turned and headed out the back side of the huge willow.

Almost immediately, he found a well-used trail that went in the direction he felt he needed to go. He began to follow it, thankful for the easy going it provided. He paused from time to time and listened into the night for any sounds that might indicate the threat of danger.

The further along the trail he went, the more he could hear the babbling of voices coming from somewhere up ahead. He could also see the orange glow of a brightly burning fire. He rightfully put the two together and decided that there was some kind of a get-together going on up ahead. He veered away from the trail and headed in a more direct line toward the activity.

No sooner had he arrived at what he felt was an opportune watching spot, than he was alarmed to see a Comanche brave unexpectedly appear from behind a nearby lodge. Sam instinctively ducked down right where he was. To his relief, he found himself behind a small bush that was sufficient to hide him, if he remained perfectly still.

The Indian walked only a short distance into the woods and paused to relieve himself. Sam waited patiently until the brave had finished. As the man turned and headed back toward the fire, Sam breathed a thankful sigh while counting his blessings that that was all the fella had to do.

He settled in and went back to scanning the area around the fire, but saw nothing that gave him any indication of what might have happened to Birdsong. There were mostly just men gathered around the fire. The fella they had held captive was among them. Sam watched as the Comanche was helped to his feet and escorted away from the fire and into the nearest of the lodges. Shortly after his departure, the rest of the Indians began leaving in ones and twos until everyone had disappeared into the night. "Looks like the party's over and done with," he whispered softly.

He remained right where he was until the last sounds of the departing Comanches had died away.

With his mind now full of unanswered questions, he remained low to the ground by carefully duck walking backwards until he came to the trail. Once back on it, he turned and straightened up a bit. He followed the trail all the way to the edge of the camp.

On his way through the groves of trees, he took the time to attempt to reason out what the meaning of what he had seen might be. It seemed to him that if Birdsong had been killed, there would have been a whole lot more commotion then what he'd seen and heard. No...it made more sense that she had been discovered and taken prisoner. *At least she'll be some comfort to the children*, he thought. He then said a brief prayer for her safety as well as the safety of the captive children.

From where they lay, there was no way Charlie or Stretch could hear even a smidgen of what was being said in the Comanche village. They had to be content with just watching. Whatever was being said seemed to include another fella who was sitting next to the fella they'd previously held captive. Eventually, Birdsong was led away and taken to a lodge that was not too far away. That was the last they had seen of her.

They remained on their guard while they waited for Sam's return. If there had been even the slightest sign of one of them Injuns lighting out in their direction, they'd have been out of there like a shot. But things remained amiable as the activity continued around the fire as if nothing out of the ordinary had happened.

The whole thing was a puzzlement to Charlie, but he figured the longer they put off killing Birdsong, the better. "Sure don't understand why they just took her off to that lodge," he said while scratching the bald spot under the back of the coonhide cap. He got a little vigorous and the hat fell off forward. He picked it up while he continued, "Seems like they weren't none too upset about things, though. No, sir...don't make a whole lotta sense ta me." Although he was unable to see anything clinging to the hat, he swatted at it a few times, anyway, before fitting it back onto his head.

The two remained silent for a spell while they continued to watch the village. Then right out of the clear blue, Stretch changed the subject, "Charlie?"

"Yeah?"

"You ever been married?"

"Yeah, but only one'st."

"Did you like it...I mean...having a wife 'n all?"

"Nope."

"Why not?"

"Well, mainly because she couldn't cook worth a plug nickel. Oh, she was an alright sort, but I reckon just didn't have no idea about how ta get around a kitchen...or a cookin' fire, neither, for that matter." He paused, remembering back. "That's about the closest I ever did come to starvin' to death...and with food all around me, too."

"I'll bet Mary Jane's just about the best cook around these parts."

"Don't be bankin' on that, boy. Why, I knowed a fella one'st what thought the gal he was sweet on was a real good cook, so he up and married her. It weren't more'n two...maybe three months before he was so skinny that he hired hisself out as a hitchin' post."

Stretch had been listening intently until that point, figuring Charlie was telling him a true story. "Don't you ever—?" Stretch halted in midsentence as one of the horses nickered softly. "Someone's coming," he whispered and hunkered down in the grass.

"I didn't hear nothin'," Charlie said softly, but drew his pistol anyway. "What makes you so sure someone's comin'?"

"You could say a little birdie told me, but then again I don't understand bird talk," Stretch whispered.

"Huh?"

"Nevermind. Just keep quiet."

They listened into the night, until presently, they heard the soft plodding sounds of an approaching horse walking slowly through the buffalo grass as it was headed straight toward them.

Charlie beckoned through his teeth. "Pssst." When he had Stretch's attention, he motioned the youngster to spread out, thereby assuring that the approaching rider would have to pass directly between the two of them. They waited with drawn shooters.

Once Charlie was sure it was Sam, he rose, and letting the

pistol slide into his holster, said, "Nice evening for a ride."

Sam's horse was caught off guard and shied, but he managed to pull the startled animal under control. "You sure don't think anything of giving a fella heart failure, do you?" Sam asked and swung down.

Stretch replaced his six-gun. "Did you see her? Did you see Mary Jane?"

"Nope. Plus I lost Birdsong, too."

"Yeah, we seen that," Charlie said.

"What'd you see?" Sam asked as he began loosening the cinch on the appreciative animal.

"Seen an Injun gal bring her inta that gatherin' around the fire and after a spell of parlayin', seen her escort Birdsong off to one of them lodges. That's the last we seen of her," Charlie offered. "So I reckon you're saying you don't know nothin' neither...that right?"

"Yeah. I dozed off for a spell and when I came to, I realized she should have been back by then. So I snuck my way up real close to the fire for a look, but that must've been after they'd already taken her to the lodge because I never did see any sign of her."

"Did you see Mary Jane then?" Stretch asked hopefully.

"Nope, or any of the others either. I don't have the slightest notion where the youngsters are being held, or if they're even in the camp at all."

❦

The ride back to the wagon train was a solemn one as each of the dejected trio was lost in his own thoughts about the recent developments. Stretch was the hardest hit by the failure to find the captives. His love for Mary Jane was growing by leaps and bounds, as was his need for her. In the privacy of the silent ride across the moonlit prairie, he prayed to himself for her safety and found himself wondering if praying about things really did any good.

❧Chapter 20☙

The only one who didn't seem to have much of a problem with Birdsong having been captured was Noah. His exact words were: "Once an Injun, always an Injun. She probably just ran off and joined up with them heathens."

This didn't set well with the other members of the train. Even Wayman and Rip shunned him for a while, but with a more pressing matter at hand, Heck called a meeting to explain the water situation—not that it really needed explaining. They all had eyes and could see that at the rate they were going, the supply wouldn't last much more than another two or three days.

"We need to go easy on what little there is left," he said, addressing the gathering. "Until we find more, we need to assume that what we got is all we'll have until it rains real good or we manage to make it to the river."

"And what happens if we don't find water before then?" Noah asked.

"That question don't need much of an answer, but I'll give you one anyway, that is, if you really want a description of what a human looks like with his tongue all swolled up so big it won't fit into his mouth no more."

Noah was just fixing in his mind what that might look like when the pastor spoke, "No thanks. That won't be at all necessary. The Lord will provide."

"Too bad that savage ain't here, "Noah said sarcastically. "She could do a rain dance or something. Why, I hear tell—"

"Why don't you just shut yer face 'til ya got sumthin' to say what's worth listenin' at?" The words came from Kyle Hendricks and were accompanied by a scornful look that said he meant business. "I reckon I heard just about all I care to hear outta you. That little ol' Injun gal done risked her life an' maybe even give it up, too, just ta help find them young'uns. The way I figger things, that makes her worth a whole passel more ta the survival a these families then you or me." He waved at the expanse around them. "Or any of the rest a ya that let her go out there in yer stead. Now I ain't much on speechafyin', but this here was somethin' what needed sayin'. So if I was you, Baxter, I'd be countin' my lucky stars an' be down on my knees askin' the good Lord ta bring her back safe 'n sound, and with them young'uns taggin' right along behind her, too."

An uneasy silence followed as no one dared to speak for fear of getting Kyle started in on them. The stillness was finally broken as Wayman began clapping his hands, slowly at first, then as others joined in, faster, until the entire group was applauding Kyle's speech.

Noah fumed as he turned beet red. He sputtered helplessly while trying in vain to find the necessary words with which to defend himself. Unable the come up with any that were suitable, he did the next best thing and stomped off toward his wagon with the applause still ringing heavily in his ears.

Once he was well on his way to his wagon, the hand clapping quickly died down.

Heck looked at Kyle's downcast eyes and said, "Not that I'm partial to giving a fella what for, but that was a right accurate speech from where I was listening."

"I'm sorry I felt the need ta say it," Kyle said. He looked at Wayman and Rip. "I'm especially apologizin' to the both a you boys. I don't figger it made ya feel none too good, neither."

Wayman was the first to speak up, "My pa's been a bigot for as long as I can remember and most likely way before that. I only wish I'd been the one to say what you just did." He placed an arm around Rip's shoulders. "You won't be getting no hard feelings from us. That right, Rip?"

"Yep. Reckon I feel about the same as you, Wayman. And don't none of you be worryin' about what'll come of this. Pa's an alright sort. He'll most likely be sore for awhile, but he ain't a violent man. What he needs is a little of what most all of you folks have."

"What's that?" Heck asked.

"I reckon I'm figgerin' he could use a real good dose of religion." He placed a hand on his brother's shoulder. "Me 'n Wayman here ain't never been what you would call churchgoers, but we been keeping our eyes and ears open on this trip and there's a kinda peacefulness about folks what...what—"

"Love the Lord Jesus?" Pastor Jenks asked with a smile.

"Yeah, I reckon that's exactly what I'm saying...them what love the Lord Jesus. And I 'spect that if you folks don't mind too much, me 'n Wayman here'll be paying closer attention whenever there's preachin' going on."

"We'd be happy to have you," Pastor Jenks said. "And don't give up on your pa, either. Just because he has a hard spot in him doesn't mean the Lord doesn't love him, too. You try your best to get him to come and listen to the preaching right along with you. In fact, if you're of a mind, I'll be happy to come talk with him about it, myself."

"How about we not push our luck," Wayman said. "Some folks is just plain 'n simple, sour, and I 'spect Pa's just one of them. But that don't mean we won't work on him from time to time."

Heck stepped forward and pulled his hat. "Good. Now that we got Noah's road to salvation all planned out, how about we do some planning for our own benefit about finding water while we still can?"

After a short discussion, it was decided to take Kyle's suggestion and send two riders out in an attempt to locate an adequate source. George and Rip volunteered to make the ride. Fay was not at all happy about her husband's willingness to leave her, especially with the attacks seemingly coming at will, but she was a considerate woman and understood the urgency surrounding the needs of the folks in the wagon train.

With the knowledge that the Comanche village lay to the south, the riders were to be sent out to the north and northwest with instructions to not venture any farther than seven or eight miles. That way they would be able to return by nightfall, or shortly thereafter.

George kissed Fay tenderly, and headed out to the north. Rip veered off northwest and both riders were soon out of sight; the prayers of the entire wagon train went with them...with the exception of a few that is.

৵

Birdsong awoke to the familiar sounds of a Comanche village. As she lay on her sleeping mat, she remembered when those sounds had been common to her. But now, she was filled with an uneasiness that told her she was far from being out of the woods, that is, as far as her being accepted by these Penateka Comanches was concerned.

She rolled onto her side and looked at Running Antelope's broad back as he slept on the far side of the lodge. There was no one else present. That meant he did not have a woman. The idea of being his woman appealed to her, but she quickly forced it from her mind. *My man is only two days gone and already I am thinking of another.*

She then centered her thoughts on the things around her. She was pleased to see that the lodge was neat and well kept. His war bonnet was perched atop a lance that stood propped against one side of the enclosure. His other weapons of war were stacked neatly in another area, with his extra clothing piled alongside. She could not remember ever hearing of a Comanche warrior, who was without a woman, who kept his lodge as organized as this one. It pleased her. *He has a good heart and is not a lazy man,* she rationalized.

She rose from the mat and crossed to the opening where she knelt and peered out. Just outside was a young man who was standing guard. He had heard her approach, and with folded arms and a stolid expression, turned his head to look her way.

"You are so young to look so serious," she whispered and glanced back to make sure her words had not awakened Running Antelope. Again speaking in a hushed tone, she asked, "What is your name?"

Bear Cub ignored her question and returned his gaze straight ahead. She crawled out of the opening and rose. He unfolded his arms and turned toward her. He placed a hand against her shoulder and said through his stoicism, "You will not leave."

"I understand," she said looking into his eyes. "I will not leave," she assured him. She placed the palms of her hands against the small of her back and twisted the stiffness away. "My name is Birdsong," She smiled into his face. "I would like to be your friend. What is your name?" she asked again.

"I am called Bear Cub," he said, while managing to keep his gaze forward and his stoic demeanor intact.

"That is an unusual name for a Comanche brave." She knew this would get him to talking; all Comanches enjoyed talking about how they had been named, especially the men.

The beginning hint of a smile graced his lips. "Long ago when I was young..." He paused long enough to allow her to understand that that had indeed been a very long time ago. "As I was walking with my mother through the woods, we came to a place where a bear had been brought down by a hungry lion. It had killed the bear and had eaten her belly. My mother told me that we must leave quickly, before the lion returned. When we turned to go, a sound from high up in a tree stopped me. I looked up and saw a cub. My mother tried to make me leave, but I would not go without knowing the cub was safe from the dangers of the lion. I climbed the tree and removed it. My mother allowed me to take it home. It was then that my father gave me the name Bear Cub." He again paused and another smile came to his lips. This time he did not try to stop it. "My father said that when I became a warrior, my name would then be Angry Bear."

"That is a good strong name for a warrior," she assured him. "I can see that it will happen very soon." The flattery worked as the smile remained and grew even more genuine.

A noise from behind her drew their attention. "What have we here? Are you two old friends or something?"

Bear Cub lowered his gaze out of respect for this man. "No, Chief Running Antelope. We were only—"

"We were trying very hard to become friends," Birdsong said and quickly added, "He was doing his job and would not allow me to leave."

"Did you want to?" Running Antelope asked. "Nevermind …do not answer that. I think I would rather not know."

"If it will make you feel better, I will tell you anyway. Your people are very nice to strangers, your father is a wise man, your lodge is very neat and clean, and I have made a new friend."

She smiled at Bear Cub and he started to return the smile, but remembered that Chief Running Antelope was nearby, and because of that, what had been the beginnings of the smile quickly disappeared.

She turned to look again at Running Antelope. "My man

has been gone for only two days." Pausing, she waited for the words to come to her. "I am in mourning but I do not want to leave this place." She lowered her eyes to the ground, hoping he would understand that she was drawn to him but needed more time to properly mourn her recently lost husband.

"Bear Cub...you may leave," he said to the young buck. "I think she will remain in the village and no longer needs to be guarded."

Bear Cub nodded, grabbed his lance from its position against the outside of the lodge, and walked away.

"Thank you, Running Antelope. You will not be sorry for believing me," she said.

They looked into one another's eyes and it became clear to them that each was enticed by the other.

"What do you have that I may fix for you to eat?" she asked sheepishly, after finally regaining her senses.

༄

Mary Jane peered out through the entrance, and picking up a pebble, tossed it in front of the guard. Through the use of hand gestures, she got him to understand that she had a need to relieve herself.

He grunted and motioned her outside.

She got to her feet, hurriedly exited the lodge, and headed for the woods. She was thankful that he let her go into the trees by herself. She enjoyed the brief respite from the confines of the lodge, but also knew that if she lingered too long he would come looking for her.

She finished quickly and was making her way back toward the lodge when her attention was drawn to what appeared to be a familiar figure on the far side of the main clearing near the center of the village. She stopped and shielded her eyes against the morning glare. A smile came to her face as she realized that it was indeed Birdsong. She wanted to call out but quickly realized what a mistake that would be.

As she returned to the lodge where the others awaited, her

heart was filled with happiness at the possibility of finally being rescued. Her chest was nearly bursting with excitement as she ducked through the opening and returned to the shadowed interior.

❧

Concerns for the missing children continued to grow as the small group of men discussed the situation. Although none of the returning threesome had seen the children in the Indian camp, they had also seen nothing to the contrary, and because of that, there remained a general feeling that they were indeed being held there.

"So what'dya figger, Heck? We can't just sit here until we run clean outta water and die of thirst," Charlie said. He looked around at the faces before continuing, "Them Injuns ain't showed at all today. I figger they maybe ain't willing to lose anymore braves for the sparse pickin's they been gettin' in return."

"Maybe you're onto something there, Charlie, but we can't just run off an' leave them young'uns," Heck said.

"Mary Jane neither! I ain't leaving Mary Jane!" Stretch said, with a not-to-be-denied fervor.

"My sentiments exactly," Sam agreed. "And the rest of those children, as well. It makes plenty of good sense to pack up the train and head for water, and so be it, but—"

"You saying that if we was to pull out, you two wanna stay behind and go after those youngsters all by your lonesomes?" Heck said.

"I don't relish the notion," Sam said, "but if that's the only way, well..." His voice trailed off as he realized the implications of what was being proposed.

"That's exactly what we're saying!" Stretch said and set his mouth in a thin line of grim determination.

Heck bowed his head and studied the grass in front of his cross-legged positioning on the ground. He pulled a blade and placed it between his teeth. He fingered the blade while he remained deep in thought. Finally, he removed it and raised his gaze. "I don't cotton none to leaving any folks behind, but that goes double for them kids."

Stretch right away figured he knew what Heck was about to say and an excited grin quickly replaced the resolve.

He listened respectfully while Heck continued, "If those riders return tonight without findin' water and the Comanches stay off our tails, then we'll look at moving out first thing in the morning. If you two have a notion to try for rescuing the kids, well...God bless you. But I hope you come to your senses before mornin'."

"Make that the three a ya," Kyle said. "That's my boy out there. I figger his ma'd be givin' me what for if I was ta just up an' let them heathens have him. 'Sides, I'm right handy with a six-gun." He then proved it by pullin' his hogleg with a flash of movement that surprised everyone present. "Done me a stint as a lawman back home in Tennessee. About four years worth ta be exact."

"I'm staying too," Jacob said and rose to stand beside the others.

Stretch looked at him and the sincerity was evident as he spoke, "Mister Greenberg, we appreciate the offer, but I ain't allowing it."

"What'dya mean, *you* ain't allowin' it? *You* ain't got no say-so over what I do."

"No, sir, I reckon I don't...but I'm asking you to reconsider. I'm promising that I'll be doing all I can to bring Mary Jane back safe 'n sound. The good Lord willing, I'll be having the pastor here," he gestured toward Pastor Jenks, "marry the two of us, just as quick as the law allows."

Pastor Jenks smiled. "I'd be honored to, Mister Henderson."

Jacob eyed Stretch, appearing to decide if he was liking what he was hearing or not. "That your last name... Henderson?"

"Yes, sir, that's about it."

"Alright, boy. If you got that much interest in her, I reckon I'd most likely just be in the way. You go on about your business and bring her back to her ma 'n me...an' her brothers."

"And me," Stretch added.

"Yeah...and you."

"Glad that's all settled," Heck said. "We'll assign some of the extra fellas to drive your wagons. Shouldn't be much of a problem. We'll also be needing to get someone for Willie's wagon as well."

Charlie pushed a hand against his knee and rose, "Don't forget about mine, too," he said. "If it comes down to needin' a tracker, I figger that's where I'll be of use...and not ta mention that I have a particular way of knowin' things about Injuns."

"Okay...that's four of you, and that's the end of it!" Heck said adamantly. "I ain't allowing no more than these here fellas." He motioned to the four standing in front of the rest of the men.

❧Chapter 21❧

The mood the next morning was one of heartfelt relief and genuine concern: relief that the train would be pulling out soon, and concern for the four men who would not be going with it. George and Rip had returned just after dark the night before without so much as seeing even a puddle of water, let alone enough to do the train any good.

Jay had not been at all pleased with Sam's decision to remain behind. She had hugged young Tom to her bosom and cried nearly all the while as she tried her darndest to talk him out of his foolishness.

But with Stretch's help, he was able to finally convince her that it was the right thing to do. The clincher was when he asked her if she would favor the idea if it were Tom who had been taken and needed rescuing.

She resigned herself, but cried softly the rest of the evening, and even well into the night.

Ronnie had volunteered to share the driving with Jay, while Danny would take on the task of driving the Conestoga all by his lonesome. With the loss of the gray mare, Stretch rearranged the remaining horses in such a way as to compensate for the missing animal. The vacant slot was left to the right hand side, next to the wagon.

"Now remember, Danny, you ain't to change this setup for no reason," he said as the two of them were making the final adjustments to the harnesses. "That blaze faced bay is the best of the lot and will take charge when the need arises." He buckled a strap and fed the end of it through its retainer. "Keep the other bay right behind her, and —"

"Look, Stretch, I understand what you got going here and I'll not change a thing. The best you can do would be to get your mind right with the Lord and start storing up all the help you can get for what's facin' you."

"What'dya mean, get my mind right?"

"If I was you, I'd be having me a talk with the pastor about trusting in the Lord and knowing for sure I was goin' to heaven if this whole rescuin' business was to fall through. Without accepting the Lord Jesus as your personal Saviour, you'll be going straight to hell if those Comanches get you. No, sir...without the Holy Spirit setting up camp inside of your soul, you'll not like where you'd be headed."

Stretch hadn't suddenly become blind or deaf since they'd started the trip. He had seen and heard things and was getting a pretty good handle on knowing what it meant to be saved by grace and washed in the blood of Jesus. He had also realized that it was something that was truly necessary if he and Mary Jane were to ever get hitched and live a good Christian life together as married folks. Then there was the undeniable fact that Danny was right as rain about having the Holy Spirit take up His abode inside of him before it was eternally too late.

Stretch let fall the part of the harness he had been fiddling with. "You reckon now's as good a time as any?" he asked.

The makings of a grin appeared across Danny's face. He stacked his forearms on the rump of the sorrel, rested his chin atop the arms, and looked across at Stretch. "There ain't never been a bad time to decide to go to heaven." He spread the grin even wider.

"You willing to finish things up here?"

"I'll take care of what needs tending to here," Danny assured him and pushed away from the sorrel mare. He then busied himself with a piece of the harness. "You just go find the pastor and take care of what needs fixin' for your soul," he added.

"Believe I'll do just that," Stretch said resolutely, and turned away. After taking just a few steps, he stopped and turned back to Danny. "And Danny...thanks."

"I appreciate that, but I'm thinkin' that when I see you again you'll be understanding that I ain't the one who's deservin' of the thanks. I'm of a mind that by the time you get back here, you'll be knowing that all the thanks goes to Jesus for all the suffering He did for us sinners. And Stretch, this might be a bit early, but welcome to the family...in more ways than one."

Stretch nodded his thanks, sucked in a deep breath, and headed out to find Pastor Jenks.

Sam and Jay were silent during their final preparations, as was Ronnie. The silence was even to the point of being awkward, especially for Ronnie. Sam noticed Stretch as he was leaving the Conestoga and heading across the circle. He wondered what was so all fired important that it would take him away from completing the task of hitching up the team.

He dismissed the thought as Ronnie interrupted the silence, "You know what? I'm of a mind that you folks is havin' a difficult time with this and I can fully understand that, but—"

Jay looked up from her packing. "I-I'm sorry, Ronnie. It's just that...well, I'm just not at all partial to having Sam put his life in jeopardy by going out to face those horrible Indians. Why, there's a good chance that—"

"Ma'am, 'scuse me fer interruptin', but there's a good

chance that my sister is in need. I done me a heap a prayin' yesterday that the Lord would find a way to bring Mary Jane back to her family where she rightfully belongs."

Jay started to interrupt, but thought better of it as Ronnie raised a halting hand toward her. "I'm sorry to not let you get a word in edgewise right this minute, Mrs. Bartlett, but ma'am...I'm figgerin' those prayers were being answered when I found out last night that Mister Bartlett and the rest of those fellas had volunteered to stay behind and see what they could do about the situation. Now I understand that you rightfully got some concerns about your husband as well as yerownself and young Tom there, but ma'am, the Lord has ways of making things work out for the better, and—"

"Okay, okay, I get the picture," she said and placed a hand on his upper arm. "You ever think about becoming a preacher?"

He grinned sheepishly. "No, ma'am, I ain't."

They resumed the packing and final preparations with a slightly more at ease atmosphere than before. There was even a bit of small talk, but it was still plain to see that Jay was certainly anxious about the safety of her man.

Once everything was in order, Sam gathered everyone together and they headed for the Greenberg wagon. Once there, they joined with Jacob and Mabel while Sam prayed for the safety of the train and the safe return of the captives. Just as he was finishing up, Stretch approached with a huge smile spread across his face, and it was easy to see that a bouncing gait had been added to his step.

"What's got into you?" Sam asked.

"You'll see. C'mon. The pastor wants everyone to gather for a blessing."

They all headed for the center of the circle. Word of the meeting had spread quickly and in short order, every member of the train was present.

Heck stood in the middle of the assemblage with hat in

hand. "Folks, as you all know, we're gonna try to make a beeline for the Arkansas. We're gonna be doing some hard pushin' and I ain't about to tell you that it'll be an easy push, because it won't. I've asked the pastor here," he wagged the hat toward Pastor Jenks who stood right beside him, "to say a blessing on our wagon train and a prayer for the young'uns we're being forced to leave behind...Pastor." He motioned him forward.

Pastor Jenks slowly stepped forward and stood with a forearm cradling his Bible against his chest. His face was filled with a wretched sadness that made it plain to everyone present that his heart was heavy. "Folks," he finally began, "the past couple of days or so have been trying ones for all of us. We lost Bill Hawkins. We lost Jack Walker. And...and we have some folks wounded." He walked over and placed a compassionate arm around Harry Carter's shoulders.

Agnes brushed at a tear as the pastor gave her husband's shoulder a couple of sympathetic pats.

"But probably the most devastating thing we've been asked to endure is the capture of our beloved children."

He looked at the tear-streaked face of his beloved wife as she pulled their remaining three sons closer to her. "As you know, I have been seriously hampered by the loss of my youngest. As for the rest of you, who also have children being held captive, I want to assure you that I share in your sorrow, as I'm sure we all do. Nevertheless, we must keep the faith and trust in the Lord to work things out. I think that's why He has dealt with four of our men to stay back and attempt a rescue." He glanced around at the faces. "At this time, I'd like those four Christian souls to step forward."

While he waited patiently, Sam, Stretch, Kyle, and Cottonwood Charlie stepped out and gathered on either side of him. The pastor placed a hand on Kyle's shoulder. "These brave souls are what loving thy neighbor is all about. They have committed themselves to the possibility of giving up their very lives in an attempt to return our children to us. They have also committed themselves to the Lord."

Sam turned a sideways glance at Stretch and was pleased to see him return a wide, toothy grin. He knew at that instant what it was that had seemed so different about the boy.

The pastor then placed his arm around Stretch's shoulders and for the first time since the start of the get together, a smile appeared on the pastor's lips. "At this time I am pleased to tell you that Stretch Henderson here has just this very morning accepted the Lord Jesus Christ into his heart and is now a child of God."

The amens. were heartfelt with everyone genuinely praising the Lord for harvesting yet another soul into His flock. That is...everyone except Noah. He stood toward the outside of the circle shaking his head in pure wonderment. *Sure don't have me the foggiest notion what all the hullabaloo is about with this bunch of Bible-thumpin' idiots.*

His thoughts were interrupted as the pastor continued, "Let us pray."

Noah watched the bunch a hypocrites as they did their praying. He heard snatches of what the preacher was saying, but it didn't send a blessing through him, in no way, shape, or form. It was just words asking for God's protection on the wagon train and the captured children, plus some gibberish about protecting those idiots who were fool enough to stay behind to go out after the young'uns. Even before the praying was done, he shook his head with disgust, spun on his heel, and headed for his wagon.

Heck broke up the meeting by instructing everyone to go to their respective wagon and prepare to get under way.

Sam and Jay walked with their arms around one another's waist and Jay's head resting against his shoulder. Stretch tended to Tom, which gave him a chance to say good-bye and tell the boy to mind his ma. Across the circle, Heck was pumping Charlie's hand, while two wagons away, Kyle was having a tearful departure from his wife and family.

Finally, Heck mounted and shouted the order for everyone to climb up.

Jay kissed her husband with a tenderness that had him wondering why he was being fool enough to stay behind.

Ronnie extended a hand down and pulled her up onto the seat next to him.

From somewhere off in the distance Sam heard Heck give the order to "Head 'em west!", but his attention was glued to his beautiful wife as he held her hand and gazed up into her tear-streaked face. Tom sat on her lap as she held him close. All too soon, it was their turn to head out and Ronnie snapped the reins along a couple of rumps.

"Hee yaw! Get up there!" he said and snapped the reins again.

The wagon lurched forward and Sam took a couple of steps alongside, not wanting to let go. Finally, their fingertips separated, and as the wagon pulled away, Tom leaned out over the side and waving, said, "Bye, Daddy."

He raised a tentative hand in return, and with the tears streaming freely down his cheeks, said softly, "Bye, son."

Charlie sided up to him as the wagon pulled away. "Mite hard on a fella ta watch his family disappearin' right in front of his eyes," he said. "I reckon there's somethin' to be said fer a fella being a loner. Never did have no family of my own ta speak of... leastways that I can remember."

No one responded; they were content to just watch in silence as the wagons rumbled toward the horizon. None too soon, the tail end of Pastor Jenks' wagon disappeared over the crest of the last hill.

The silence continued a while longer, then Stretch put it all into perspective, "Sure is a good thing that little hill was there, otherwise we might've been standing here most of the day watching those wagons until they pulled clean outta sight."

That brought Sam back to his senses. "Eh...yeah...eh,

what'dya fellas say to us maybe getting away from this spot in case the Comanches decide to come back?"

"I'm thinkin' that'd be a fairly sensible move," Charlie said and looped the reins over his horse's head. "Ain't no sense endin' our little adventure before it even gets started real good."

❧

Mary Jane's excitement at seeing Birdsong earlier that morning was infectious to the other children and she had her hands full trying to keep them from getting overly exuberant. "You mustn't let on that I even saw Birdsong," she said as she hugged Charlette against her chest and lightly stroked her tangled blonde hair. "If the Indians even think there's a chance that she'll be rescuing us...well, I shouldn't have to tell you that our chances would pretty much disappear right out from under our noses. Just keep on the same as you have been, but deep down inside it's okay to know that the Lord is doing what it takes to get us out of here."

"I sure do hope Him and Birdsong hurries up and gets it done," Josh said. "I've had just about all this kind of fun I can handle," he added and grinned.

"Well...you can call it fun if you want to, but all I can say is that I never in all my borned days thought I'd be happy to see them ugly faces of my brothers again," John commented. "Shoot...if I was hardpressed, I expect I'd even admit to missing 'em."

Josh playfully shoved a hand against John's shoulder and tipped him over. "Now, that's *really* sick," he said and giggled as John also snickered his giddiness.

Abruptly, the entrance flap opened and the guard stooped his way into the confines of the lodge. He said something that none of them understood and gestured toward the outside.

"He wants us to go outside," Mary Jane said, wondering at this sudden new development.

They rose and filed out through the opening. Once outside,

they shielded their eyes against the bright sunlight until eventually Mary Jane was able to make out an ugly man with a very big mustache and an oversized hat that had the brim curled up all the way around. He was walking straight toward them, accompanied by an old Indian man and Birdsong.

"Don't act friendly toward Birdsong," she said under her breath.

"But—"

"Just do like I say. If we seem too friendly to her, she might get in trouble. Trust me," she whispered just before the ugly man came to a stop right in front of them.

He had a heavy accent as he spoke, "Hello, little one. You are very happy to see Sancho, no?" he said, resting his gaze on Charlette. She didn't answer. "How about you, Señorita?" he asked, hooking a knuckle under Mary Jane's chin and lifting her face until their eyes met. "You are not happy to see Sancho? You do not want him to take you away from this place?"

Mary Jane, too, did not answer his questions. She instead closed her eyes as the tears welled up and spilled over.

"Do not be so sad, Señorita. I will not hurt you. Sancho will soon be your very good friend. You will grow to like him very much." He emphasized the words by running his hand along the side of her face.

"Leave her alone," Josh said, taking a threatening step forward.

Without warning, the Mexican lashed out with a backhand that sent the boy sprawling. "I will talk with you later, insolent one. But for now you will shut your mouth and say nothing."

"It is not good to be mean," Birdsong said as she decided she had already put up with just about all she cared to. "These children do not threaten you. You do not need to hit them."

The fire in her eyes surprised him. He was not at all used to a woman, any woman, telling him what to do. He turned to face One Eye and spoke in Spanish, "Does this worthless squaw have the freedom to make decisions for the mighty Penateka chief?"

"She has always spoken true to me. I have no reason to distrust her," One Eye replied.

Birdsong was able to understand enough to get the gist of the conversation and smiled at the comment from One Eye.

"She tells me to not hit the boy. I do not like a squaw who tells me what to do."

"Ummm..." One Eye responded, then turned to Birdsong, and knowing that the Mexican did not understand Comanche, spoke freely with her. "Why do you tell this pig to not hit the boy? Did not the boy say something disrespectful to him?"

"No, he did not. This filthy animal was being suggestive with the young girl, and the boy told him to leave her alone."

"And that is the only reason for hitting him?"

"Yes."

One Eye then turned toward Sancho and went back to speaking Spanish. "I have been told why you hit the boy. I do not think you deserve a good price for the White Eye children. Now, you will pay more."

Anger flared in Sancho's eyes. "What? You cannot do that! We have an agreement!

"I am the one to say what the price will be. You will pay more...*much* more."

Sancho turned to face Birdsong. "What did you tell him?" he asked angrily.

"I only spoke true to him."

Sancho's anger increased and he started to tremble with rage. "You have shamed me. Now, I will—" He raised a hand to strike her.

One Eye may have been old, but he retained the reflexes of a cat. He quickly grabbed Sancho's wrist and gripped it tightly, while showing a fire in his eyes that was not to be taken lightly.

The children drew back from the confrontation, not understanding exactly what was going on, but knowing that things were getting out of hand.

Mary Jane protectively pulled them together around her.

Continuing to hold tightly onto the man's wrist, One Eye said softly, "Now you do not have enough to trade for these captives. They are no longer for sale to you."

Sancho had never before heard of such a decision as this. He wrenched free from the old man's grasp. "We had an agreement! You will keep the agreement!" he said, glaring his true hatred at the chief.

One Eye suddenly assumed a threatening demeanor and spoke with ominous intent, "If you value your life, Mexican pig, you will speak no more and leave my village before I feed you to the dogs."

Sancho may have been a fool, but he was not completely stupid. He knew the chief had reached the end of his rope. He glared first at the old chief, then at Birdsong. He then moved his gaze to Mary Jane and said, "I will see you again, my sweet Señorita...of this you can be sure." He pursed his lips and smooched a mock kiss to her. She felt repulsed as his face erupted in a wide grin that showed his decayed, brown-stained teeth.

"You will leave now," Birdsong said flatly.

"You too will see me again someday," he said with a vengeance that left no doubt about his dislike for her.

Miguel Sancho spun on the balls of both feet and stomped away toward his horse.

Mary Jane watched him and his friends leave the village while she continued to hug the children to her. Once they had disappeared from her view, she breathed a deep sigh of relief and closed her tear-filled eyes. *Thank You, Lord*, she said to herself.

❧Chapter 22❧

Birdsong had scrutinized Sancho's every move as he mounted his horse and rode out of the camp at the head of his band of filthy banditos.

"He is not a man to be trusted," One Eye said. "If you meet him again, do not turn your back to him."

"I too think he will be trouble for me some day," she responded. "He does not like for someone to speak true of him."

One Eye smiled. "I think maybe you are a wise woman."

She bowed her head to him in respect. "Thank you for speaking well of me." She glanced at the children who were huddled off to the side. "May I speak with these captives?"

"Why would you speak with them?"

"Because they were afraid of the Mexican pig and did nothing to deserve such fear. I think they would be more at ease if I could tell them what has just happened. But…if you do not trust me to speak with them, I would understand and accept this."

"You will do nothing to help them escape?"

"I will only attempt to make them feel at ease."

He nodded thoughtfully. "I believe what you say is true. I will let you speak with them." He then turned and left.

She watched him go before turning toward Mary Jane and the children. She spoke hurriedly, "We have little time together. Say nothing…only I will speak. Do not get excited at anything that I will say to you. You were nearly sold to that filthy pig of a man. But the chief decided not to sell you, because—"

"Never mind that," Mary Jane said. "What are you doing here? Is my pa here, too? Is Stretch here?" She glanced around.

"Please do not get excited. I will continue to speak quickly. You must listen. Last night we came to rescue you. I was captured. The others got away. I was not killed after I was captured because I cared for the wounded leg of the chief's son after he was taken in an attack on the wagons. His name is Running Antelope and he has been given permission to have me share his lodge with him."

Mary Jane was incredulous. "But you're *married*."

A heavy burden appeared across Birdsong's eyes. "My man is dead," she said sadly. "He was killed during the second attack on the wagons. He died as a true warrior."

"I-I'm sorry, Birdsong. I liked Willie. He will be truly missed."

The sound of approaching footsteps made Birdsong realize that her time for speaking with the captives was up. She glanced at the approaching brave and spoke quickly, "Do nothing to upset these people and do not show them your fear. They will understand this as a sign that you are weak and may decide to kill you because of that weakness."

Charlette couldn't hold her curiosity in any longer, "Is my ma and—?"

"Your family is well; as are all of your families," she assured the others.

A smile came to each of the faces at this bit of good news.

The brave stopped immediately behind Birdsong and spoke, "Tell them to return to the lodge," he said flatly.

"He wants you to return to the lodge where you were being held," she said in response to their inquisitive looks. "Do it without question."

She watched as the children obediently returned to the nearby lodge with the brave close behind. She then returned to Running Antelope's lodge. He was lying on his sleeping mat, but was not asleep.

"How is your leg?" she asked, genuinely concerned for his wellbeing.

He grimaced as he swung it around for her to see. "It is painful. Perhaps it is not healing as well as it should."

Birdsong was apprehensive as she carefully began unwrapping the bandage "I will see why this is so," she said.

Once the final wrap had been removed, her concern deepened in the form of lines of wrinkles appearing across her brow. There was an angry redness around the wound that indicated a dangerous infection. "I will go to make a medicine that will make the redness be no more," she said.

He nodded slowly. "Bear Cub will go with you to carry what you need. Go quickly," he said and squinted as a stab of pain shot through the tenderness of the infected wound.

"I will return very soon," she assured him. She then disappeared out through the flap.

꒰ꕥ꒱

The quartet of hopeful rescuers had settled themselves on their bellies along the crest of the small hill just to the north of the Comanche village. They had arrived in plenty of time to witness the entire scene with the Mexicans.

"Sure is good ta see that all four of them young'uns is alright," Kyle said with a measure of relief that didn't escape anyone's notice.

Stretch was as thankful as could be that his Mary Jane appeared to be not only safe, but uninjured as well. Now, more than ever, he wanted to ride headlong down the hill into the Comanche camp and hoist her up behind his saddle and then head lickety-split back to the wagons. But with anything akin to such foolishness as that not being even a remote possibility, he resigned himself to the bunch of them coming up with a more sensible approach.

Sam pulled his hat, rested it on the ground, and ran a palm over his hair. "Just don't seem like Birdsong's a prisoner," he said. "Kinda looks to me like she has the run of the camp. Anyone see it any different?"

"Sure does look like maybe she went right back to bein' a Comanche," Charlie observed. "Kinda sorry ta see it, though. Wish she'd a waited 'til after we had them young'uns safely outta there. Oh well...I reckon there ain't no use to reminisce about things what mighta been. I reckon what we gotta do now is to figger a way to get 'em out of there without her help."

"Look...look at that!" Stretch exclaimed as he pointed toward the camp.

Birdsong had just emerged from one of the lodges. She carried a basket as she and a Comanche brave disappeared into the nearby trees.

They continued to watch while wondering what the heck was going on.

It was a good ten or fifteen minutes before Birdsong and the brave reappeared, with him now toting the basket. She took it from him and sitting in front of the lodge, busied herself with mixing something together, using the contents of the basket, some water from a container on the ground at her side, and a handful of dirt every now and then. Presently, she rose and carried it with her as she disappeared into the lodge.

"What'dya figger that was all about?" Kyle asked, looking at Charlie.

"I ain't real for sure, but if I was ta make a guess, I'd say she just mixed up a batch of medicine. I'm of a mind that that fella, what we had prisoner, is havin' a peck of trouble with that leg of his. I'd say she's tendin' him," he concluded.

"Maybe...just maybe, that's why she's got the run of the place," Sam offered thoughtfully.

"You mean because she's been working on that fella's leg they figure she's worth keeping around?" Stretch asked.

"That plus the fact that he's most likely told 'em that she helped him when he was in need back at the wagons," Charlie answered.

"Would that be cause to give her the run of the place?" Sam wanted to know.

Charlie thought for a moment or two, rubbing his chin all the while. "I'd be inclined ta say that's exactly what's goin' on. If that wounded fella is as important to them as I think he is, and if she's tendin' him an' maybe keepin' him alive, that'd surely make her a mighty important person, as well. Didn't she say that he was the chief's son?" he asked, looking at Sam.

"Yep, she sure did."

~

Birdsong had easily found the needed plants and leaves and sat in front of Running Antelope's lodge with the mixing bowl nestled securely in her lap. She steadfastly worked the concoction of herbs, leaves, water, and soil to a mudpack consistency. She had been taught these things by her mother's brother when she was still very young. She finished her preparation, rose, and carried the medicine into the lodge.

Running Antelope forced a painful smile as she entered. She placed the remedy on the floor and began examining the wound.

"Why do you not have your healing one tend this wound?" she asked.

He flinched as her probing fingers touched a tender spot. "Because he is very old and will soon die."

"The wound is very painful for you. This medicine I have made will very quickly bring happiness to you."

She had no sooner said the words, while tenderly spreading a handful of the concoction on the area, than he felt a soothing coolness that did in fact bring a smile to his lips.

Pausing her healing hand above the wound, she looked into his face and saw the smile. "See, you are being happy already," she said and continued with the soothing application.

He watched as she deftly applied the remainder of the mixture and covered the area with the same bandage she had removed originally. When she had finished, she picked up the bowl and started to rise.

He placed a hand on her arm and said tenderly, "Birdsong...do not go. I wish to speak with you."

A constricting tightness gathered in her chest, as she felt certain she knew what was coming. She let the bowl rest back to the ground and lowered herself next to it. She slowly raised her gaze to meet his and let him see her tears.

"Why do you cry?" he asked as he brushed a thumb across her cheek.

"Because I know what you will say and I am still in mourning for my man."

"After you have finished your mourning, I would ask that you be my woman," he said softly.

Just being in the Comanche village for such a short time had already brought back fond memories of her childhood. She had nothing left to make her want to return to the white man's wagon train. Her man was gone and so was her desire to be a part of the white man's world. Although she had hoped for and expected to hear those words from him, she had not expected them so soon. She was pleased that he had offered her the time to mourn her man. She smiled, closed her eyes, and nodded slowly. "I will tell you when it is time," she said simply.

She kept a close watch on his wound throughout the rest of the day. Toward evening, she replaced the remedy with a fresh, but slightly different one that she had collected and mixed. During those times together, he was very respectful and did not speak again of the commitment that had been suggested.

As she sat across from him, sharing his evening meal, she wondered about the captives. "Now that the Mexican pig cannot have the captives, what will happen to them?" she asked, managing to keep the question in a matter-of-fact tone.

He was not at all fooled. "I understand your concern for the white maiden and the little ones," he replied. "I do not understand why my father refused them to the Mexican, but someday he will tell me."

Although she knew the reason, she did not offer it to him. It was not her place to get involved in such matters. "I am sure that is so," she said.

"You have great concern for the captives?" The inflection in his tone indicated that it could have been either a question or a statement.

Taking it as a question, she replied, "Yes, they are my friends. Just as you are my friend and this village is my friend. I have a troubled heart because they will not see their families again." She set her food aside. "I remember my own family and often wonder if my life would have been better if I had been allowed to remain with them." She watched as his face took on a vacant look. "You are troubled?" she asked, reaching a hand to his arm.

"Yes, I am troubled because I, too, have felt this way. Although I have many friends in this village, and my adoptive father and mother have treated me well, I still think of what might have been if I had been allowed to remain with my people."

"But you have said that *these* are now your people."

"That is so...these *are* now my people, but things are in my head that will not go away; things that you have returned to my memory. I sometimes wonder if my sister is pretty. I sometimes wonder if she has a good man and many children. I sometimes wonder of what could have been." He took her hands in his. "I am happy that you are here. I am pleased that we are of the same people. And I am happy that someday you will be my woman."

Their eyes met and locked in a joining of souls that both knew would be a long-lasting relationship. A soothing warmness descended from the sky and surrounded them as they enjoyed the special moment together.

Birdsong realized an opportunity to further touch his heart and maybe plant a seed as well. "The young captive maiden, too, has a man waiting for her," she said tenderly, and watched his eyes. "She has been promised to a young man who is also my friend."

He squinted a questioning look her way. "Are you saying that these captives should be released and allowed to return to their people?"

"I am saying that they are people just as we are people. They have families who love them. The young maiden has a man waiting for her who will someday make her a good husband. She has two brothers...just as the others have brothers and sisters." She looked again into his eyes. "Just as you once had a sister." She released his hands and took up her plate of food. "I am just wishing out loud. I understand that the captives will be sold to another tribe someday soon. But I have a heavy heart wondering if they, too, will someday sit in a lodge and speak of such things as we have done today."

"I understand what you are saying, and I, too, feel in my heart a hurt for them. I will speak with my father and ask if they may return to their people now that he is unwilling to sell them to the Mexicans."

Chapter 23

As they continued their vigil from the crest of the hill, the men again saw each of the captives at least once. The Comanches seemed gracious enough and allowed them to go off into the woods unattended to do what needed doing. They were brought food periodically, alleviating any fears the onlookers may have had about them being starved. There was also no sign of abuse and that served to lessen the feelings of haste and apprehension the rescuers had been experiencing when they'd first set out to find them.

Sam lay with one fist stacked on top of the other and his chin propped on top of that. He watched with peaceful contentment, thinking of his wife and son. He wondered if they were safe and how far they had traveled before stopping for the night.

Kyle interrupted Sam's thoughts, "Should be about anytime now," he said as he glanced skyward at the waning daylight. "By the time the two of ya get down to the south end of the camp it'll already be dark."

They had decided earlier that once it got dark enough, Sam and Charlie would sneak into the camp and see if there was any way they might be able to pull off a rescue.

As the pair prepared to leave, Stretch and Kyle swallowed the last drop of the contents of their canteens. Sam had assured them that he would be able to refill them in the brook he'd found on his previous trip to the Comanche village.

Sam slung the carrying strap of Stretch's canteen around his neck and stuck an arm through, positioning it on the opposite side from his own. Charlie did the same with Kyle's. Once they were all set, they shook hands all around and mounted. Sam then tipped his hat and without another word, he and Charlie reined around and coaxed their mounts into a slow canter while keeping the horizon between themselves and the Comanche village.

They rode slow and easy until Sam figured they were far enough to the southwest to safely skirt the village. He motioned and they turned southward.

In less than half an hour, they were nearing the stand of trees where he and Birdsong had parted the night before. There was still maybe an hour or so of moonlight left when they reined up under the expansive branches of a huge cottonwood.

They dismounted and kept their voices to a whisper as Sam gave Charlie the lay of the land, "Just a ways northeast of here is a clearing that leads to another grove of trees. Once we get across that, the Comanche lodges start pretty much right away."

"Where's that trail you was talkin' about?"

"After we make it to the second stand there's a large willow with branches that touch the ground. That's a good spot to settle for a while and decide what our next move should be. The trail is just to the east of there. It pretty much runs the full length of the camp. There's places where it gets mighty close to the lodges and I'm hoping maybe it'll get us near the one where the children are."

He could just make out Charlie nodding his understanding

in the shadows.

"The stream is right over there." Sam pointed. "Let's fill the canteens first and leave them with the horses. That way, if we need to get outta here in a hurry, that won't be holding us up."

"Good idea."

They made their way to the edge of the gently flowing stream and submerged the mouths of the four canteens under the surface of the water. After gurgling the containers full, they took the time to drink a sufficient amount of the refreshing water.

Once they had quenched their thirst, they topped off the canteens, carried them back to the horses, and draped the straps over the saddlehorns.

With the water supply now safely tucked away, Charlie felt for the haft of his knife, and satisfied that it was indeed where it belonged, said, "Okay...let's go see this Injun camp."

They cautiously made their way through the trees and halted once they reached the edge of the clearing. Scanning the expanse that stretched before them, they decided it was indeed safe and hastily crossed to the security of the foliage on the other side.

Once there, they knelt and listened for any sound that might indicate the presence of any nearby threat. They heard nothing, so they crept their way to the protective branches of the huge willow. As soon as they were safely inside the confines of the tree, they began to breathe easier.

A dog barked somewhere off in the distance, but not close enough to threaten discovery.

"Which way's the nearest lodge?" Charlie whispered.

Sam pointed. "Should be right over there," he said in a matching whisper. "The trail is right over that way." Again he pointed. "Let's head that way and see what turns up."

Sam led the way as the twosome quickly made their way to the back side of the willow. They ducked through the branches and disappeared into the blackness of the surrounding forest. After just a short distance, they came to the pathway and knelt to get their bearings.

Sam again spoke in a soft whisper. "It'll angle off to the northeast for a ways. After that it turns back toward the camp. Last time I was here they had a bonfire going up by the north end of the camp, but near as I could figure that's a good ways away from where Mary Jane an' the young'uns are most likely being held."

They continued along the trail until it swung around back toward the camp. They then hunkered down while Sam tried to make heads or tails out of the layout. But try as he might, it was next to impossible to get his bearings; everything seemed completely different from this new point of view.

"I just can't tell," Sam admitted, while glancing around. "I think the problem is that we're a lot farther back in the trees then we realize. I'm thinking the camp is a whole lot bigger than we might expect."

Charlie, too, was at a loss. Nothing looked familiar as he craned his neck to see around the bush immediately in front of him. "I think you might be right. Things just ain't the same from down here. We might do well ta head back an' do some real close payin' attention from up on the hill after first light. Kinda looks like the part we seen from up there is just the beginnin' of what's really here."

"Let's get out of here then while the gettin's good and get on back to the horses," Sam suggested dejectedly.

The sound of someone approaching demanded their attention. They made themselves as little as possible, scarcely daring to breathe as a Comanche brave walked past not more than six or eight paces away.

Once the sounds of his presence had diminished enough to ensure their continued safety, Sam heaved a huge sigh of relief. "That was a mite closer than I like," he whispered, and took yet another deep breath. "C'mon, let's get out of here."

The trip back to the horses was cautious but uneventful. The animals appeared undisturbed and the canteens were as they had been left. Satisfied that their visit had gone undetected, the duo mounted.

మ

The morning erupted in a blaze of sunlight as the shadows of the night gave way to the rising orange globe. Birdsong had prepared a breakfast fit for her chief. He had devoured it hungrily and feigned disappointment when she told him there was no more. His protruding stomach attested to the fact that he had indeed ate more than his share.

"You have a good sense of what a man's needs are," he said, resting a hand on his belly. "The food was very good. You are an amazing woman, Birdsong."

She smiled at his appreciation. She had feelings for wanting to please this man and it seemed as though she was being successful. "How does your leg feel today?"

He moved it with the assistance of a supportive hand. "It is much better. I have very little pain. It seems as though the redness will be gone if we opened the cloth and looked inside."

"We will wait until I prepare more of the healing things. Then we will look for the redness and I will again change the medicine."

She rose and disappeared outside. She found her ingredients just as she had left them and began mixing the plants with water and dirt. When she had the mixture at just the right consistency, she brought the bowl into the lodge, set it down, and began to carefully unwrap the wound.

Running Antelope had been right. The redness was nearly gone. It was plain to see that the danger had passed. "You were right. The redness has almost gone. I am pleased," she said. She also noted that he was being less jumpy about her touching the area around the wound. She smiled her success. "When will you speak to your father about the children?" she asked, not looking up.

"I will speak with him today."

That ended the conversation.

She expertly cleansed and repacked the wound before again securing it with a fresh bandage. Once she had cleaned up the mess that had been made, they talked of things such as: how old each of them had been when they were taken from their parents, how he had grown into becoming a sub chief of the Penateka, and why he had never taken a wife. All these things were of interest to her as she watched his face while listening to him talk. She was pleased to see that his eyes spoke true when he said he had not found the one special person to share his life with...that is, until she had come to him. She knew in her heart that it would not take long before they would be forever together.

༄

The area under the overhanging ledge was comfortable enough. Once daylight had spread across the land, a cooking fire was built. Charlie did the honors, saying, "I've been eatin' my own cookin' for longer than I care to admit an' I ain't near come close ta givin' up the ghost from it yet."

He did a real good job of warming up some of the bacon they had brought along, and they ate it along with some hardtack. Not wanting to use any more water than was necessary, they decided against making coffee. That decision didn't sit too well with any of them, as they were all partial to sipping a cup first thing in the morning. But they mutually agreed that doing without the coffee was a sight better than doing without water, if it came right down to it.

Once they had finished the breakfast, they cleared up the eating utensils, and while using sand to scrub the frying pan, managed to do a tolerable job of cleaning it. After wiping it out with handfuls of grass, they packed it away along with everything else they had gotten out.

They smothered the fire with sand, saddled up, and

headed out for the Comanche village. The trail took them through a narrow passageway between two large rocks at the bottom of a dry wash. No sooner had they entered the cut, than a whooshing sound reached their ears that right away got everyone's attention.

The arrow hit Stretch high in the left arm but it missed the bone as it passed through, stopping with just about equal lengths sticking out on either side. As they struggled to control their horses, another arrow took Sam's gelding in the neck and he reared, throwing Sam to the ground. He hit hard and rolled while pulling his pistol. He hastily threw a shot at a figure that had appeared from around the edge of one of the larger rocks. The Indian cried out in pain as his bow and arrow went flying.

By then the rest of the fellas, including Stretch, had managed to pull their guns and were already giving a good accounting of themselves.

As near as the whites could see, there were just three Indians taking part in the attack. The arrow that had found its mark in Stretch's arm was the only one that did any damage to the white men. The one that put Sam's gelding down was the only other one to stop short of burying itself in the sand of the dry streambed.

With all four of the White Eye sending bullets their way, the trio of Comanches smartly broke off the attack. The fella that Sam had winged was not hurt so badly that he couldn't swing up onto the back of his pony and ride off with the others.

The aftermath was one of confusion as well as relief that no one had been killed. Sam was certainly shaken and slightly dazed from his fall, but all things considered, he remained relatively unhurt.

Kyle rode to the crest of the wash to make sure the attackers had indeed left the area. "They're hightailin' it in the direction of the Comanche camp!" he hollered, looking down into the wash where Sam and Charlie were helping Stretch down off his sorrel. They carefully propped him up with his back against a boulder.

"Looks like I picked up a souvenir," he said and grimaced, as the feathered end of the arrow brushed against a small uprooted bush.

"Ain't gonna take much ta pull that little ol' stick outta there," Charlie said and reached for the shaft.

"Wait just a danged minute! Just because you say so, don't make it so! It's my arm and I say it's gonna hurt more than just a wimpy little bit!"

"I ain't sayin' it ain't gonna hurt. I'm sayin' the point ain't stickin' inta the bone is all. It's gonna hurt like the dickens but that stick still needs ta come out, and the sooner the better."

With that, Charlie quickly averted his gaze off to one side as if something had suddenly demanded his attention. No sooner had Stretch fallen for the ploy, than Charlie drew back and uncorked a Sunday punch to the point of his jaw that knocked Stretch about as unconscious as the rock he was situated against.

"Nice punch," Sam commented. He then held Stretch steady while Charlie first snapped off the feathered end of the shaft and then yanked it on through the wound from the backside. Once that was done, Sam rose and retrieved his spare shirt from the saddlebags that were still behind the saddle on his now dead horse. He tore off three strips, wadded two of them, and placed them against the holes on either side of Stretch's arm. While Charlie held them in place, he used the third strip to bind the makeshift bandages against the wound.

Satisfied with the job they had done, Sam said, "Let's bring him around and get out of here before those heathens return with their friends. Once we get to somewhere that's safe, we might want to think about cauterizing that with gunpowder."

Charlie nodded and retrieved his canteen. He then poured

a small amount of water into his cupped palm while letting it dribble between his fingers and into Stretch's face.

The youngster jerked awake.

"What the—?" he said and glanced around. "What happened? Who hit me?"

"Ain't nobody hit cha," Charlie lied. "Why…you just up 'n fainted dead away from the pure pain that little bitty stick was causin' to ya."

"No I didn't. Someone hit me." He looked from one to the other. "Why else would my jaw be so sore?" he asked, rubbing the spot on the point of his chin where the punch had landed.

"Well, whatever happened," Sam said, "the arrow's gone and so are we." With that, they each got a good hold under an arm and carefully helped Stretch to his feet and onto his horse. Not wanting to risk causing any more discomfort to Stretch's wound than was absolutely necessary, Sam got up behind Charlie and they rode out of the wash, joining up with Kyle who had continued to keep watch.

They rode for a spell until they felt secure enough to stop and give Stretch a breather. His wound was serious and he was obviously in a lot of pain. They all realized that they needed to keep a close watch on it and get him to the wagons as soon as possible. They knew that there were enough medical supplies in the wagons to allow him a good chance of keeping the arm.

After talking the situation over, they decided that their chances of sneaking up on the Comanche camp had dropped down to right around zero. They reasoned that the Indians would now know that some of the white men had remained behind to rescue the children and because of that would therefore probably strengthen the guards around them.

It was especially hard on Kyle to own up to them abandoning the rescue attempt. Stretch also was opposed to calling it quits. But after promising that they would form another rescue attempt after getting him back to the wagons, common sense won out and they headed west-northwest in search of the train.

❧Chapter 24❧

They had just completed the noonday meal. Bear Cub patted his full stomach while belching appreciatively. Birdsong had invited him to join them, and after being assured that it was all right with Chief Running Antelope, he had gladly accepted.

"Bear Cub, I have need to speak with my father. You will go tell him so."

"You want *me* to speak with Chief One Eye?" Bear Cub asked with a wide-eyed expression that pulled a couple of amused smiles from Birdsong and Running Antelope.

"Yes. Tell him that I have a proposition for him and cannot yet walk well enough to come to him. Tell him that if it does not please him to come to me, then I will wait until my leg is better."

"You are sure that he will not think badly of me if I speak these words to him?"

"I am sure. Now go."

Bear Cub reluctantly headed for the exit, but before ducking through he looked back at Running Antelope and asked again, "You're sure?"

"Yes! Now go before I..." Running Antelope's meaning became clear soon after he had picked up a moccasin and good-naturedly flung it at the young Comanche. It missed its mark, but Bear Cub, being the type of fella that could pick up right away on a subtle hint such as that, disappeared through the opening and headed off to find Chief One Eye.

Running Antelope lay back on his sleeping mat and watched Birdsong as she gathered up the remnants of the meal and began straightening up the lodge. He centered his attention on her profile while she worked. He watched with favor as she brushed an unruly lock of hair away from her face.

The effort caused her to turn her head slightly, enabling her to notice his attention on her. "I am sure there are better things for you to do than watching this worthless squaw while she works."

"You are probably right, but at this moment I cannot think of a single one. I would, however —"

The conversation ended as the entrance flap flew open and One Eye ducked inside. He stood with his arms folded across his broad chest. He looked first at Birdsong, then at his son. A concerned expression wrinkled his brow. "You are not happy with this woman?"

"Why do you ask such a question?" Running Antelope asked.

"Because she is over there," he motioned with a tilt of his head, "and you are over there." The tilt went in the opposite direction.

Birdsong decided it was time for her to intervene, "Chief One Eye, I am very happy and honored to share this lodge with your son, but..." A tender sadness appeared in her eyes, and Running Antelope quickly came to her rescue.

"Father, this woman will someday be my woman. Of this we have already spoken...but for now we will wait."

"Why do you wait?"

"Because she is mourning the loss of her man. He was a White Eye and his life was taken during the final raid on the wagons."

He looked down at Birdsong. "Is this true?"

"Yes, it is so." She wiped an escaping tear from her cheek and continued, "My husband was a brave man but he rose with the smoke and is now gone to a place he called heaven. I have been in this village for only a short while but am now ready to spend my life here...if you will allow this. I, too, am of the northern people, just as your adopted son was from the northern people." She paused, and turning her gaze to Running Antelope, was pleased to see a smile in his eyes.

One Eye glanced at his son, then returned his attention to Birdsong. "He has told you of this?"

"Yes, but—"

A wide grin spread across his face. "This pleases me. Long ago, his adopted mother once told me that I would know when the proper woman comes into his life because he would keep no secrets from her. Maybe you are this woman."

A silence hung in the air as no one spoke. Finally, Birdsong said in a very soft voice, "Yes...I am this woman."

"Uhh...this is not why I asked to see you, my father."

"Why then did you send word for me?"

"Because I...ahh...because *we* have an offer to give to you."

"An offer for what?"

"For the release of the captives," Birdsong said, and was immediately sorry for speaking out of place.

One Eye quickly moved his gaze from his son to her. "What is this offer?" he asked, while eyeing her closely.

"I am but a female. It is not my place to speak. Running Antelope will speak for us to his father," she said, and looking at Running Antelope, assumed the proper submissive posture by folding her hands and placing them in her lap while she lowered her gaze.

"I say again, you are a wise woman," One Eye said, smiling

his satisfaction.

Running Antelope took up the cause, "As you can see, my leg is much better today. This is because I was able to have use of the healing powers possessed by this woman." He gestured toward her with a wave of his hand. "She has a gift and great knowledge of the healing plants that is better than anyone I have ever seen before. Even better than Buffalo Horn when he was young."

One Eye could not believe what he had just heard. Buffalo Horn, although he had grown very old now, was legendary among all the Comanche tribes as the best to ever understand the use of the healing plants. "Where have you learned about the healing plants?" he asked, looking at her.

She raised her eyes. "My mother's brother was our tribal healing one. He had much patience and took the time to teach me these necessary things."

"What has this to do with the release of the captives?"

"Birdsong has agreed to become our new healing one if you will set the captives free and allow them to return to their people."

This was indeed a bold proposition. Chief One Eye did not indicate his pleasure or displeasure with it. Instead, he focused his attention on Birdsong. "Why do you think I would feel the need to make such a trade?" he asked and again folded his arms across his chest.

She rose and walked to the front of One Eye. Fixing an unwavering gaze on his, she said, "These children were taken to sell to the Mexican pig that shows no respect to you. You wisely did not sell to him. I think that now they are either to be traded to another tribe or you will keep them to use as workers in this village. But..." She took a deep breath that did not escape his notice.

"Continue," he said.

"I was taken from my village when I was very young, as was Running Antelope. I had brothers and sisters, just as he too had a sister." She looked at Running Antelope and saw a hint of sadness in his eyes that quickly disappeared.

One Eye, too, looked his way and was again pleased that he kept no secrets from this woman, and because of that, had told her about his long-ago sister.

Birdsong continued, "These children who have been taken from their families also have brothers and sisters. The young White Eye maiden has a man who she would soon marry if she were allowed to." Taking a dramatic chance, she reached a hand to the side of One Eye's face. She spoke with tenderness, "You have a son that loves you very much but he has never forgotten that he was taken from his sister. He will never know if she is a beautiful woman. He will never know if she has married a brave warrior. He will never know if she has many children." She removed her hand from his cheek and looked down at Running Antelope. "He will only know that if you give these children back to their brothers and sisters, it would be the same as giving him back to his sister." She then paused as the realization of just how bold and outspoken she had been gave her cause for great concern. "Please excuse me for speaking out of place," she said and lowered her eyes to the floor.

"Are these your true feelings, as well?" One Eye asked his son.

"Yes, my father. These are my feelings. She has spoken well."

"I will think on it," One Eye said resolutely, turned, and ducked his way out through the exit.

A silence filled the air between them as Birdsong and Running Antelope sifted through their thoughts. With a sigh that came out much louder than intended, she knelt beside his wounded leg and started to unwind the bandage.

"He is a fair and wise man. He will decide quickly," he said.

"I am afraid I have made him angry. I am but a woman

and should not speak directly to him as I have. I am sure he does not like me anymore." A tear rolled down her cheek as she paused in her removal of the bandage. She then looked into his eyes. She scooted closer to him and with a tenderness that touched his heart, said, "Please hold me. For now I am truly afraid."

Miguel Sancho sat on the back of his horse and watched the approach of the small group of riders. He had split his band into two parts in an effort to cover more territory. Pickings had been slim as of late and tempers were short. The episode back at the Comanche village the day before had left a bad taste in his mouth and he was itching for a fight.

"We will stop these gringos," he said. "Diego...you take the woman into the trees and keep her away from the eyes of these worthless gringo dogs."

Diego nodded and motioned to her. "Come, Señorita... come with Diego. We will go into the trees and have some fun, no?"

"I will go nowhere with you," she said and set her jaw in strict defiance.

"Sancho...she say she will not go."

"You will do as I say!" Sancho ordered, as he threw a stare at her that accomplished nothing in the way of its intended intimidation.

"You maybe can make the others to be afraid of you but I am not afraid. You have killed my family but I will not do as you say." She returned the stare and added a hatred to her glare that angered him.

"You are making a very big mistake, Señorita. After we rob these gringos, I will make you sorry for your insolence to me. You will say nothing or we will kill these gringo dogs...and you, as well. You understand?"

She did not acknowledge his question. Instead, she smirked and tossed her head in defiant loathing.

As the small group of riders neared Sancho and his men, it became clear to Sancho that one of the horses was carrying double and another of the riders was dangling a wounded arm. The gringos waved a greeting as they reined up.

Sam was leery of the bunch of Mexicans because of the stories he'd heard back in Independence about the bandits that had been robbing travelers along the Santa Fe Trail. Even though they were a good ways north of the usual route, it didn't pay to get careless. As soon as they had gotten close enough to recognize the riders ahead as possibly being Mexicans, he'd suggested that everyone be on their guard and ready to pull down on them at the slightest indication of trouble. Sam himself had pulled his pistol and held it hidden from view between himself and Charlie.

"Howdy, fellas," Charlie said cheerfully, as they reined to a halt. "Bit of a lonesome spot to be out sightseeing. Wouldn't be that yer out lookin' for your lost dog, now would it?"

Sancho tipped the front of his sombrero with a gloved finger. "Hello yourself, Señor," he replied with a hint of amusement. "The only dogs we are looking for are gringo dogs who have more food and water then they have use for. Have you seen such gringos as this?"

"Nope. Can't say as I have."

Sam had been watching the young woman's face, as she seemed to be a mite on the nervous and apprehensive side of things. Her eyes darted from face to face with what seemed to him to contain a plea for help. Feeling uneasy about how this conversation between Charlie and the Mexican was going, he leaned back slightly, allowing both Stretch and Kyle a gander at the pistol. Once he knew he had their attention and they would back any play he made, he leaned forward and again hid the gun from everyone's view.

"I think maybe you are such a gringo as this," Sancho was saying.

"You'd be wrong about that, Mex. Fact is, I'd say it'd be a

big mistake on your part for you to be thinking thataway."

Sam caught a slight movement out of the corner of his eye and realized that one of the Mexicans was making a slow play toward his pistol. Deciding to keep the upper hand, he pulled the six-gun from its hiding place while at the same time earing back the hammer. "Now, I figure that that would be a fatal mistake on your part, hombre," he warned the Mex and leveled the barrel at him. Kyle, Stretch, and Charlie also pulled their hardware.

"You are no being very friendly," Sancho said as anger began shrouding his face. "It is not a good thing to point a pistola on someone who is wanting to be your friend."

"If I thought for even one measly little second that you were of the friendly sort, why I 'spect I'd be apologizin' all over myself an' askin' for your forgiveness," Charlie said, while keeping his six-shooter leveled at the Mexican's chest. "But as you can see, I ain't neither apologizin' nor askin' for no forgiveness."

Sam turned his attention to the woman. "You look like you might be having a bit of a problem, young lady," he said.

He kicked her horse forward. "Not no more, Señor," she offered, as a lovely smile began gracing her beautiful features.

"You will stay where you are!" Sancho ordered, and reached for the passing horse's bridle. He managed to hook it with a fingertip and held on.

"You will let go of my horse!" she protested and slung the end of her rein, slapping it against the back of his hand.

He was probably figuring he was lucky to have been wearing the gloves.

"You little..." Sancho reached out for her but he changed his mind as Sam fired off a shot that immediately shifted his attention to a more pressing problem.

"I'd say she doesn't have much of a desire to remain with you fellas. Would I be right about that, ma'am?" Sam asked.

"Yes...that is so. These men are filthy pigs who have killed my family and have made me to be a prisoner. I will be very happy to come with you now, Señor."

"Sounds good to me." He looked in the eyes of the Mex. "Let go of that bridle, hombre," Sam said with deadly intent and raised the pistol to eye level...Miguel Sancho's eye level.

Sancho was fuming, but he was no fool and realized the position he now found himself in. He smartly released his hold on the bridle. "It is not right for you to steal my woman," he said, while scowling his displeasure into the end of the barrel. "She is mine and I will find you and kill you someday because of what you are doing."

"That may or may not be true," Kyle interjected. "But fer now, you fellas just pull them hoglegs and let 'em settle in the dust." Noting the hesitation on the part of the Mexicans, he thumbed back the hammer and added, "I'd be advisin' you ta do it right quick. This here trigger finger of mine is startin' ta pull tight. I'm figgerin' that the longer ya take ta get shed of that hardware, the tighter it'll get. Then...next thing ya know...BOOM! and there goes some poor fool's head...if ya get my drift."

The bandits begrudgingly lifted their pistols from their holsters, but not without more than one thought of trying for the upper hand. But the thoughts were just that and nothing more. Each of them finally unloaded his hardware into the dirt and waited for the gringos' next move.

Kyle continued, "Now...turn them sorry excuses fer horses ya got 'tween yer legs, and don't look back 'til ya figger the rest of us has been disappeared fer quite a spell."

The band of would-be robbers reined around and kicked their horses into a slow canter, glad to be away from those crazy gringos. The foursome replaced their guns as they watched the Mexicans ride away. Kyle dismounted and collected the pistols. He slipped them into his saddlebag and buckled it shut.

Sam slid off the rump of Charlie's horse and looked up at

the girl. "What's your name?" he asked.

"Constance Maria Consuelo Valdez," she replied as a huge smile spread across her grateful face. "But from now you can call me, Lucky."

"Well then, Lucky, how about you an' me sharing your horse and giving Charlie's here a breather?"

She slid back onto the brown mare's rump and said, "Come, Señor. You can have this horse. I will ride behind you."

Sam mounted, swinging his leg forward over the horse's neck. Once he was firmly in place, she circled her arms around his waist and wrapped the fingers of one hand around the wrist of the other.

"You have saved my life, Señor," she said as they started forward. "I will always be grateful and will always be your very good amigo."

A smile graced Sam's face as he kicked the mare forward and they resumed their attempts to cross the trail of the wagons.

&Chapter 25&

As Bear Cub approached, Birdsong looked up from her sitting position in front of Running Antelope's lodge. There was a sense of urgency in his voice as he said, "Come…Chief One Eye would speak with you."

She hastily set aside the mending of Running Antelope's deerskin trousers and rose. A feeling of anticipation accompanied her as she followed Bear Cub to One Eye's lodge. Upon arriving, she stood before the opening and exhaled heavily in an attempt to calm her nervousness.

Bear Cub leaned down toward the entranceway and announced, "She is here, my chief!"

"You will come inside, Birdsong," One Eye invited from within.

Bear Cub motioned her into the lodge with a sweeping motion of his hand. "Good luck," he whispered as she passed by.

One Eye sat cross-legged on the far side of the enclosure. His hair was untied and hung over his shoulders. A young maiden was sorting through the tangles and rattails with the help of a wide toothed comb that had no doubt come from the

White Eye.

Birdsong stood silently before him with bowed head and downcast eyes. She clasped her hands together in front of her and waited for him to speak.

"Leave us, Spotted Fawn," he said, and waved the young maiden away.

She released the comb, leaving it imbedded in his flowing hair. She then worked her way to her feet, and with a pleasant smile to Birdsong, obediently ducked her way out through the opening.

One Eye gestured to the place at his left. "You will sit here."

Birdsong remained apprehensive while she did as she was told. She crossed her ankles, lowered herself to the ground, and with practiced ease, pulled them in toward her. "You have thought of this thing?" she asked.

"Ummm...I have thought of this thing. I have decided that if you are as knowledgeable of the healing plants as my son seems to think you are, then it would be a good trade."

Her heart jumped at this good news. A pleasant smile appeared. "You say 'if'. That means you are not convinced. What must I do to convince the wise chief of the Penateka?"

"You will talk with Buffalo Horn. He alone will decide if you are to be the healing one that will someday take his place. If he says no, then the agreement is off and we will speak of it no more. Do you agree to this?"

"But if he says yes?" she reminded him.

"If he says yes...then the captives will be set free and you will return them to the White Eye wagons."

Birdsong smiled. "Then I agree to these conditions. Where will I find the great healing one, Buffalo Horn?" she asked, eager to prove herself.

"His lodge is in the trees along the side of the village where the water runs. You can find it by...wait." He leaned toward the opening. "Bear Cub...come inside!"

The young buck appeared almost immediately. His nervousness was evident as he swallowed with wide-eyed apprehension. "Yes, my chief. What is it you wish of me?"

"You will take this woman to see Buffalo Horn. You will remain there with her and when she is finished, you will return her to me."

"Yes, my chief."

"Now go...the both of you." He dismissed them using the back of a shooing hand.

୭

Birdsong's meeting with the Buffalo Horn had gone well. The old man was indeed good at his trade. He knew of remedies that she had never before even heard of. But she too knew of things that had escaped his many years of learning. Their time spent together was one of respect on her part and a pleased wonderment on his.

He inquired as to how she had learned of the healing plants and was pleased when he was told of her mother's brother, Crooked Foot. Buffalo Horn had remembered Crooked Foot from the days of long ago, before the tribe had split into the northern faction and the southern Penateka. He asked after his health and was sorry to learn that he had passed to the spirit world many years before.

The meeting lasted nearly two hours, but seemed to her to have been much shorter. She enjoyed talking with this old man who seemed to know how to heal every ailment. She asked him if he would teach her more about the healing plants, and he agreed. But all too soon the time had arrived for her to return to One Eye's lodge.

୭

"Did your time with Buffalo Horn go well?" Bear Cub asked as the two strolled amongst the trees toward One Eye's lodge.

"Yes. I think it was a good meeting." Stopping, she waited for Bear Cub to also stop and return to her.

"Why do you stop here?"

"Do you understand why I have been to see Buffalo Horn?"

"I sometimes can hear parts of what is being said and think you want to remain with our people and become the healing one once Buffalo Horn has passed to the spirit world."

"That is true. But more importantly, if I do become the healing one, Chief One Eye will release the captives and I will be allowed to return them to the White Eye wagons."

"Ummm..." he said, with a thoughtful nod. "Why are you telling me of these things?"

"Because I would ask that you accompany me on my journey to the wagons."

"I do not think—"

"Good. Then it's settled," she said and resumed her trek to the chief's lodge with a finality that left him standing open mouthed and scratching his head.

၈

Mary Jane and the children were barely able to contain themselves. Nevertheless, at Birdsong's insistence, they managed to keep their questions bottled up until they were well out of the camp.

"Now will you tell us how we were set free?" Mary Jane asked as she pulled her pony alongside of Birdsong's.

"It is a long story and you will hear it in time, but for now you will need to understand that there are dangers for us out here. I am sure the wagons have left the place where you and the others were captured, and we will have a long ride to find them. It will take many days. We will be hot and thirsty, but with Bear Cub's help we will find them and your families. Now, you will ride in silence. Talking will only make you thirsty. Even though we now have much water, it will not be so in a few days if we are unable to find more along the way."

They rode the rest of the day with little conversation. After making camp that evening, the questions and answers flew until well into the night. Once everyone understood the circumstances surrounding their release, they were at ease and slept peacefully for the first time since their abduction.

∽

Two days passed with the dryness of the weather taking its toll on each of the groups wandering the plains. Water had indeed become a scarcity for everyone involved and had understandably been forced to the forefront of everyone's mind.

Birdsong and the children were in the best shape because they had been on the trail for the shortest period of time.

However, the rescue party was not as fortunate. Stretch's wound remained painful and required constant care and attention. They had taken the needed time to cauterize it with the gunpowder from a rifle shell and that seemed to have helped...at least it wasn't bleeding and didn't appear to be dangerously infected.

Even though Stretch insisted that it was alright, the immediate area around the wound was dried and cracked and needed to be kept moist. That of course used up a good portion of the water supply. No one complained. They would have expected the same if it had been one of them who had suffered the unfortunate wound.

Constance did her best to keep him as comfortable as possible under the circumstances, and it no doubt would have been tougher on him had she not been around; a woman's touch just naturally seemed to help keep the hurt to a minimum.

Miguel Sancho and his men met up with the other half of their band and intensified their search for the gringos who had stolen Sancho's woman and humiliated him. His anger was such that he would not rest until he had cut their ears off and fed them to the dogs.

The real problems were with the wagon train. The journey had gone well enough after leaving the site of the attacks, but the "well enough" had lasted barely a day or so. On the second day out, Harry took a turn for the worse and died from his head wound. He needed to be put to rest and that took the better part of an entire afternoon, costing them almost a half-day's progress.

The only one who seemed to have a problem with it was Noah. Not at all willing to jeopardize his chances of getting to the Arkansas, he had gone to voice his displeasure to Heck.

"Ain't there any way we can just leave him? It'll take up valuable time ta plant him in the ground, and that's time we ain't got. In case you ain't noticed, we got barely enough water left to fill up a termite's swimmin' hole"

"Noah, I can understand your position in this, mainly because of your beliefs, or should I say non-beliefs. However, there's no way a Christian man would leave another to be eaten by the coyotes. If you have a problem with that, well, I'm truly sorry, but you'll just hafta deal with it."

"I'll deal with it alright. I'm takin' me 'n mine and headin' out for the Arkansas," he said with a vengeance.

"I can't let you do that. You hired me to bring you and your boys out here and I'm responsible for all three of you as well as your wagon. I can't let you go out on your own."

"Well then, I'd say that's easy enough taken care of...you're fired! Now, I'll be gettin' my boys together and pullin' out." He spun angrily and headed for his wagon. "Wayman! Rip!" he hollered as he stormed away.

It was just a matter of a few minutes before Noah had pulled his wagon out of line. With folks on both sides of the wagon doing their darndest to dissuade him, he whipped up his team and the solitary wagon left them behind and rolled westward and out of sight beyond a slight rise in the prairie floor.

All in all the burying took the better part of three hours and then another ten minutes or so for Pastor Jenks to say a farewell to the dearly departed. Once the ceremony had been completed, there was still another fifteen minutes or so of dishing out the necessary comforts to Mrs. Carter. She had already lost her son, Joshua, to the heathen Comanches and now her husband was gone, as well. Her faith had been badly shaken and she had no desire to continue the journey.

Pastor Jenks did his best to console her and provide her with the needed strength, but his efforts proved to be to no avail. Finally, Mrs. Jenks was able to get through to her by having a no holds barred, one on one with her about how she was not the only one who had lost a child on this trip. Although losing both a husband and a child in just a matter of a few days was significant, it was not the end of the world. She was finally able to reach her by saying, "The Lord never gives a person more then she can handle. You just need to keep the faith in Him."

Agnes reluctantly accepted her plight and the train again got under way, some three and a half hours behind the Baxters.

They had gone less than a mile when, while making its way through a skinny passageway between two closely spaced boulders, the lead wagon dropped a wheel into a deep hole and snapped a couple of spokes.

Spirits had already reached a low point because of all the delays that seemed to be plaguing the wagons, but their faith in the Lord won out and the men went to work in an attempt to get the wagon out of the hole and the damaged wheel repaired as quickly as possible.

They worked diligently but their efforts were hampered because of the close proximity of the boulders. Unable to pull the wagon from the hole because the twisted, broken wheel was lodged against the rock, they steadfastly levered the corner of the wagon up with a tree limb and painstakingly worked their way through the difficulties.

Eventually the wagon was pushed and pulled out of the gaping hole and the wheel was finally repaired. While the repairs were being made, the crevice was filled with dirt and stones to a level that allowed passage of the rest of the wagons. Only then was the train able to resume its journey.

෧

Sancho smiled his pleasure as the group rode past his position of hiding. He could not believe his good fortune. He sat silently and watched the insolent squaw, along with the pretty young Señorita as they continued toward the trap he and his men had hastily prepared for them. Although the prizes were accompanied by the other children and a Comanche buck, Sancho paid little attention to them and instead focused his attention on his sought after prey.

As soon as the riders drew abreast of Sancho's men, they rode out from their places of hiding. A minor confusion ensued as the Indian woman's horse reared, causing a diversion that allowed the young buck to slam his heels into the sides of his pony and quickly disappear into the surrounding brush.

"Well, well," Sancho said as he approached from behind the children. He was barely able to control his delight. "What is this? My beloved pretty Señorita is come to find her Sancho, no?" He rode to a position alongside Mary Jane's horse and showed his brown teeth as he gave her his best smile. "I am very happy to see that you have missed me so much."

Mary Jane watched the expression on the filthy pig's face as he leered at her. The tears ran freely down her cheeks.

"Aww, my little Señorita cries tears of joy to see her Sancho once again." He reached a hand out to touch her, and forgetting her fright, she brushed the hand aside and glared at him through the tears.

"Don't touch me!" she ordered, hardly believing the determination of her own voice.

"Oh...I will touch you alright," he said, the smile fading. "But only when the time she is right."

"You are but a filthy pig," Birdsong intervened. "Why do

you feel the need to frighten this young girl?"

Birdsong was within Sancho's reach and he shot out a backhand that caught her on the side of the face, sending her pitching headlong from her pony. She landed hard and glared her defiance up at him. "You are *still* a filthy pig," she repeated through clenched teeth, as she used the back of her hand to wipe away the blood from the corner of her mouth.

Looking toward one of his men, Sancho said, "Pablo...kill the insolent one."

Birdsong quickly gathered her thoughts and immediately sprang to her feet. She glanced at Mary Jane then bolted for the nearby bushes. As soon as she reached the brush, she began looking around frantically for a suitable place to hide.

She heard the leader of the Mexicans say, "Go after her!"

Almost immediately, she found a dense scrub oak thicket and ducked into it. She was oblivious to the pain as it scratched her arms and face. Once she felt as though she were safely hidden, she crouched low to the ground.

She had chosen well. The bush was very close to the clearing where the ambush had taken place. *The Mexicans will not think of looking for me this close to them.* She was right. The one called Pablo passed by without so much as glancing her way. A smile came to her face as she remained perfectly still.

She listened intently to the sounds around her. The searching one was making a thorough inspection of the surrounding area, but not the bush where she lay hidden. Suddenly, a muffled cry reached her ears from the direction Pablo had taken. It was followed by silence. A smile crossed her lips as she realized that Bear Cub had found the man.

"Pablo!" The call came from the filthy one. "Pablo!" he repeated, this time with more urgency to his tone His apprehension was met by a Comanche war cry from the lips of the victorious Bear Cub.

Birdsong smiled her pleasure as she listened to the orders being given for the rest of the Mexicans to spread out and search the bushes for the pair of escaped Comanches. She reached to her side and drew the knife from its sheath. She remained motionless as the first of the searchers passed by. The next one, however, did not assume the bush was empty and after stopping, stuck the barrel of his firestick into it and moved the branches around. His search turned out to be haphazard, and he continued on as she relaxed her previously white knuckled grip on the handle of the knife.

The search continued while the sounds grew progressively fainter. Once she felt sure that it was safe to do so, she eased her way from the hiding place and glanced around the open areas. Not seeing or hearing anything that would indicate a nearness of the searchers, she quietly made her way back toward the clearing.

When she reached it, she saw what she had hoped for...the lone filthy pig was keeping guard over Mary Jane and the children. She was to the left side and slightly behind him. She eased back into the bushes and circled around until she was directly to his back. She inhaled deeply, gathered herself, and with the stealth of a determined Comanche, silently sprang from her cover.

She charged at the horse and drew the blade of the knife along its back leg, cutting it deeply. The animal screamed its fright at the suddenness of the attack and reared, throwing the unsuspecting Miguel Sancho to the ground.

She was on him with the swiftness of the puma and watched as his expression turned from first surprise, then to fear as he realized he was about to die. Without a second thought, she thrust the knife blade into the front of his neck. The blood gushed out and covered her hand. She released the handle, leaving the blade imbedded. A smile crossed her face as she listened to the life gurgling from the lips of the soon to be dead man.

Almost immediately, she was drawn back to the problems at hand, as the sounds of an approaching rider demanded her attention. She looked at the frightened faces of Mary Jane and the children. "Ride quickly! I will find you! Go!"

The urgency in the tone of her voice, along with the insistence of her pointing finger, served to answer any questions that had sprang into the minds of the children. They reined around and disappeared from the clearing just before the approaching rider entered.

Seeing the Indian woman standing over his fallen leader, Jose drew his pistola and pointed it at the now defenseless Birdsong.

Just when she was sure he would kill her, an anguished pleading cry came from the edge of the clearing behind him.

He twisted in his saddle and fired at Bear Cub. At nearly the same instant, Birdsong leapt forward and pulled him from the back of his pony while at the same time removing the knife from the sheath at his waist. As soon as he hit the ground, she plunged the knife into the man's stomach. She then pulled the blade sideways. Seeing the entrails beginning to appear, she did not wait for him to die. She instead ran to her pony, and grabbing a handful of mane, deftly swung herself up. She took one last look at the motionless body of her beloved friend lying at the edge of the clearing. She was flooded with pangs of sorrow for the loss of this brave warrior. "You will always be in my heart, Angry Bear," she said lovingly, and kicked the pony toward an opening between two of the bushes.

She gripped the sides of the animal with the insides of her knees and thighs as she rode hard to escape the dangers behind her. Her heart pounded with the ferocity of remembered war drums. Holding tight to the pony's mane, she twisted around to look back. She was relieved to see that she was not being pursued.

She continued her escape with a sense of urgency that slowly evolved into one of relief. *Their leader is dead. They will not come after me*, she realized and allowed the beginnings of a smile to come to her lips. *They have no more reason to risk their lives.* The smile grew even wider as she spotted the cloud of dust a good ways ahead that she knew would turn out to be Mary Jane and the fleeing children. Encouraged at finding them so soon, she leaned forward and rubbed the pony's neck, urging her even faster.

&Chapter 26&

Heck shaded his eyes and squinted into the setting sun. Wisps of blue smoke curled lazily into the evening sky. He twisted around in the saddle. "Circle the wagons!" he ordered as he circled a hand high overhead.

He waited patiently as the beleaguered drivers did their best to coax the exhausted, thirsty teams into a formation that only vaguely resembled a circle. He removed his hat and haphazardly hooked it on the saddlehorn...it fell to the ground. He just left it there. His wounded arm remained in a makeshift sling and was still pretty much right next to useless. With his good one, he wiped the sweat from his brow by ducking into the bend of the elbow. He then glanced wishfully at the clouds that floated lazily overhead. Judging them to not be anywhere near of the rain producing variety, he didn't hold out much hope.

He turned to look at the approaching Jacob Greenberg who was keeping his sagging bay gelding reined down to a slow walk.

With great effort, Heck got down and retrieved his hat.

"Seen the smoke," Greenberg said as he reined up.

"What'dya figger it's from?"

"I'm thinking it's what's left of the Baxter wagon."

"Now, that'd be a cryin' shame. I didn't much care for Baxter's outlook on most things, but..."

"Me neither," Heck said. "How about you riding over there with me to make sure it's them?"

"Ain't partial to doin' it, but I reckon it's better than not knowin' for sure. C'mon, let's go get it over with."

"Just a minute," Heck said. If they found what he expected to find, it would take the rest of the day and then some to bury the Baxters. While Jacob waited, Heck gave instructions for the train to make camp for the night and to post a guard. He then tiredly climbed aboard his horse.

They were in no hurry and rode slowly until they arrived at what were indeed the remnants of the Baxter wagon and the remains of the Baxters. Although all three men were lying dead with their scalps removed and their bodies riddled with arrows, there were signs that not a one of them had gone easily.

The bodies of the attackers had been carried off, but the splotches of blood that dotted the buffalo grass indicated at least six Indians had been taken down. The wagon had been ransacked, its contents thrown around haphazardly and the whole thing set on fire. The horses were gone.

"Ain't a pretty sight," Heck said as he bent down and retrieved an arrow. He turned it over between his fingers as he went about examining it closely. "This here's Ute. See the markings...right here?" He held it out toward Greenberg while he pointed at the cresting on the upper portion of the shaft. "Them's also Ute designs in the feathers." He tossed the arrow away in disgust. "Ain't we got us enough troubles to deal with, what with the children being stolen, the Comanches killin' our folks, and the water being gone?" He drew in a deep breath and exhaled slowly. "Now we gotta put up with the Utes out roaming the countryside an' treating folks thisaway." He indicated the bodies with a sweeping hand.

Jacob had seen enough. "C'mon Heck, let's get on back to the wagons and get some fellas together to do the grave diggin'."

❦

Mary Jane and the children continued to ride hard to escape the dreadful confrontation back at the stand of scrub oak. Her thoughts had never left Birdsong as they rode without looking back.

After what seemed to her to be an eternity, she thought she heard a faint voice mixed in with the drumming hoofs of the running horses. She glanced behind her and saw Birdsong riding swiftly and catching up to her and the children.

Mary Jane hollered at the children to stop and pulled hard against her pony's mane. She was relieved when the animal finally began to slow.

The children were having some difficulty, but they, too, eventually managed to get their horses under control as one by one they brought them to a slower pace, then finally to complete stops.

"Look! It's Birdsong!" Mary Jane said excitedly, as Josh and the others rejoined her.

"I can see that," he said. "I ain't entirely blind, ya know." Even though the words indicated a bit of sarcasm on his part, the grin on his face gave him away. "Sure is a sight for sore eyes, though," he finally admitted and changed the grin into an all-encompassing smile.

Birdsong reined up and slid from her pony. "Is everyone okay?" she asked.

"I think so," Mary Jane said, looking around at the nodding heads.

"Did you kill those men back there?" Charlette asked.

"Yes...I took the life of two but they killed my friend Angry Bear."

"I-I'm truly sorry, Birdsong," Mary Jane said.

"It is alright. Even though he is gone to the spirit world, he has made the journey as a warrior. That is what matters most to a Comanche. He died an honorable death."

"So what now?" Josh asked. "We just going to sit here like a passel of lost children, or are we gonna go find them wagons?"

"I am thinking it would be a good idea to go and find them wagons," Birdsong said, mocking him.

"I sure will be glad when we finally do find 'em," Mary Jane said. "I miss my family...and Stretch," she added, wondering if he missed her, too.

ೲ

Sam and the rest of the fellas, including Lucky, had been making good progress. Fact is, unbeknownst to them, they were within a mile and a half to two miles of the wagon train when they made their camp for the night. The rolling hills that made up the distance between them not only kept the two parties hidden from one another, but neither was able to catch a glimpse of the glow from the other's fire.

The water supply was bordering on critical as Sam unscrewed the cap from the last of the canteens and handed it to Lucky. "How's it looking?' he asked, watching the pain in Stretch's eyes while feeling more than just a little bit sorry because of the discomfort the youngster was being forced to endure.

"He is doing well. I think the wound she is very painful, but it will no make him to be sick." She accepted the canteen and held it to Stretch's lips, keeping a cupped hand under his chin to catch any that might spill.

He took a small sip and pulled his mouth away. In doing so, a small amount leaked into her hand. She brought it to her lips and licked the wetness from her palm.

"You must drink some more," she urged, again offering the canteen to him.

"Naw...I figger I've had about enough. I'm plumb full

clean up to my eyebrows."

Sam decided to try his hand at getting him to see reason, "Stretch, it might not be such a bad idea if you were to take just a little more. I reckon all the blood you've lost hasn't done your body much good. I'm sure there's a need for keeping some moisture inside of you."

"Thanks, Sam. I think that what you're saying is probably true enough, but I won't be taking away from the rest of you just so I'd stand a better chance of making it through this mess. I'm thinking that right now I'm in about as good a shape as any of you. That means we're all on equal footing around here until something drastic happens that says different."

Sam nodded while reluctantly accepting what Stretch had to say. He admired the boy's spunk, but truly wished he would drink a little more than the rest of them. He rose and walked away, knowing there was no way he could change the boy's way of thinking.

Lucky bathed the wound sparingly before carefully rewrapping it with some fresh pieces of cloth she had torn from the bottom edge of her dress. "You have a pretty Señorita who waits for you, no?" she asked as she gathered up the soiled bandage for disposal in the fire.

"Yeah, but I ain't even sure if she's still alive or dead or maybe somewhere in between," he said, as despite his efforts to the contrary, he lost control of his bottom lip and felt it quiver slightly.

She noticed his show of emotion, reached out, and tenderly took his hand in hers. "Your sweetheart, she is safe." His gaze met hers and she saw a glimmer of hope in his eyes. In an effort to make him feel even better, she continued, "You will see her very soon...of this you can be sure."

৽

The general feelings back at the wagons were those of hopelessness, anger, and despair. Folks were worn to a frazzle and outright bone tired. They had been keeping the faith as well as could be expected, but their faith was being sorely tested and the discovery of the Baxters had removed just about any lingering hope they may have had of getting out of their mess safely.

The lone exception was Pastor Jenks. He refused to give in to the worldly happenings and prayed all the harder.

Mrs. Jenks, however, was also having her faith sorely tested and seemed to be losing the battle right along with the rest of them.

"We must keep the faith, Maggie," he urged. "The Lord will not abandon His children. You see those clouds up there?" He pointed at the soft wisps of fluffy white clouds as they floated overhead. "The Bible says that that's the dust from God's heels as He walks around an area He has created. It's my contention that the Lord is here with us right now and will not let us give up."

"I truly do love you, Mister Jenks," she said, and rubbed a single tear from where it had slid down onto the lower portion of her cheek. "You are a wonderful man and the Lord has blessed you in many ways." She then went to him and draped her arms loosely around his neck, clasping her wrist with the fingers of the other hand. "And you know something else, Pa? I have a feeling that He's not done with you yet." She pulled him to her and kissed him gently on the lips.

"Maggie, stop that," he said good-naturedly. "What will folks think?"

"I would hope they'd think that I've got one heck of a good man here. Now shut your trap and kiss me back."

He did.

৯৹

A fire was built and the beleaguered men of the train worked well into the night digging the graves for Noah Baxter and his sons. Although it was generally felt that Utes wouldn't attack after dark, there was no sense in taking any unnecessary chances and a guard had been posted as a precaution. Once the graves had been dug, the bodies were laid out alongside and the men returned to the wagons. It had been decided to have the burying and the accompanying service early the next morning.

ॐ

The following morning was not much different from the one before. A few high clouds greeted the early risers as the sun peeked its brow above the eastern horizon.

Sam sat on the edge of his blanket and pulled his boots to him. After turning each upside down he thumped them against the ground. Satisfied that they were truly empty, he pulled them on and stood. He then stomped his feet into a proper fit and gazed out across the sunlit prairie. A movement far off to the south caught his eye and he instinctively crouched. He said a silent prayer and continued to watch as the string of figures moved slowly along the distant horizon. He figured it would be best to wake the others just in case a hurried exit might be in order. He nudged the figure nearest him. "Charlie...wake up," he urged in a hoarse whisper.

Spending the majority of his life in Indian country tended Charlie toward being a light sleeper and he was instantly wide-awake. He sat up. "Yeah...what is it?"

Sam pointed. "There's a line of riders over that way."

Charlie nudged both Kyle and Stretch. "Get up, fellas. Sam says we got company." He then reached over and jostled Lucky awake as well.

"What kind of company?" Stretch asked as he one-handedly rubbed the sleep from his eyes.

"Don't know for sure," Charlie said.

In no time at all, everyone was up and watching the line of figures that were silhouetted along the distant horizon.

"What'dya make of it, Charlie?" Stretch asked.

"It's sorta hard ta say from this distance but I'm inclined toward it bein' Injuns." He continued to squint off in the direction of the movement. "Yep. I'm pretty sure from the way they're trailin' one another that it's Injuns alright. Might not be such a bad idea if we was ta get the horses saddled and be ready to hightail it outta here if we get spotted."

"Sounds like a good idea to me," Sam said. "Stretch, you and Lucky keep an eye on those fellas while the rest of us saddle up and break camp."

Stretch nodded and winced as the slight movement caused a stab of pain to shoot through his arm.

"Are you okay?" Lucky asked as her concern for him furrowed her brow.

"Yeah...just a mite tender in spots is all," he said and closed his eyes, as yet another sharp pain took a toll on him.

She continued to watch him closely and thought she detected a slight lessening in his pained expression as he raised his forearm up to where it was angled across his chest.

"Does that make it hurt less?"

"Yeah...seems to."

She then pulled the bottom of her dress up, exposing more leg than he had ever seen in all his entire borned days. A hot flush of red started from somewhere down under his collar and spread upward to his cheeks and beyond. He quickly averted his eye as she began tearing strips from the dress. Once the tearing sounds had ceased, his embarrassment eased as well.

The smile across her face said that she had enjoyed his uneasiness. "You are very bashful, no?"

"Ah...yeah. You might say that."

"You no have to worry. I will no bite you." She quickly went to work and used the strips of cloth to fashion a sling that she passed under his wrist and knotted together behind his neck. Once it was securely in place, she looked into his eyes. "What do you think? Does it make your wound feel better now?"

He tested the sling by first pushing against it with the

injured arm, then swinging it around in an arc away from his body. After not feeling any major discomfort to speak of, he replied, "Yep. Don't seem to hurt none at all now."

"Maybe it was looking at my pretty legs that make it to no hurt no more."

The flush returned as he rose and headed for the horses. "Ain't you fellas finished with those horses yet?" he asked, with the sounds of her soft chuckle easily reaching his ears.

"Just right this instant as a matter a fact," Kyle answered. "Somethin' ailin' ya, boy?" he asked, seeing the flushed appearance of Stretch's face. "Yer lookin' a mite reddened."

"No, I ain't ailing! So whyn't you just go on and mind your own business!"

Kyle lifted his hat and went about scratching his bald spot.

Sam had been looking off to the north. "Charlie, what'dya say we walk these horses a ways off that way?" He pointed. "The prairie slopes in that direction and if we can get just a little ways down that hill those Indians will never see us."

"You might have somethin' there, Sam. I reckon it's worth a try."

Without another word, they led the horses down the gently sloping terrain until they felt safe enough to mount. Once the decision was made to make a break for it, they urged the badly worn horses into motion and finally into a gentle lope.

After less than a half hour, they topped a gentle rise, hauled up alongside one another, and sat speechless. There on the prairie below was the lopsided circle of wagons. Off to one side were the remains of a burned-out wagon. That was also where most, if not all, of the members of the train had congregated.

"Well, well. Would you just look at that," Charlie said and kicked his horse forward.

As they rode slowly down the hillside, it became increasingly apparent that the gathering was for the placing of more than one body into the ground.

"Looks like they've been having a few troubles of their own," Sam commented.

❧Chapter 27❧

Sam and the others dismounted and approached the beleaguered group of travelers just as Pastor Jenks was finishing up. "And so, we offer the souls of these two young men into Your kingdom, Lord. Although Noah wasn't saved and will spend the rest of eternity burning in the rages of hellfire and damnation, I thank You for sending Wayman and Rip to me to receive You into their hearts." He looked up to see the returning rescuers. Sam and Kyle were already hugging their wives, while the rest of them looked on from a short distance away. "Amen," he said hurriedly.

"Well now," Sam said, "peers like we got here at just about the right time."

"Kinda depends on what your line of thinking is," Heck offered. "We got Injuns killing folks, the water's gone, and spirits around here are just about at rock bottom. I can also see that the children didn't return with you. Kinda makes a fella wonder what else could go wrong."

"I don't think you really want to know," Sam said as he bent down and hoisted Tom up. "But I'll tell you anyway. Not more than a half hour ago, we spotted a good-sized band of

Indians headed this way. I expect they'll be showing themselves along the top of that ridge most anytime now." He motioned toward the ridge to the east with a slight tilting of his head.

That announcement brought gasps from the women and more than one hand found an open mouth. The men were slightly more under control, but mumbled cussing could be heard coming from a few of them.

"All ya'll listen up," Heck said. "If it's the same Utes what done this here killin' of the Baxters, then we got us a real problem headed our way and need to get back to the wagons and prepare ourselves for another fight."

The graveside service was forgotten as the members of the train hurried toward the wagons while pushing and herding their children in front of them. More than one of the youngsters suffered a swat on their backside if they failed to keep a good distance in front of their parents.

SWAT! The sound of a hand placed strategically on a youngster's backside could be heard above the low-toned conversations of the weary travelers. "I said..." Sam heard a concerned mother say, "get yourself to them wagons or I'll just leave you to them Injuns, and you can spend the rest of your days doin' for those heathens. And I mean right now, boy!" SWAT! The second one did the trick and the boy skipped ahead with both hands rubbing his rump and tears streaming down his cheeks.

Sam carried Tom and took Jay by the hand as he led her over to where Stretch and Lucky stood. "Jay...this here's Lucky. I mean...ahh—"

"Hello, Señora. I am Constance. I am very happy to see you."

"Hello, Constance. I'm Judith, but please call me, Jay." She extended a hand and the young Mexican woman accepted it gladly.

"And who is this?" she asked, looking at Tom.

"This here's my son, Tom," Sam said with more than just a little bit of pride showing through.

Jay noticed Stretch's sling. "Stretch...you're hurt." She quickly brushed past Sam and stopped in front of him. "Is it bad?"

"Naw," he replied, trying to appear tougher then he really was. "Just a little ol' arrow hole is all."

"Oh my goodness. Sam...? What happened?" she asked, looking from one to the other.

"It's a long story," Sam said. "I'll tell you later, but for now, how about we get on back to the wagons with the others?"

They hastily made their way to the circle of wagons where Jay went about tending to Stretch's wound, while Constance broke the ice with young Tom. She liked children and Tom seemed to take to her as well. While she was occupying him by taking off some of her bracelets and showing him how to clank them together, Jacob approached and asked the obvious, "No luck with getting Mary Jane and the rest of the youngsters out of that Injun camp, huh?"

His sorrowful expression touched Sam's heart to the point of making him feel even guiltier about not having brought them back. "No, Jacob. I'm sorry to say the whole rescue attempt was doomed right from the start. We couldn't even get it straight in our minds where they were being held, let alone make a decent attempt at getting them out of there. But you need to know that it wasn't anyone's fault. We were doing the best we could. Then when we got ambushed and Stretch took an arrow, we figured it'd be best to get him back here to the wagons before going back for another try."

"What?" Jay said as she hooked his arm and pulled him around to face her. "Did I hear what I thought I did? You aren't really thinking about going back there?"

"Jay, honey, those youngsters are still in the hands of those heathen Comanches. I just don't know how I'd ever be able to live with myself knowing that I'd given up on the lives of those children." He placed a hand on each of her upper arms. "Please try to understand that my life would be worthless knowing I hadn't given this my all."

She fell against him and rested the side of her face against his chest while his arms went around her. "I understand what you're saying, Sam, and know that I must let you go, but why you? I just wish this was all over and done with," she said resignedly.

"Thank you for understanding, Jay," he said and kissed her on the top of her head.

"When will you be leaving?" she asked after they had parted.

"Just as soon as we do what we can to help get this train the rest of the way to the Arkansas."

"Who's we?"

"Me 'n Charlie an' Kyle have decided that the three of us can pull it off...with a whole lot of God's help, that is. But we'll deal with that later. In the meantime, tell me what's been going on around here. It looks like the stock is just about done in."

She waved her hand in an exasperated arc and said, "The water's all gone, the delays have been coming faster then can reasonably be thought possible, and now the Utes have attacked and killed the Baxters who had set out on their own. Heck seems to think that it'll take a miracle to get us out of this fix. He says we're still about a day and a half from the river and...and..." She wiped her brow with the sleeve of her dress and sighed heavily. "And he doesn't see any way the horses can make it. He says the best we could hope for is that these few clouds," she glanced skyward, "will amount to something and produce some rain before it's eternally too late." The look in her eye suggested that it had gotten close to that point already.

"The Lord won't let us down," he assured her. "He knows

His children are down here and in need. He'll do what needs doing."

At that point, their conversation was interrupted as Danny hollered, "Heck wants ever'one together at the center of the circle!"

"Sounds like Heck might have a plan," Sam said. "C'mon."

Heck smiled and acknowledged Sam with a nod as they arrived. "As you folks already know, Sam here..." he indicated him with a tilt of his head, "and Kyle 'n Charlie all say there's a whole passel of Injuns just southeast of here. That's more than likely gonna mean trouble. I know that you folks have come through a whole lot already, but there's still more what needs dealing with."

He paused to wait for the gentle mutterings to die down. Holding a hand high above his head, he continued, "You all know that the water's all gone and the animals ain't got a whole lot left in 'em, but what you may or may not know is that the Lord hasn't given up on us. We just gotta hang on until He decides our trial is over and it's time to bestow a blessing on the whole bunch of us."

He then looked from one face to another until his gaze came to rest on Pastor Jenks. "Maybe the pastor here can say it better than me. Pastor would you give it a try?"

Pastor Jenks smiled and stepped forward. He remained silent to those around him while he said a brief prayer to himself. Once the Lord had given him the needed words, he looked at the faces around him. Some showed apprehension, while most were filled with outright trepidation. "You folks have a right to believe that the Lord has abandoned you, but trust me when I tell you that that is indeed not the case."

Sam knew the importance that hinged on the words the pastor would give to these harried folks. He closed his eyes and spoke silently with the Lord. *Father, please give this man of God the power and liberty to say what needs saying in such a way that'll reach an' encourage 'em...amen.*

Pastor Jenks continued, "Now I know that there's been more than one occasion when I've been a mite windy with both my preaching and praying."

The mumbling and chuckles attested to that statement as being a true fact.

"Well, this time I'll be short and to the point. I told my missus earlier this morning that those clouds up there," he pointed, "are the dust from God's heels as He passes through these parts. That means that He's here and He's watching over us. In the book of Deuteronomy...in Chapter thirty-one, it says; *Be strong and of a good courage, fear not, nor be afraid of them: for the Lord thy God, he it is that doth go with thee; he will not fail thee, nor forsake thee.*"

Sam smiled his approval. "Amen," he said softly, and again smiled as the pastor returned to his place among the others, accompanied by a chorus of hardy "Amens".

"Sounds like some words for a fella to take ta heart," Heck said as he again took charge of the meeting. "With Him here and on our side, how can we even think of givin' up?"

The question didn't require an answer, and it was a good thing because no sooner had he gotten the words out, than Ethelda Mae Hendricks said excitedly, "Look...over thata-way!" She pointed to the southeast.

They all turned toward the indicated direction. Along the crest of the nearby hill sat a line of about twenty-five or thirty Indian braves astride their ponies. A controlled kind of pandemonium broke out as mothers scurried off to find their young'uns and fathers brought their rifles to a more handy position...that being right about chest level.

"Don't no one make any stupid moves," Heck warned. "Keep those guns handy but don't shoot until I give the word." Looking around, he spied Cottonwood Charlie. "Charlie, come on over here."

Charlie quickly moved next to Heck and rested the butt of his rifle on the ground in front of him. He then placed a forearm on top of it with his gaze never leaving the band of Indians.

"What'dya make of it, Charlie?"

"I ain't real fer sure, but..." He picked the rifle up and cradled it in the crook of his elbow. "C'mon," he said and started forward.

As the two walked toward the wagons that lay between them and the Indians, Charlie told Heck his suspicions. "I'm thinkin' these redskins ain't lookin' fer no fight. They seem ta be on the friendly side. Look real close...they ain't wearin' no paint and neither are their ponies. That's makin' me figger they's just passin' through and they fer sure ain't Ute, neither."

"So, what now? We gonna go have a parlay with 'em?" Heck asked.

"That's exactly what we're gonna do."

They climbed over the barricade and continued out onto the prairie toward the group of Indians. As they neared, Charlie was grateful to see one of their number slide off his pony and approach on foot, unarmed.

Seeing this, Charlie lowered his rifle to the grass and indicated for Heck to do the same. They continued their approach until they stood face to face with the very same Arapahoe they had, what now seemed so long ago, given food to.

Charlie and the Indian greeted one another, and he and Heck were both surprised to learn that the warrior knew a whole lot more English than he'd previously let on. From their brief conversation, they learned that his name was Swift Claw and that he was in fact the chief of the whole Arapahoe bunch that claimed this part of the countryside as their own.

"I am happy to again see the White Eye who gave my people the much needed food," the chief said. "I can see from the burned White Eye wagon that you have found trouble. You will tell me about this trouble." He crossed his arms and waited.

Charlie filled him in. "I, too, am happy to once again see the mighty Arapahoe Chief, Swift Claw. We have no more water. The wagon that was burned was one that had left the safety of the others and was attacked by the Utes."

"Ummm..." The chief nodded his understanding.

"We wish only to be left alone and wait for the sky to open and drop some water on us. We do not want trouble with the Utes."

"Your trouble is easy to fix. There is water very near. We will take you. The Utes will not come back. We will go with you until you reach the big river. If they return, we will kill them."

Heck spread a wide grin and slapped Charlie on the back. "Well now, don't that just beat all?" he said, barely able to control his delight. "Ain't it amazing what kinda rewards a fella can get just from parting with a little grub ever' now 'n then? Why the next thing you know, he'll be telling us—"

His line of reasoning was cut short as he noticed movement along the crest of the hill. Looking up, he finished the sentence, in a kind of absentminded manner, while not at all believing what he was seeing, "he'll be telling us that they've got the children with them."

Charlie looked up the slope. Sure enough, there was Birdsong leading Mary Jane and the three youngsters down the hill toward the three of them. He pulled his coonhide hat and rubbed his bald spot. "I'd say that preacher sure does know what he's talking about," he said and replaced the hat. "Yes sir...right down to a gnat's eyebrow, I'd say."

The reunion with the children got everyone to rejoicing. However, the news of there being water nearby, plus the escort to the Arkansas and protection offered by the Arapahoe chief, got them all to giving thanks and praising the Lord.

Stretch and Mary Jane were unashamed as they fell into

one another's arms. Jay smiled at the sight and nudged Sam with an elbow. "I'd say there's most likely going to be a wedding before we even reach the river," she said, and wiped away a tear of thanksgiving. She couldn't remember ever having felt a more satisfying feeling in her whole entire life.

Sam patted the back of the man standing next to him and said, "Well, Jacob... you about ready to turn loose of her?"

Jacob took note of the happiness in his little girl's face as she clung to her beau. "I don't think I'll be havin' any say-so in it."

Sam grinned. "I'd say *that's* a true fact."

ഔ

Sam and Jay sat atop the seat as they waited their turn to move forward. Lucky and Tom sat on the lowered tailgate with their feet dangling over the edge. Sam looked back through the wagon and said, "You two all set back there?"

"Yes, Señor. We are all set, thank you very much. We are ready to go find a place to live."

Then turning to Jay he smiled and asked, "How about you?" She smiled up at her husband, contentedly, and he knew he'd done his job. He pecked her on the cheek. "See...I told you I'd take care of you out here."

There was a smile on both of their faces as he snapped the reins along the backs of the team. "Hup! Hup! Get up there!" he said and whistled through his teeth.

THIS IS NOT THE END, BUT RATHER JUST THE BEGINNING.

ഔ

Preview:

The following is a preview of book two of the Arkansas Valley Series:

UNCERTAIN TIMES

❧Chapter 1❧

Sam shoved a booted foot against the brake handle and leaned back hard on the reins. The prairie schooner creaked and rattled to a stop. He straightened up, draped a half hitch of leather straps around the handle, and slid an arm around his missus' waist. He couldn't help but feel a sense of adventure. *Well, Lord,* he thought, *now that You've got us here, all safe and sound, I'd appreciate it if You was to not quit on us now.*

He looked lovingly at his beautiful wife seated on the wagon seat next to him. She brushed aside a wayward wisp of her auburn hair before resting her head against his shoulder. They sat in silent contemplation taking in the layout of the oblong stockade that lay situated just beyond the base of the hill the schooner now rested atop.

Two circular bastions adorned the tops of the southeast and northwest corners of the thickly walled structure. The walls themselves appeared about fifteen feet or so in height and were lined along the tops with ominous-looking cactus plants, no doubt to help ward off intruders. The area inside the perimeter was made up mostly of a courtyard and corral of sorts that was surrounded by what looked to be general storage facilities. Midway along the eastern wall was a massive gateway that was fitted with two plank doors that appeared to be heavily plated with sheet iron. This seemed to be the only way in or out, except for a small wooden door at the base of the bastion on the southeast corner.

"Well, what'dya think, Jay?" he asked as they eyed the outpost. "At least it's a *measure* of civilization," he added, not at all sure what her reaction would be, but certainly willing to try to coax her into a favorable one.

Judith Bartlett was not exactly taken with the dismal, drab appearance of the trading post. Neither was she anywhere near becoming ecstatic over the scattering of cone shaped teepees that were situated just outside the north and east walls of the mostly adobe outpost. She raised her head and faced him squarely. She loved her husband dearly. The fact that he was extremely handsome didn't hurt matters none either.

His eyes were of a hazel color that would seemingly change shades as his mood dictated. His rugged features were chiseled to a handsome perfection, punctuated by a square jaw that indicated a man who was apt to stand up for what he believed. A distinctive cleft in the front of his chin only served to add favorably to his rugged features. There was also a genuine good-natured set to his mouth that implied a willingness to smile easily if something pleased him. His hair was thick, wavy, and a sandy-brown color that did justice to his hazel eyes.

She sighed heavily. "That's it? That's what we came

through all that bad weather and high water for?"

He had the feeling that she was fighting valiantly to hold back the tears. "I'll admit the first impression isn't much, but—"

Sam's feeble attempt to smooth things over was mercifully interrupted as he saw the wagonmaster, Heck Yeah, slowly riding their way—the moniker was short for Hector Yallow, but he preferred being called Heck to most anything else.

Heck reined his dust coated, sorrel mare to a halt, swapped the chaw over to his other cheek, and after pulling his hat, gestured with it down the slope before saying what Jay already knew, "Ain't much…but that's it…what they is of it anyways. We'll be making a circle an' stayin' the night. If you folks are of a mind, you might want to go on down and have a parlay to see if this is for sure where you're gonna call it quits."

Sam pulled his arm from around Jay's waist and leaning out offered it to Heck. "Thanks, Heck. We'll do just that."

After releasing the hand, Heck ducked his sweat-streaked forehead into the crook of an elbow He replaced the hat and touched a fingertip to its pushed up front. "Let me know what you decide. The train'll be pulling out first thing in the morning." He reined around and lightly nudged the mare's flanks with the heels of his trail worn boots.

Sam began to climb down stiffly. "I'll just take a minute to let Stretch know what's going on," he said and stumbled as his foot slipped off the hub. He caught himself, smiled sheepishly up at his wife, and then headed toward the Conestoga that had drawn to a stop immediately behind the schooner. As he drew near, he cleared his throat to warn the newlyweds of his approach.

Stretch Henderson—his given name was Darrell—and the former Miss Mary Jane Greenberg, had been married just the week before. Even though by all accounts they had begun the journey as a pair of extremely bashful seventeen-year-olds, it hadn't taken long before they'd somehow managed to put all that aside and fall hopelessly in love.

Their relationship had gotten a healthy boost of sorts right about the time Stretch had saved her life after she had been washed away in her pa's wagon during the fording of a particularly ornery river. It had then quickly blossomed into a genuine yearning after he had taken an arrow while trying to rescue her and those three youngsters after the Comanches had made off with them.

In any case, as nature has a way of working through those issues of the heart, they had Pastor Jenks say the words on a particularly delightful Sunday morning along the banks of the Arkansas.

"Howdy, Stretch...Mary Jane," Sam said, nodding his greeting. "I'll be taking my wagon on down to the fort there." He waved in the general direction of the trading post. "Me and Jay are going to check into the prospects offered about setting up housekeeping hereabouts. You two go on and include the Conestoga in the circle for the night and we'll get together after we return. Save us a spot for the schooner while you're at it."

"Sounds good to me," Stretch said. "You figuring on leaving Lucky here with us while you go about your business?"

"Yeah, believe I will." The area between Sam's hazel eyes narrowed as he grew thoughtful. Tapping the cleft in his chin, he decided, "Nooo...on second thought, she has a stake in this same as the rest of us. I believe I'll take her along."

"Alright then. See you when ya get back."

Sam returned to his wagon and climbed aboard. He unwrapped the bundle of reins and expertly sorted them between his fingers. "Well, the Lord has called us out here...so I guess we ought to go down there and see what He's got in store for us!" he announced.

He released the brake and snapped the reins along the

trailing pair of rumps. He whistled loudly. "Get up there!" he commanded and at the same time pulled hard on the left handful of reins.

The wagon lurched forward while he stole a sideways glance at the woman who had been following him ever since day one. Thankfully, she was turned away from him, tending to something in the bed of the wagon. Feeling some better, he snapped the reins again.

The schooner rattled and shook its way down the decline and was soon nearing the open gate of the Fort Bent Trading Post.

The opening was generous enough, but what with the hustle and bustle of all the foot traffic heading in and out, Sam took care to keep the wagon centered. As soon as they were safely through, he spotted a likely looking spot and guided the team around toward it. Once there, he hauled back on the reins while at the same time jamming the boot against the brake handle. The effort locked the rear wheel, causing the wagon to slide sideways slightly. When it had safely come to a stop, he again bundled the reins in their customary place around the brake handle and climbed down. He looked up at Jay and was relieved to see a gentle smile grace her beautiful face. Hoping against hope, he asked, "What's the grin for?"

"Let's just say that you haven't led me astray so far and I've decided to continue to reserve judgment on this latest whim of yours...at least until I see something that causes me sufficient enough concern to think differently about it."

Sam knew that she was referring to their whirlwind marriage. Then, barely a scant year later, how he had managed to convince her to leave the high society debutante way of life she'd been accustomed to in upstate New York and travel with him to Independence, Missouri, where they shared their lives while building a successful livestock business.

The hardest part for her had been having to make the difficult trip while pregnant with their son, Tom. Then, to top it all off, she had later agreed to pull up stakes from Independence and make the current journey all the way out here to the heathen-infested grasslands along the western edge of the Great Plains. It was an area that folks were calling the Arkansas Valley, but because of its lack of any good-sized hills or mountains to speak of, didn't resemble any kind of valley either of them had ever laid eyes on before.

He returned the smile. "I surely do love you, Mrs. Bartlett," he said and reached out for her hand to assist her down from the wagon seat.

"I think that is enough of that kind of talk." The heavily accented words had come from the interior of the wagon, just behind Jay. "If you are so much in love then maybe you want to be alone, no?"

"Why don't you just go on and mind your own business, Lucky?" Sam said as he pursed his lips and narrowed his eyebrows in playful scorn.

The well-put-together face of the Mexican woman was that of Constance Valdez. Although barely twenty-years-old, she could easily be judged four or five years older. However, the appearance of the extra years had not proven unkind. Her features were those of a woman who, despite the no-nonsense set to her mouth, could melt the frost off a pumpkin in late October. Her raven black hair and sparkling eyes, that appeared nearly as dark, would certainly demand the attention of any man with any sense about him.

Sam had only recently rescued her from a band of opportunistic marauding banditos who were being led by a ruthless man, Miguel Sancho. Although her full name was Constance Maria Consuelo Valdez, she had been so grateful to Sam for having rescued her that she had informed him that he could call her Lucky. And so, the nickname had been created and was now sticking like fleas on the back of a Bluetick hound dog.

"*You* are now my business, Señor Sam," she informed him

with the beginnings of a mischievous grin caressing the pleasant features of her lightly browned face. "When you save my life from those banditos you make me to be very happy. So now you are my business."

Sam knew he couldn't argue with the reasoning she was dishing out. The truth be known, he didn't want to either. She also seemed to be a godsend when it came to helping out with tending to their three-year-old son, Tom. Plus the fact that whenever Jay would let her get close to the cooking pans, she was a right tolerable cook as well.

"I guess what you're saying is true enough but that doesn't give you the right to interfere when me and my missus are being lovey-dovey, now does it?"

"I would think that our romantic relationship is better kept private," Jay said with what seemed to him to be more than just a small dose of consternation. Of course, he had no way of seeing the furtive wink she had tossed Lucky's way.

Feeling duly chastised, he rightfully reasoned that it would be best to just let Jay's comment fall by the wayside while he went about handing her down from the wagon. Looking up at Lucky, he said, "Well, you want to come, too, or would you be satisfied to stay here and mind *your* own business?"

"I will come with you, Señor. That way you will no have to worry about how to find me when you are need my help."

"Fat chance of that ever becoming even a remote possibility," he said. He then reached for his son as she held him suspended out over the side of the wagon. He gently placed Tom on the ground then helped her down, all the while feeling a sense of satisfaction that she truly wanted to be a part of what was going on.

Once everyone was out of the schooner, they looked at their surroundings, taking in the activities and structures that were all around. There seemed to be busy folks just about everywhere.

Situated around the central court were rows of low slung,

open fronted rooms with dirt floors. The roofs were barely six foot off the ground, made of both clay and gravel, and supported by pole beams about every eight feet or so. They made up what appeared to be a warehouse, a cooking area and some general living quarters.

There were also a number of sheds that were being used to provide storage for ox yokes, harnesses and various other pieces of caravan equipment. The entire layout was one of a place for everything and everything in its place.

Sam pulled his interest away from his assessment of the layout as his attention had been drawn to a weather-beaten old timer dressed entirely in buckskins and heading their way. When the man was within easy distance, Sam reached out and gently placed a hand on his arm. "Excuse me," Sam said cordially.

"Fer what?" the man replied forcefully. He spit a squirt of amber tobacco juice that glanced off the toe of Sam's left boot, ricocheting into the dirt right alongside.

Sam was taken by surprise by the trapper's unexpected response and raised the boot up behind his right leg where he slowly and deliberately worked the toe up and down against the back of the pant leg. "Well, for —"

Lucky came to his rescue; well…sort of anyways, "For thinking you have the brains enough to answer some questions…that is *for what!*"

Sam rolled his eyes then closed them momentarily. His next concern was to place both feet squarely on the ground about a shoulder's width apart; he was fully expecting Lucky's remark to start trouble and was getting prepared for it. He ventured a peek and was pleasantly surprised to see the grizzled oldtimer showing the beginnings of an amused grin.

"Like me a señorita what's got 'er some spunk! You wanna sell 'er?" he asked, turning his full attention on Sam.

"How much you got?"

"Not much more'n a dollar 'n a half, but I do have me a —"

"You will not sell me!"

Maybe it was the fire that now blazed in her intensely narrowed eyes that grabbed Sam's attention. Of course, it could have been the clenched fists perched steadfastly atop her hips, or maybe it was the fervor with which she had just delivered the words. In any case, he got the message and figured the fun was over even before it got started real good.

He poked a fingertip into his right ear and wiggled it at an imaginary itch while he briefly went about pondering the situation. "Yeah, maybe you're right," he said while looking at her. Turning to face the fella, he said, "Thanks just the same, oldtimer, but I think I'll keep her for awhile. I need her around so she can mind my business for me. What I do need from you, though, is some information."

His disappointment was evident as he turned a longing glance her way. "About what?" he finally managed.

"About where I need to go to talk to whoever's in charge around here."

"Well now…" The fella paused in his response by turning to the side and spitting again. This time he landed the squirt a safe distance away from Sam's feet, probably figuring this gent was a mite particular about the appearance of his boots.

"That'd be Bent himself," he finally offered after swapping the chaw. "He's most likely over to the general store." As the trapper spoke, he also pointed a stubby, work worn finger across to the opposite side of the compound.

Sam's gaze found the intended target as it came to rest on a slightly bigger shed that was separate from the others. The dead giveaway was the boldly lettered sign above the door that read:

GENERAL MERCHANDISE

There was additionally some smaller lettering along the bottom edge of the sign that Sam couldn't make out from this distance. "Much obliged," he said and touched an index finger to the brim of his hat.

The trapper gestured toward Lucky. "You sure about not sellin' that purty little señorita? I could maybe throw in my —"

"He is sure!" Lucky said adamantly, and fired a squint at Sam that caused him to break out in a wide grin.

"Okay, but if'n ya was to change yer mind, anyone kin tell you where ta find Beaver Tail Jack."

"I'll keep that in mind," Sam said while managing to keep his grin somewhat under control.

Beaver Tail Jack went on his way while Sam slipped an arm around Jay's slim waist and started to gently nudge her toward the general store.

"You will wait just one more minute, Señor!" Lucky said angrily. The fists were again perched menacingly atop her slender hips.

Sam stopped and faced the defiance that was glaring straight back at him.

"You will tell me right now that you will *never* sell me to some of these people. You will tell me right now that you will..." An angry tear had appeared. She quickly wiped it away just as it had started to slide down her cheek.

"Lucky, I have no intentions of ever selling you," Sam said. "Why, I don't think I could get much more than Beaver Tail Jack's offered dollar and a half, or maybe a couple of dead skunks for you, anyway."

The stern look slowly transformed from what was at first an expression of uncertainty to one of relief. "I think..." she rubbed a flattened palm against her cheek. "I think maybe you are someone that will need me to stay very close to him. I think you are someone that is no have very good stable thinking."

"What'dya mean, not very good stable thinking? Why, I'll have you know that I'm of sound mind and —"

"That is no what I say. I say you no have, how you say, good horse sense. You know... *stable thinking*." This time it was her turn to break into a smile, "Come...now is time for we go to the store."

Books by r William Rogers
For information on any of these book, visit my website at:
http://bobthebookbuilder.com

Arkansas Valley Series
Toward A New Beginning - Book 1
Uncertain Times - Book 2
Shattered Dreams - Book 3
Mustang Justice -Book 4
Shiloh Ranch - Book 5
Rails Along The Valley - Book 6
Kindled Faith - Book
(end of series)
Cripple Creek mining District Series
Poverty Gulch - Book 1
Cripple's Golden Pioneers - Book 2
From The Shadows of Mount Pisgah - Book 3
(more on the way)
Settlers of South Park Series
A Dream Fulfilled - Book 1
Divine Discovery - Book 2
Turmoil - Book 3
The Redemption of Arnie Bradbury - Book 4
An Unlikely Friendship - Book 5
Wesley and Little Fawn - Book 6
(more on the way)
The Saga of Willard Hansel
Trooper Hansel - Book 1
Trail To Washoe - Book 2
(more on the way)
Journeys of The Heart Collection
Stanton
Gideon Hartman
(more on the way)

Stand Alone Books
Birdsong of The Penateka
She Wore It Tied Down
Ordeal On Elkhorn Peak
Minor League Misfits

CPSIA information can be obtained
at www.ICGtesting.com
Printed in the USA
LVOW04s1706070916

503615LV00023B/1069/P

9 781508 413356